PHALLUSY

Character illustrations
Indiana Vaynman

Object/creature illustrations
Muamer Cajic

Cover art
Roderick Frost Photography

PHALLUSY

THE HAMMER OF CASTRA,TION's ANVIL

RODERICK FROST

Contents

The Orchard

Milfandria seemed destined to be the prettiest woman in the Queendom. Then a horse kicked her face at age nine, in the equine equivalent of a high five. The impact to her delicate bone structure was calamitous, like a glass sculpture speed dating an extinction grade asteroid.

As she grew, her kind nature, can-do attitude and physique could have attracted a suitor. She hid these qualities though, under coarse hessian clothing, in the family orchard on the outskirts of an insignificant hamlet. So well hidden, her only sexual experience wasn't with a man at all.

It was with an orc.

As a child, Milfandria had imagined the orchard's apple trees were her protectors, ready to uproot and attack invading monsters. This notion had comforted her after her parents' death. However, one evening at the age of twenty, the leader of an orcish raiding party exposed her naivety by ripping off her door and destroying her innocence.

He'd left her screaming silently at the ground, wracked by pain. Her only consoler, the empty hug of a cold floor and darkness creeping into her tiny hut. The whole encounter took a handful of minutes, but changed her life forever. Outside her apple trees stood silent, revealed as false guardians.

Eight months later, reports reached as far as the Citadel that something extraordinary had happened.

A Half-Orc child had been born.

This momentary fame did nothing for Milfandria. During the pregnancy, she'd occasionally thought of the growing creature inside her as a parasitic invader. This feeling disappeared when she first held the defenceless child, looking into her large innocent eyes.

Though now powerless, she knew her daughter would possess great strength in time. A strength that could protect her. Thinking of the brutish orc barbarian who'd fathered her, she'd named the girl "Barbidon" in a moment of reproductive Stockholm Syndrome. It was soon shortened to 'Babs' for all but the sternest of parental rebukes.

The young mother politely answered the questions of a physician from the royal court, but when he left, life returned to normal. Albeit, with the huge additional burden of a rapidly growing child. Breastfeeding proved particularly difficult as the child's not-quite-human teeth grew.

There was one exception to this normalcy. When Babs was still a toddler, Milfandria awoke one morning to find a monstrous, matt black great sword placed on her doorstep. It was wrapped in a crude blanket, with no note.

Milfandria had struggled to pick it up, for it was taller than her. She'd stood confused, examining the way light died on its surface as utterly as life would on its edge. Taking it inside, she put it under the bed shared with Babs. Brought out occasionally to inspect, it was eventually left dormant, gathering a caked-on layer of dust.

The growing Barbidon had some contact with children her own age. In childhood, Trill, Jacinta and Arque did not display the same racism as adults, many of whom remembered the raid that 'brought her' to the Hamlet. This reprieve of judgement was temporary. As her Orcish blood matured her faster, the differences were stark to her peers. By fourteen, she was a towering adult, and by sixteen, was stronger than any male in the village.

She had become fascinated with the Great sword, and practiced swinging it against imagined foes whenever she had time. Milfandria would marvel at her physical presence when the last rays of sunshine silhouetted her sword swinging daughters' form.

The villagers never saw Babs in this endeavour. Milfandria had drilled into her from an early age to never show signs of aggression. People were already distrustful of her father's heritage, so swinging a great sword around was deemed unwise.

Yet inside that 6'4 body was still a naïve, uneducated girl with no book *or* street smarts. This was hardly surprising given the absence of books in her life.

Or streets.

She had occasional contact with the three other children, who she rapidly outgrew. With surging hormones, Barbidon fell in love with one of the boys. The whole notion was slightly ridiculous given she was a foot taller than her prospective lover.

Trill was kind in his rejection of her, but young love burns like a stone in a supernova, and the opened wound seemed so deep it would never heal.

Another boy, Arque - whose father had always disapproved of the 'stupid orc calf' increasingly took on his father's views. When he heard from Trill about the "declaration of wuv" as Arque mockingly pronounced it, he thought it hilarious. Flirting with Jacinta one afternoon, the pair passed Babs on her way to town. It was just two days after the breaking of her heart.

Babs ambled down the path with her head down. She didn't notice Arque until he called out to her.

"Hey Babs, found a lover yet?"

"Go away."

Delighted at scoring a hit, it emboldened him to go further.

"Why don't you try the paddock? You might have a better chance at seducing a bull."

Women usually pick up on emotional cues quicker than men, and at that moment Jacinta saw something in Barbidon's normally placid eyes. It gave her pause. She reached out a cautionary hand to Arque's forearm, but he had already prepared his next taunt.

"After all, it worked for your mum!"

After an awkward moment without response, Arque's sneering face turned uncertain. Nobody was reacting to his amazing wit. Not even his victim.

Barbidon's body surged forward. There was little warning of her newly discovered rage. Her green tinged hands reached out with blinding speed and crushed Arque's windpipe in an instant. His eyes bulged wider than a methamphetamined owl. The bones in his neck cracked, head flopping comically to one side - like a confused dog struggling to understand a new command.

Hands shaking, Barbidon let go of Arque's corpse. It crumpled unceremoniously, face and knees on the dirt with arse pointing to the heavens. A whimpering posthumous fart escaped, perhaps his soul, attempting to depart the body with an upward trajectory.

Barbidon and Jacinta locked eyes, mouths agape. Jacinta didn't scream, she bolted.

Bab's blood pulsed so hard in her temples it felt like her heart had traded places with her brain. She may have been simple, but as she stared at the dust kicked up by Arque's rapidly retreating girlfriend, she comprehended the event's gravity. His father and older brother would be out for her half-cast blood. She turned back towards the orchard, almost colliding with Milfandria as she burst through the door of their tiny hut.

"What is it?"

"I have to leave."

"But why? Wait. Why are you grabbing the sword?"

"I love you mum." Barbidon sobbed, "But I killed Arque."

"What? How? Why?!" Milfandria pivoted wildly, as her daughter grabbed a blanket, then some apples. Soon she was out the door with a final good-bye hug.

"I love you... I have to go."

Barbidon turned to leave, heading for the forest. Tears streamed down her face as she passed the sign her grandfather had built twenty years ago. It was a simple sign with one word on it: 'Orchard'.

Milfandria watched in utter devastation as sixteen years of beloved parenting sprinted away from her.

2

Girls meet, dog's meat

Vaginia stood at the dusty patch of ground that was her brother. It was only family she had to say goodbye to. Seeing his murderer's symbol patronisingly adorn the small grave stone filled her with fresh anger. The screams of Gaymax and his lover burning at the stake still echoing in her mind.

Even 6 months later, Vaginia wanted to charge at Father Vindictus of the Cross'ed Legs Church with a knife and fury so fresh that 'cold blooded' would have been a misnomer. However, the likelihood she would succeed was slim, and the likelihood it would make a tangible difference was nil.

Vaginia was far from the first youthful person to look at the calcified morality of her elders with anger. But anger without power is just insomnia. She therefore clutched the letter from the dwarf tight. It held the hope to cure her lack of knowledge, to lift the veil of encumbering impotence.

She did not actually *say* goodbye, Vag was rational enough not to talk to dirt. Lifting her pack over one bony shoulder, she headed north into the forest.

Vaginia made steady progress over the coming days. Young and diminutive, she was not comfortable travelling alone. Vag had abilities to draw upon if attacked, but they had their limits and there were many potential dangers in the wild.

Her anxiety, normally kept hidden around others, was now unchecked out here alone. It caused her to swivel her head in exhausting hyper-vigilance.

In her weaker moments, Vag would question whether she should turn back. But a glance down at her dress, a birthday present from Gaymax drove her foreward. Unbidden and unwanted, it invariably led to her thinking of Father Vindictus.

He had made the arrest along with two guards. Now in his fifties, he must have lost a lot of weight since his youth. His loose jowls made his face looked like a melted candle. The man was the worst kind of priest. Hateful, yet keen to sanctify the negative emotion by wrapping it in the trappings of piety. He had smiled with malevolent contentment at the burning of Vaginia's brother. Vindictus had not even noticed the then dishevelled, skinny nineteen-year-old girl, sobbing at the spectacle, but she had not forgotten him.

A distant noise brought Vaginia back to the present. She stopped and listened for almost a minute.... nothing. Tomorrow she would rendezvous with the Dwarf. He could provide some protection against monsters or brigands, though where they were going, she wondered if even his fighting skills would be enough. A sun shower started, and she was grateful to see a rock formation ahead which would afford cover.

Barbidon had no plan, just to run. As she entered the foothills where the woods started, she thought she heard barking dogs. A search party. Sweat ran down her body and her thighs ached from the uphill run. She considered dropping the sword for greater speed, but could not bring herself to part with the weapon, so she continued on, grateful for a brief shower that came in spurts, penetrating the majestic forest canopy in accumulated heavy droplets that dripped down her face.

The dog's barks seemed to close. They'd been sent off, ahead of the men. Considering her options whilst running at pace, she went past a rocky cropping and almost ran into a very startled, black-haired young woman.

-

The rain was loud, and Vaginia was completely taken off guard. A huge humanoid with... Orcish features? came barrelling around the outcropping, directly towards her. In the humanoid's hand was the biggest, night black sword Vag had ever seen. Three days of tiring alertness had given her only eight metres warning for this terrible threat. She held out her staff shouting,

"Stay back! I can defend myself!"

She continued evaluating the situation in micro-second steps. Her assailant was female, with almost comically sensual proportions. Finally, Vaginia saw her eyes. They were filled with fear. This monstrosity of a girl wasn't a hunter, she was *being hunted.*

-

Barbidon came to a sudden stop, looking over her shoulders at the approaching dogs. "Get beside me!" Vaginia commanded in a tone that Barbidon felt compelled to follow. They both saw the dogs now, four of them, with teeth bared in anticipation.

It didn't take long for the distance to be closed, but it gave Barbidon crucial time to steady her breath. As she raised the massive sword in front of her, light crackled and shot from her new companions' hand, hitting the lead dog. Astonished, but with no time to marvel, the second dog leapt at her.

She swung up, striking under its body - causing a gash, but also aiding its leap to a comical degree. The dog flew high, landing upside-down on a boulder with a sickening crack. Another spark flew out whilst Barbidon spun around, ready to thrust out her sword like a spear at another dog.

It too leapt at her, but this time she aimed point first for the dog's open maw. Its momentum, combined with Barbidon's powerful thrust, meant that it didn't stop until its mouth hit the cross guard.

The immediate threat was over. The lightning-struck dogs were still alive, but sufficiently shocked that they had run off, terrified. Vaginia looked over, about to admonish the pneumatic, barbaric girl for bringing this threat to her, but instead, she burst out laughing.

Barbidon had skewered the last dog from its mouth to its butt, with more than a foot of sword emerging out of its anus. Babs looked down at the source of her amusement. It was a bewildering simultaneous lesson in physics, anatomy and BBQ preparation.

"Nice swordswomanship." Said Vag, extending a tiny hand. "What's your name?"

"Oh, I'm Barbidon. Babs for short." she said, in a voice juxtaposing cuteness and gravel.

"Vaginia. But call me Vag. I think you're going to need to wash your sword."

"And, th... the lightning? I didn't know Magic was real!" Said Babs

"It is, though don't get too excited. I'm weak at wielding it."

This fascinated Barbidon. She peppered Vaginia with questions, forgetting about the villagers until they were almost upon them.

She had also forgotten to de-skewer the dog.

When she quickly raised her sword on instinct at the men's approach, she raised the dog with it. They rounded the outcropping and were greeted by a dog's bleeding sphincter with a great sword protruding from it. They stopped dead in their tracks as a momentarily distracted Babs struggled to unmake her kebab.

"What the?!"

They had not expected to find Barbidon armed with a six foot sword, all four hunting dogs dead or fled, nor a strange woman with lighting starting to crackle from her fingertips. They unanimously decided their afternoon fun run had reached its halfway mark and that it was time to turn around and head home. One of them, the dead boy's father, yelled over his shoulder once they had some distance. "You're going to pay for what you've done if you show your face again cow!"

"Charming." Said Vag, as the men retreated.

Barbidon looked at her hands which shook as if asking for attention. Her legs crumpled and she allowed herself to collapse on the rocky ground.

"Thank you." Babs managed, as her breathing calmed.

"You're welcome." Vaginia said as she looked down. The huge woman now looked more like a girl than a monster, with legs tucked up to her chin. A single tear formed then escaped down her cheek as her eyes closed. She shut her eyelids so tightly, it looked like an attempt to escape reality.

Vag was not sure what to make of her, but an idea formed in her mind. She crouched beside the girl and put her hand on her shoulder, summoning a latent motherly instinct.

"Where are you heading warrior?"

"No idea... and I'm not a warrior."

"Well, we are what we do, not what we call ourselves, and...." Vag took a moment to look up at the canine corpses despatched by the black weapon. "you swing that sword better than a lot of men who call themselves one."

Barbidon blushed and opened her eyes. "Thanks."

"So, let me guess, those racists drove you out of town and you now have nowhere to go?"

"Um... something like that. There was this boy and..." Babs paused, uncertain whether she should finish the sentence *'I snapped his neck.'* She decided against it.

"Ah... I understand completely." Said Vag, not understanding at all. "The church of the Cross'ed Leg forbids relationships between races, and I see you are not entirely human?"

"My father was an Orc."

"I see." Said Vaginia. "Well, you look exhausted, and it is late in the day, so let's find a spot to make camp."

3

Maiden's man

Clamax "the quick" as his friends called him, hadn't liked human society at the best of times, but under young queen Chastidia's rule, it had grown almost intolerable. As a newly divorced middle-aged dwarf, he was sure her conservative rule was thwarting his potential as a young 'maiden's man'.

He could no longer use 'Kindling' the bulletin boards for romance seekers. Chastity Priests had torn those down, along with the lesser used "Grindstone"- a similar tool for men seeking men. They viewed both as 'beyond sinful'.

And so, he sat at the Thirsty Beaver tavern, intensely aware of two robed men's disapproving eyes upon him and his, unusual, war hammer. Ignoring them, he did his best to charm two young women at the bar. It seemed to be working. Witty anecdotes were rolling off his tongue and the girls (aided by wine) were giggling hysterically.

Well, what do you know, he thought to himself, I may not be the youngest colt in the stable, but the girls still love Clamax.

One of the maidens was trying to compose herself after the last expertly delivered punchline. "Oh Clamax, you are hilarious!" She put her hand on his thigh. Leaning forward, her tipsy eyes smiled seductively at him. *Oh boy!* Thought the dwarf... *this is... this is really going to happen!*

"I wish my father was a funny as you!"

It was perhaps the worst compliment he'd ever received. She delivered the line with warmth, though his heart sunk through the floor, even as he threw back his head in a good-natured laugh. "Well, it looks like my meal is ready now, if you'll excuse me, it was a pleasure chatting with you ladies". Teasia - The thigh grabber, affected a pout before smiling and thanking him for the wine and stories. She was oblivious to the fact she had just ripped out his heart of hope, thrown it on the floor and squished it into the rough wooden floorboards.

He moved to a table, languidly finishing his meal, whilst reflecting with self-assured certainty that if only the Queen hadn't introduced her ridiculous chastity laws, his evening would have gone very differently.

He finished his gruel without ceremony and made his way into the night to his lodgings. He heard a noise as he headed down the final secluded alleyway, and any slight haze from his one ale vanished. A robed man from the tavern was in front of him, and a second noise behind Clamax confirmed where his accomplice was.

"That is a disgusting weapon dwarf, surely a cleric's weapon of the banned god?"

Clamax couldn't hold back a snort, "How do you *ban* a god?"

Without waiting for a response, he charged the man in front of him. He had no desire to wait for them to converge on him and figured it was best to fight the man ahead first.

He swung his small war hammer as he dodged a thrusted short sword. The head of the hammer connected with the side of the man's chest and he let out an unusual groan before dropping to the ground, legs convulsing. A second strike to his forehead caused another pitiful groan, and, like a cross eye school master that couldn't control his pupils, his gaze bent towards the bridge of his nose, before finally relaxing... lifeless.

The second man caught up to Clamax, attempting an overhead thrust toward his exposed back. The Dwarf half turned and jumped inside the downward arc. He gave an upper-cut headbutt. This stunned the man, who fell on his back as the lower half of his body continued its forward momentum. Clamax lifted his hammer and struck down at the prone man's groin. There was a strange golden glow as the man's limbs convulsed and his head arched back. A second powerful strike to the sternum ended him.

Silence returned to the alley. It was an almost jarring contrast to the deathly struggle moments before. There was laughter in a nearby laneway, but no calls of alarm. He looked down at the bodies. Chastity Guards, he thought with disgust. The Queen's experiment in enforcing conservative values were appearing even here in Jaldur on the edge of the Realm.

Clamax needed sleep, but couldn't leave the bodies here. The alley penetrated deep in the town's centre at one end. The other, in a large dark bush. He dragged the bodies one by one to the far side, stowing them under low-hanging branches.

He was grateful for his bludgeoning weapon. It meant no blood. The blaring, but belated odour alarm of decay did not concern him. He would leave this town in the morning.

Clamax classed himself as a lover first, cleric second and fighter third. Lately, his life had been all fight, no love. At least the war hammer granted by his deity two weeks ago was effective at disabling opponents. Bodies hidden, he moved to his lodgings, and sleep.

4

Laying out the crew

Vaginia had supplies, but not enough for her *and* a huge half-orc. Fortunately, Babs had brought a small bag of apples, but even then...

She looked down at the dog Babs had skewered. It wouldn't be her proudest meal, but the creature *had* tried to kill her. Barbidon wasn't the slightest bit squeamish about eating it. Perhaps it was her Orcish blood, or perhaps it was because she was simply ravenous after her exertions.

Vag ate, cooking additional meat until it was dry and difficult to chew. Good enough to store in her pack.

"Barbidon, do you realise they won't allow *anyone* to love or marry you?"

Babs frowned, looking up in anger, "Who won't?"

"The Church of the Cross'ed Legs."

"That's not fair." Said Babs through a mouthful of dog leg. "Is that why Trill didn't want me?"

"Possibly. Priests are imprisoning or executing people who love outside their race, or within their gender."

She reached out, putting her hand on Babs' arm. "I'm set on changing those rules, but I'll need help. I could use a warrior like you to help me, help everyone, but also to help your own cause."

Babs looked uncertainly at their surroundings, but none of the trees, or rocks, gave any counsel. "I suppose I could come with you for a bit, I don't have anywhere else to go."

"Thank you." Said Vag, trying to look reassuring. I'll be grateful for the company. Have you ever met a dwarf before?"

-

Long after sunset, they lay back with full stomachs. The uncomfortable, uneven ground was offset by the visual spectacle, a vast canopy of stars visible above their rocky outcrop. Chatting by their small campfire, Vaginia felt she had now had Babs figured out. Not the brightest spark, but she *was* slightly adorable. An odd juxtaposition of naivety, physical beauty and brutal potential violence. Perfect to work with.

The Mage closed her eyes and began to let go of her consciousness.

"So where to first?" Asked Babs with excitement, as Vaginia was drifting off.

"We'll meet up with the dwarf, A wizard turned to necromancer lived north of here, I need his spell book. There is a spell I need to learn."

"Oh" said Barbidon, pretending to understand.

Vaginia tried to let sleep take her again. Her travels had exhausted her, so it wouldn't be hard...

"....What's North?"

"It's a direction"

"And the Necrothingy?"

"Returning dead things to life to serve you."

"Oh, I see."

Vaginia went to sleep quickly. Barbidon, did not.

-

They awoke at dawn. Vaginia had them on the move soon after.

"Are we meeting the dwarf today?" asked a skipping Barbidon.

"Yes, this afternoon, at Youval lake"

There was a brief silence. "So, how do you know each other?"

"We worship the same God. Orgasmodan, giver of love *and* (she leant in conspiratorially) *pleasure!*"

Barbidon giggled. She thought it sounded a bit rude, but her knowledge of these things would not have concerned a chastity Nun.

Vaginia smiled at Barbidon's response.

They reached Lake Youval by late afternoon. 'Lake' seemed an embellishment after the dry summer. The sneeze of an incontinent hill giant could have created a comparable puddle. The watery landmark served its purpose though, as a smiling dwarf waved at Vaginia from the other side.

Clamax was relieved to see the budding mage approach on the agreed day. Then he saw the woman behind her. She wasn't Human, she was bigger, more muscular, yet with an impossible hour glass shape. "Sweet Orgasmodan." He said to himself whilst they were still out of earshot.

This was Barbidon's first introduction to a dwarf. Her first impression was that they must have trouble closing their mouths, because even after Vaginia introduced them, he still stood agape for an awkward moment.

His lock jaw passed after Vaginia help close it with a tap. He was very friendly after that, and Barbidon was glad to have met two people who didn't mind she was half-orc.

Vaginia looked down at the Cleric's war hammer, her eyes bulging wide, "Wow, I have never seen a war hammer like *that* before".

Clamax held it up excitedly. "It is a very recent gift from Orgasmodan, though she did not call it a war hammer. She referred to it as a *love* hammer."

"Ha, I can see why! It's magnificent!"

"It is amazing! I don't enjoy fighting, but it seems to make my adversaries go into a spasming fit when struck. Makes it easy to finish them off."

Barbidon looked at the hammer's business end. It was ornately carved in gleaming steel, but didn't recognise the strange shape.

"What's that supposed to be?"

"Can't you tell from there?" He held it up for a closer inspection. This didn't aid Barbidon's understanding.

"Why Lass have you not seen a penis before?"

"What's a penis?"

She looked at the dwarf, awaiting clarification. Unfortunately the problem with his open jaw had come back as he just looked up at her with a single tear running down is cheek. Babs turned to Vaginia, who rolled her eyes with a good-natured smile.

"A *penis* is what a man has between his legs. And, if you agree to it, she grabbed the love hammer for emphasis, aiming a gentle tap at Babs' Crotch, "It can go between your legs too"

When the hammer tapped against her, Babs' world was rocked by unbelievable, indescribable pleasure. She collapsed to the ground, convulsing wildly and let out a series of barely coherent "Oh wows!"

The problem with Clamax's jaw continued as he stared down at the writhing half-orc.

Vaginia looked from the hammer to Babs, and back to the hammer. After a moment's contemplation, she lightly tapped herself down below.

Vaginia hit the deck with a loud moan. Clamax turned his dumbstruck face from Babs, to Vag, then to the hammer, now at his feet. He picked it up and decided he needed to understand what his weapon could do... for research purposes.

"Oh my god!"

His hips thrust forward and his little manhood... or should we say dwarfhood? Unfurled like a miniature hose. His head arched towards the heavens while his right knee wobbled in and out of lock. He eventually flopped to the ground to catch his breath, noticing he'd made an emission in his pants.

The remains of the afternoon were not exactly productive as they passed the hammer around. Exhaustion set in and they all fell asleep, no watch, no dinner, waking well after dawn.

The next morning, they were ravenous, wolfing down a surprising amount of their food.

"What happened to us yesterday?" Barbidon got out through a mouthful of dry meat. "It was AMAZING!"

"What you experienced Lass, was Orgasmodan's blessing, an orgasm."

"Wow!" she said, wide eyed "Your god is the best! Can they be my God too?"

"Absolutely." said Vaginia "By aiding us you will be one of her favoured."

"And have more of the Gasms?"

"Yes Babs, you can have lots of orgasms, but you need to finish your food now. We're moving out."

5

Necrosexual

The necromancers abandoned keep was a full day's journey on foot. Vaginia briefed the others on route with what to expect. Rumour held that a pack of zombies still guarded the tiny stone building, even though their master was dead. They would be difficult to kill, but slow. Babs was glad to hear she would be twice as fast as their shambling frames.

In between learning how to fight rotting undead corpses, Babs also learnt about making love and where babies come from. It made her ponder who her father was. She'd heard Orcs were really scary. So how had her mother fallen in love with one?

Perhaps her misshapen face had made it difficult to find a human man that would love her. Her brow furrowed in anger as she had an epiphany, a sudden realisation as to what must have happened. Arque's dad and the other racist men in the village must have driven her handsome and unusually gentle Orc father away. It must have been young love torn apart!

Babs used the hours of travel time to further embellish her imagined narrative. It was perhaps for the best, as the others were busy talking in hushed tones of their plans. Had the young brutess been less engrossed in her thoughts, and more suspicious, she might have wondered why the dwarf and mage needed to exclude her from so much of the conversation. That was until Clamax earnestly put his hand on Vag's arm, bringing them all to a halt.

"The world is full of confident incompetence Vaginia. You have been blessed with a greater intellect than perhaps anyone I have ever, or will ever, meet. As to your doubts, they're merely are signs of an enquiring mind looking for contingencies to plan for. So, embrace them as challenges, not proof of your incompetence."

Vag paused, absorbing his words before looking at him fondly, "I wish I had a father like you."

Clamax looked up at her kindly.

"A few lines of accumulated wisdom from half a lifetime isn't the same as patiently nurturing a child for almost two decades, but thank you for the compl-"

Clamax's sentence was cut short by Babs enveloping them both in an unsolicited hug. "I think you are nice people" said Babs.

Releasing them after an awkwardly long time (actually Clamax didn't mind it *that* much), Vag looked up at her smiling. "You're ok too Babs."

They returned to their journey. Bab's now returned to the conversation, having completed the mentally prepared novella of her parents' tragic love story. It took the form of a language quiz though.

"What's a contingency?"...

"What's intellect?"...

"What's enquiring?"...

"What's incontinence?"...

Sunset was approaching by the time they reached the keep. 15 to 20 shambling figures walked aimlessly around a central stone building. Babs was told the best thing was to 'engage' (she assumed that meant hit them), before pulling back to avoid being surrounded. Approaching the nearest zombie, it noticed their presence and turned slowly toward them.

Babs wasn't prepared for the combination of rotting flesh and malevolent gaze. It locked eyes with the dwarf.

"Braaaaains." It issued in a deep raspy voice, full of hatred.

The dwarf rushed forward and connected with his hammer. Instantly the malevolence vanished, replaced with a look of serene ecstasy.

"Braaaaains?" It whimpered with a raised inflection, legs now even more unstable. The Dwarf edged back for Babs who deshoulderised the zombie. It was like a decapitation, but she accidentally struck the top of the torso. The force of the sword strike was so great that it went straight through anyway.

"Fawk!" said the dwarf, having never seen anything like it.

Barbidon turned to the 'grown-ups' (chronologically, not altitudinally) doing tiny jumps on the spot with a beaming smile and raised eyebrows. The scene was like that of a small child, eager for assurance her parents had witnessed a new gross motor skill.

Drawn to the noise, the remaining zombies converged on the trio.

"That's great Babs, outstanding job, let's pull back though."

They withdrew to a pre-arranged four metre wide ravine that would funnel the zombies in. Babs and Clamax formed a front and readied themselves. The undead came on with deceptive speed. Sparks leapt from Vaginia's fingers, hitting the lead grey-matter-glutton square in the chest at a range of twenty metres. It staggered, but kept coming.

Then the carnage began. Barbidon swung her sword in vast arcs, and the dwarf was as afraid of friendly decapitation as he was of the zombie's. Barbidon seemed to be in an aggressive trance and... *Gods that sword must be sharp!* He thought, as it sliced clean through a zombie.

Clamax struck another advancing zombie with his love hammer. Unfortunately, its crotch had rotted through, so it was unable to receive Orgasmodan's blessing. The dwarf heard a 'whoosh, just above his head, like the sound a helicopter blade would make if they existed. It was Bab's sword, on its way to decapitate the undead creature incapable of sexual release. Oh well, he chuckled mid battle, at least it could still get a great head job.

Fortunately, most of the zombies had crotches, and Clamax dished out more corpse climaxes than a necrophiliac with an epileptic tongue. When they were down to only six remaining zombies, Vaginia felt strangely anxious again, and despite the battle raging in front of her, she sensed something that caused her to look behind.

The creature had been stalking the trio for hours. After all, the green one with the long black pointy thing looked dangerous. It was going to wait for nightfall, until they attacked the creatures that stunk of death. That's when it came up with an idea. It would attack from behind while they were distracted.

The creature had soft padded feet, but Vaginia felt the foreboding tremors, inevitable given the weight of the huge predator cat bounding towards them. Her eyes went wide. It was only metres away. On instinct, she threw out the most powerful spell she knew.

"Frigidimus!"

A wall of ice went up at the last moment. The feisty feline's mouth smashed into it with more force than a passionate lover. It fell back, dazed. The boom was so loud, Babs and Climax heard it.

"Fawk!" declared the Dwarf in Groot-like repetition.

Even the zombies stopped for a moment, taking in the spectacle. The wall faltered, and as Babs looked back, she could see the oversized pussy through a large crack.

"Get behind me!" Screamed Vaginia to the half-orc, who moved to protect the mage. Vaginia found herself wedged between her stronger companions with Climax doling out whack-a-mole sexual therapy at the morgue, whilst Babs drove her sword through the crack to ward off the terrible new threat.

It smashed at a different section of the wall and immediately broke through. This started a game of deadly cat and orc. Paw strikes reached out, scoring glancing blows. Frustratingly for Babs, it was *extremely* nimble, consistently jumping back as the great sword cut nothing but whiskers.

Climax fared better, assisted by Vaginia, he made steady progress with the last of the necromancers' minions. When they were down to only one remaining shambler, a sickening thud sounded behind them. It was Babs' head, flung against the side of the ravine, hard. Her sword dropped to the ground. Climax knew he needed to act fast. He hit the last zombie with a pleasure strike, spun around and did an overhead throw of the hammer at the predator cat as it was about to pounce on Vaginia.

Praise be to Orgasmodan's clitoris, it struck between its eyes. The hammer fell to the ground as its eyes rolled back, front legs locked and back legs buckled. Clamax ran over, picked up the hammer and started hitting the Cats' front leg again and again. It meowed, again and again, but Clamax felt he was doling out all pleasure and no pain. His arms were *so* tired. "Babs! Wake up!" He yelled.

Babs opened her eyes. Everything was blurry. Beside her, she thought she made out Vaginia, beating a zombie over the head with her staff. Her vision gradually sharpened. An exhausted Clamax was repeatedly hitting a huge convulsing creature with his hammer.

She remembered where she was. Her hands wrapped around the hilt of her sword and she started a stumbling run towards the massive threat. Moments later, the huge black shaft was thrust deep inside the quivering pussy, and it finally knew peace.

Vaginia eventually hit the last zombie enough times to send it to death 2.0. Barbidon fell to her knees, bleeding from the back of her head and losing consciousness again. Clamax fought off exhaustion and ran to her. He laid hands on her wound and called on his deity's blessing. The wound healed amongst a golden glow. Barbidon's eyes shot open and her infectious smile returned. "Wow, that was exciting!"

"Hmpf!" replied Clamax. "That's one way of saying it. Let's get indoors, so another one of those big cats doesn't sneak up on us."

6

Spanked

They moved tentatively towards the stone building. It was small but conspicuous given its remoteness. Babs worked her sword through a gap in the deteriorating door, lifting the plank on the other side. They heard no noise in response to it clattering on the ground.

"We're sure this guy is dead right?" asked Vaginia, appreciating the power a necromancer could wield.

"Pretty sure Lass. The mighty Involuntus Celebitus would've surely come out and helped his pets if he was alive."

Saying this, Clamax had a disturbing thought. Every single one of Celebitus's zombies was female. He shivered, trying unsuccessfully to shake off a terrible mental image.

With night descending, the first room was dark. "Orgasmodan, grace us with your golden light." Said the Dwarf in a reverent tone. A warm glow emanated from the tip of Clamax's hammer. It showered the three tired adventurers in a golden stream of light that Barbidon observed as *"Really pretty."*

They looked around in wonder. The room was both study and library, but it was the sheer number of books and scrolls that was astonishing.

"Wow, there's so much to learn here!" Said Vaginia "We should check all the rooms and settle in for the night."

The other rooms were more typical; kitchen, privy, store room. They ascended the stairs and found only a large bedroom with a four poster at its centre. On it lay the mighty Involuntus Celebitus. Fortunately, he was even deader than his zombies, an inanimate skeleton with a trace of rotting flesh and clothing remaining around his bones. The necromancer had spent much of his life raising the dead, but alas for him, no-one had been there to return the favour. So much for 'Paying it forward'.

Vaginia declared the library the best place to sleep. There was no disagreement. Clamax chivalrously offered the ladies the couch. They both declined, so he reclined his tired body on the plush two seater and extinguished his light with a single word command.

An hour later, he dreamed restlessly, arms flopping above his head on the side of the couch.

"YOU HAVE BEEN VERY NAUGHTY! A commanding female voice shocked them all from sleep.

"Wha... What?" The awakening dwarf exclaimed. The voice belonged to a tall, sensual, stilettoed woman with greyish skin. She was undead! But not a lowly Zombie. A vampire? A wight? They had failed to eliminate all the Necromancers minions, and now it would be their doom!

"YOU MUST BE SPANKED!"

Ok. That was a bit weird. Maybe a Succubus?

"AND THEN AFTERWARDS..."

Barbidon's sword swung straight through the woman like she didn't exist, a spark from Vag had similar success, it hit a metal object on the other side of the room.

She is impervious to their attacks! Thought Clamax as he clambered to the side of the couch furthest from the Femme Fatale. His arm struck the side of the couch and the kinky assailant suddenly disappeared.

"What in Orgasmodan's name!"

"Ha!" laughed Vaginia, "She was an illusion!"

The mage went to the couch, hitting a black button on the armrest.

"YOU HAVE BEEN VERY NAUGHTY!"

They watched the illusion play out. The undead double D disciplinarian kept looking at the now empty couch, admonishing it, while removing items of clothing.

"Why is it doing that?" asked Babs with her head tilted sideways.

"It appears Involuntus Celebitus got lonely out here and created a show for himself" said Vaginia with a smirk. Commotion over, they eventually settled again. The dwarf also opted to sleep on the floor this time.

Vaginia got to work in the morning, engrossed in the books downstairs. Babs, with the least to do, explored the Necromancers Room. It seemed to hold little of interest at first, though on closer inspection the resident skeleton's finger bones had a small ring interspersed with them. It was pretty, but sadly too small for her hand. Or was it?... it seemed to grow as she held it, enabling her to slide it on.

Most things in the wardrobe had deteriorated, however a sizeable amount of the most amazing blue material that Babs had ever seen sat folded in a corner. She imagined herself in a dress made of the stretchy fabric, like a princess! Running downstairs, Barbidon searched for Vaginia in earnest.

"Can I keep this material?"

"I don't see why not. Wait a second, where did you get that ring?" asked Vag with an alarmed tone.

"I... I found it on the Negro dancer."

"*NECROMANCER*. Babs, can you take it off?"

With shaking hands, Babs quickly complied. Vaginia audibly exhaled.

"Well, if you can take it off and the necromancer was wearing it, it's probably not cursed. Can I please examine it though?"

Babs reluctantly placed it in Vaginia's outstretched hand.

They spent two long days at the Necromancers remote outpost, boring Babs. Clamax was interested in the other settings programmed into the 'couch of visions' but ultimately grew bored too. He hung out with the beautiful warrior - happily teaching her what a massage was after she complained of a sore back.

She asked if she could have another of the "Gasms". Clamax saw no harm in this, they had little else to do. He gave her a tap with the hammer, then tried to find the ceiling interesting as she moaned and writhed in hammer-induced ecstasy.

He attempted to remind Babs that orgasms were normally achieved through coupling with another person, but immediately chided himself.

Truth be told, his conversation with the young maiden Teasia in the 'Thirsty Beaver' tavern had afforded him a harsh reality reset. It now seemed ridiculous to imagine a grizzled middle-aged dwarf like him having a chance with a young woman like Babs. Fortunately for Clamax, the guileless Half-Orc was oblivious to the hint, saying only that she would like to try it one day with a tall, muscular man.

Tall... noted Clamax.

The unlikely pair also had much time for conversation while the arcane texts absorbed Vaginia's attention. Babs told Clamax about the teasing and racism she experienced growing up. She conveniently skipped the whole, 'neck-cracking' incident that had driven her pre-emptive exile. Bab's sincerity soon had the dwarf metaphorically 'opening up' wider than Orgasmodan's legs as he talked about his past without gloss.

Clamax's mother had died in childbirth. The woman he'd *called* mother was a paternal Aunt. She was kind enough, however happily handed the crying boy back to his father when he returned one winter.

Clamax spent years on the road to learn the trade of trading. This took him north, far away from the Dwarven lands. His father was an anomaly amongst a race that did not travel. As a result, he had seen no dwarf but his dad since childhood, and definitely no dwarven woman.

As he grew, so did his interest in the fairer sex. He'd been intimate with a few (all humans), but always had the sense that he was "novelty nookie". Long-term relationships eluded him.

He was a still barely out of adolescence when calamity had struck. Land pirates attacked the trading convoy their wagon was travelling with. They had set up an ambush so ingenious that the convoy's two scouts missed it entirely. The bandits had an unusually intelligent Ogre with them who stayed concealed in a trench under Autumn leaves for an entire day. He broke concealment, running down a short embankment and smashed into the third wagon.

Clamax's wagon.

They had been travelling with a group of refugee acolytes, worshippers of Orgasmodan (who was hitherto unknown to Clamax). Fortunately, a powerful Paladin of their order accompanied them. The Convoy's mercenaries would have stood no chance if it wasn't for this exceptional warrior single handedly facing off against the behemoth.

Clamax contributed little to the fight as debris pinned him down. His father fared far worse, a sickening blow from the Ogres first impact had killed him instantly. Through the first of many tears shed, he saw the Paladin fight.

It was surreal. The man surrounded himself in a blue aura and struck the beast with not just his sword but also a magical hammer. The weapon floated like a butterfly, but stung like a boulder.

For a man to fight an eleven-foot-tall ogre seemed impossible odds, and perhaps they were. For even as the mortally wounded Ogre dropped to one knee, it reached out with a desperate club swing, killing the Paladin. The rest of the convoy successfully drove the Brigands off, though Clamax now found himself fatherless.

Orgasmodan's Acolytes conducted a touching funeral for the fallen. Campfire chats with the Orgasmodanic faithful continued as they consoled him on the loss of his father.

Clamax was stirred by the heroic fight of the paladin and intrigued by their message of free love. At the journey's completion, he sold his wares and headed to their secret temple. It was in a secluded valley forty kilometres north of the Citadel.

He would never forget his first sighting of the four-storey stone building shaped like a decapitated pyramid, nor the surrounding gardens. Most extraordinary was a long rectangular body of water lined with statues. These signified the many forms of intimacy Orgasmodan blesses; female to female, male to male, Elven to Human, Gnome to Halfling and so on.

Taking pride of place at one end of the lake was an enormous statue of a vagina. Opposite was the 'Phallus of Felicity', a crystalline penis as tall as two humans. This filled with pressure each hour before releasing its fluid in a powerful stream that traversed the entire length of the lake, showering its female counterpart in glistening fluid.

Not the subtlest piece of religious artwork in the land, but the young dwarf thought it most impressive.

The High Priestess, a charismatic matronly elf named Ovula, taught him the twin laws of Orgasmodan; Openness and Consent. He also learnt the clerical powers he now wielded.

Inspired by the Paladin who'd given his life to protect him, Clamax also received martial training. This would enable him to go out into the world and preach Orgasmodan's word, whilst defending other followers against the forces of Prudishia, the deity of the Cross'ed legs church. A church whose power was growing at an alarming rate.

He had travelled east to the borders of 'Tion', a neighbouring prosperous dukedom. There he'd met and fallen in love with his now *ex*-wife. Bodyclokina was ten years younger than him and full of vigour and positivity. Whilst human, she had an alluring squatness to her figure. Clamax found it amazing that other men didn't see her beauty as he did.

Alas, their relationship did not last forever, for she desperately wanted children. Years of trying (always with great gusto on Clamax's part) forced them to concede that Dwarves and humans couldn't interbreed. He was content with this, she was not. With her children bearing years running out, Bodyclokina broke his heart and left him for a retired soldier.

Clamax's found solace in his religion, hitting the road and 'spreading' Orgasmodan's word. This was now a clandestine affair, as the new young queen Chastidia had made Prudishia the Realm's official Deity upon ascending to the throne. As a result, the Church of the Cross'ed legs soon had their noses in everybody's business, especially anything involving their genitals.

Barbidon listened, fascinated by her new friend's history. She didn't understand why the Church put their noses in people's genitals, but she didn't interrupt.

In his subsequent travels he met Vaginia, shortly after the execution of her brother. With such a strong personal grievance against Prudishia's agents, he felt confident confiding his religious beliefs. She'd been eager to join and possessed an extraordinarily rare skill she was coming to terms with, the gift of magic.

Clamax knew little of arcane arts, but on his second visit he provided her with two books. Orgasmodan's High Priestess had sourced them specifically to help the high-potential recruit learn her craft.

Vaginia had read and re-read them, learning all she could. It was not enough. Not enough to make a difference against Father Vindictus, the priest who'd arrested her brother. Certainly not enough to make a bigger difference, to change the lives of everyone in the realm. That would require a truly majestic plan.

"And so Barbidon, here we are, building Vaginia's knowledge, to make a bigger difference."

"The story about your wife is so sad, and the Paladin too." Babs looked at him with a hopeful expression. "Maybe you'll get to be a Paladin one day?"

"Not likely, Paladins are about as rare as a six foot dwarf. I'm content to serve my god as I am."

"Still," said Babs, "you never know?"

Vaginia learnt much from the Necromancer's tomes, including the money shot, his spell book. She had no desire to learn Necromancy (which grossed her out). Fortunately, it contained spells from other schools of magic, including a more powerful lightning bolt than her ineffective spark.

There was also an invisibility spell that would require further study. Most importantly, it contained the spell that formed the lynchpin of their "majestic plan".

It required spell components; a white marble and an onyx ball she did not possess, and it was beyond her powers to understand the complex symbols describing the spell, but with hours of study - she hoped, she *needed*, to learn their secrets.

Vaginia had also picked up invaluable tips in recognising arcane auras. She was starting to understand magical items. For example, the ring Babs found seemed to grant increased agility. A valuable item Vag was tempted to keep for herself, but reluctantly gave back to the warrior girl. Babs needed it more up front, protecting the mage.

She also felt the magical presence of Clamax's hammer. Her abilities in this area were weak and prone to false positives. The black sword Babs carried gave a particularly strong signal. It must have been something to do with the strange black material. It was odd enough that a poor farm girl had a Great-sword, for it to be powerfully enchanted artefact seemed preposterous.

7

Divination

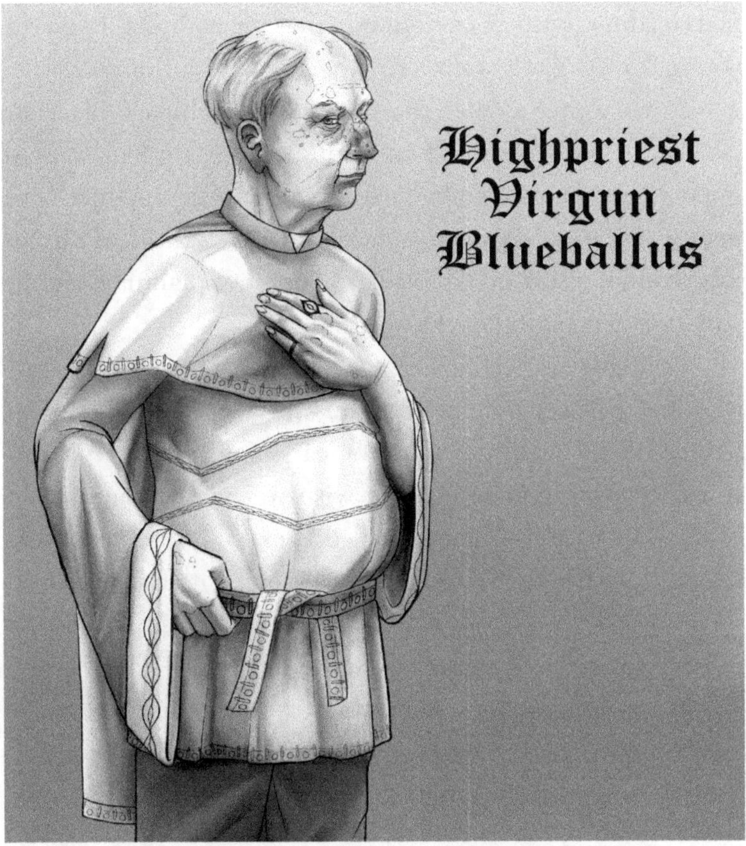

In the distant citadel, or "Del" - as its inhabitants knew it, Virgun BlueBallus- High Priest of Prudishia and head of the church of the cross'ed legs, sat in audience at the royal court. He was proud of his position. His brother Vindictus was a middle-ranked priest just returned from the provinces, meanwhile here he was, the most powerful man in the Queendom.

Beside him sat Queen Chastidia herself. Her chair (he was pleased to note), was not much larger than his own. Virgun had to admit, with an envious eye, that the embroidery on the young Royal's gown was more exquisite than his own robe.

On the other side of the Queen sat Archmage Electran. As always, He'd plastered an insufferably smug look of self-importance on his chubby face. The otherwise unremarkable man was the only known wizard still alive. This had all but assured him a seat on Chastidia's council of planning, and he still looked proudful of the position.

For all his magical powers, he had not prevented the gravitationally driven migration of his hair follicles. They'd descended from scalp to eyebrows, ears, nose and presumably shoulders. The remaining long wisps of hair at the summit of his nondescript frame travelled back and forth across his scalp like the trade routes of a spice merchant. The styling effort concealed none of his baldness, but revealed all his vanity.

Yet, as long as he commanded the 'lightning sphere of foretelling', the court would grant him respect and deference. Entirely too much in Virgun's opinion.

There were two audience chambers in the keep. The first, a grand public hall, and the second, a smaller chamber of planning where they resided today. It was a more intimate affair, suitable for regular meetings. A beautiful marble map of the Queendom formed its cool floor.

Upon entering the room, one would walk over the dwarven realms, step like a giant on the Southern provinces, until they stood over the citadel at the centre of the room. From there, a supplicant could look right to the neighbouring human dukedom of 'Tion'. To the left, well beyond lake Youval and the town of Jaldur - lay the Orcish lands. Fortunately, those brutish warriors had turned their attention to the Northern Elven realm over the last decade.

Virgun and the Queen sat above the vast forests between the citadel, with the sea of Goman behind them.

A messenger from the border post near Castra now stood facing the triumvirate.

"Your majesty, I have received two separate reports of Orcish raiding parties from hamlets west of Jaldur."

"Orcs? Are you certain" asked Electran with an incredulous tone.

"It's hard to confuse an Orc with anything else." said Virgun, eyes rolling at the insufferable wizard.

"Well yes, it's just that they have been engaged with the northern Elves for ten years. It makes no sense for them to make an enemy of us again whilst still at war."

"Just because you can't think of a reason doesn't mean one doesn't exist."

"Gentlemen." said the Queen curtly but softly. "Perhaps we are trying to ascribe too much rationality to these brutish creatures. Electran, could you consult your sphere of foretelling on this subject?"

"Of course your Majesty" Said the wizard, rising from his chair with an unnecessary flourish. He whispered to an aide with oddly muscular legs who discretely exited the room ahead of Electran. Chastidia and Virgun followed at a more leisurely pace.

They converged moments later in another modest sized chamber. Electran had overseen its construction immediately upon his appointment to court. Runic banners hung on the wall, looking very arcane. But the centrepiece of the room was, well, it's centrepiece. A large glass orb on a stand with a much smaller metal bulb in the middle.

Electran stood next to it, holding his arms out wide and chanting.

"Futuro expectan revealioso."

Virgun heard a strange squeaking sound that seemed to emanate outside the room. A thrumming, that Virgun thought sounded more mechanical than magical accompanied the squeak.

There was no doubting the magical power of what happened next though. Small sparks of lighting arced erratically from the inner metal orb to the outer transparent orb. Virgun begrudgingly admitted to himself that it was impressive spectacle.

Electran dramatically placed his hands on the outer orb. They immediately attracted the lightning, which had hitherto seemed directionless. The energy coursed through his body. The hair from the back of his head and temples now stood comically erect, as did those from his bushy eyebrows and ears.

The Wizard raised his head upwards, his eyes rolling back, so that Virgun saw only white. He continued chanting for a few moments before almost yelling –

"Expellus."

The whirring sound ground to a halt, as did the lighting from within the Orb. Electran composed himself and his hair before giving a triumphant look to Virgun, and a submissive look to the Queen.

"Well?" she asked expectantly.

"There is no need for alarm. They were isolated, opportunistic raids and do not presage war with the Orcs."

"Hmpf" snorted Virgun. Having Electran use his device to dismiss the threat seemed like getting an unscrupulous student to mark his own homework. But, the Queen trusted him, and that was where it would end.

"Well, that's a relief." She said. "Shall we return to the chamber of planning gentlemen?"

"After you your majesty" said Virgun, gesturing the same.

They took their respective seats again before hearing some comparatively boring disputes over the next hour. When the end of proceedings finally drew near, the door swung open in a manner that commanded the attention of everyone in the chamber.

Virgun was impressed by the confident stride of the dashing, lithe man that entered, back-lit dramatically by a coincidental positioning of the afternoon sun. He wore his shoulder length honey blonde hair loose, though it was still kempt and shevelled. His asymmetrical dark grey cloak over a white cotton shirt was effortlessly stylish. As the doors shut, Virgun's eyes adjusted, finally recognising the man's face.

"Fellatio Jackhammer! You are a sight for sore eyes! Why, I heard you had drowned in the sea man?"

"Your Majesty, Your Grace, Electran." Said the handsome man who could have easily graced the cover of 'Swordsman's monthly'. With a quick bow, he displayed subservience and confidence in one gesture. "My ship was lost, though I managed to shed my vestments and pop my head up for breath. I swam for two hours before emerging from the sea of Goman dripping wet and without a single garment to hide my modesty."

At this point Virgun noticed that he was biting his lip rather hard, so he stopped and moved back from the edge of his chair. He saw Electran was looking at him rather than their guest, an infuriating smug little grin on his face. Prudishia alone knew what he found funny about this exchange though.

Fellatio continued, not pausing for a breath.

"Not wanting to offend our wonderful deity, I immediately secured some clothing and a pitchfork from an obliging farmer and started on my journey through the great northern forest".

"When I was but forty kilometres from the Citadel, I made a miraculous discovery. One I can only assume occurred under the guidance of Prudishia herself." He now paused for dramatic effect, edging his audience.

"What was it?" asked the High Priest, the loose jowls that were a family trait flapping in excited expectation.

Jackhammer looked at Virgun directly.

"Your Grace, do you mind if I approach?"

"Um...certainly."

Felatio was Colonel of the army and a regular at court. He had proven his loyalty to both crown and church many times. Virgun therefore had no fears for his safety. He was however, surprised that this presumed discovery was for him, and not the Queen. She had no insecurities and indicated she was happy for Virgun to take the first look.

The Swashbuckler stepped diagonally forward, directly in front of the slightly unsettled Virgun.

"This is where I found the phallus you have searched so long for." Jackhammer triumphantly declared, directing his gaze downwards.

Virgun followed his gaze and ended up staring at the man's impressively sized cod piece.

Gosh, was it getting warm in here? Thought the Priest. Confused, he stared back up at Fellatio.

"I'm sorry, what?"

Jackhammer frowned. "My lord, I was referring to the map on the floor. I believe I have found the secret location of the Phallus of Felicity, unholy relic of the demon god Orgasmodan."

The Queen and Virgun's heads synchronously snapped to the floor in shocked understanding, examining the marble map at Fellatio's feet.

"But... that is so close to the Citadel?" stammered the vexed Virgun.

"Indeed your grace. A protective Highmana barrier masks their temple and sacred fluid feature."

"Is this 'Highmana' barrier magical? How were you able to penetrate it?" asked the Queen, the conversation now being worthy of involvement.

"It was no problem for a Jackhammer your majesty, all it took was a gentle push. Barrier is perhaps the wrong word. Its power is hiding through illusion, rather than physically barring entry. I did not spend long there. Make no mistake though, I saw both the temple and the disgusting 'Phallus of Felicity'."

"This is excellent news! Wonderful job Fellatio, though don't let it go to your head."

"No job ever goes to my head your grace."

Virgun could hardly believe this turn of events. For years he had dreamed of having the Phallus of Felicity within his grasp, and here it had been all along. He need only have looked down, right between his legs.

He turned to the Queen excitedly. His jowls followed a moment later.

"We should send a force immediately to destroy this disgusting relic of Orgasmodan and the followers of this filthy excuse for a religion, would you agree your majesty?"

"You have my permission to use whatever force is necessary. Make it happen gentlemen. Quickly."

8

❧

49

Hunting with a bang

The next morning, Vaginia announced they could move out. Having determined what was needed, she recruited Barbidon to carry the large spell book. She also carried the high quality fabric found in the Necromancer's cupboard. At least there was limited food left to haul, though this gave rise to a fresh problem.

Clamax hadn't brought enough supplies from Jaldur, and Babs ate like a Rhino trying to bulk up. It was a simple equation, they would have to ration.

None of them came close to the title of 'ranger' or 'hunter'. Their survival skills were on par with a narcoleptic Giraffe's ability to hold military parade attention. Babs and Clamax did not even have bows, so Vaginia realised it would be up to her if they spotted wild game.

The problem could have been avoided if *any* of them had thought earlier to dry some meat from the 400 kilo predator cat, but it had sat in the sun for a day before Vaginia had thought of it. She'd been distracted by the Necromancer's spell book, Clamax had been distracted by Babs, and Babs, with the cerebral power of a gifted fruit fly, didn't need distraction to *not* think of something.

Their next stop was two days on foot. Babs did not know where they were going, and was happy without the detail. Most people would insist on knowing the 'why'. Her mind did not need second order reasons, blissful ignorance was fine.

The first part of their journey was across a long grassy plateau. Clamax's loud armour would scare off any potential prey, so Vaginia walked ahead with Babs for protection.

Whilst keeping an eye out for anything edible, Babs asked Vaginia what she'd learnt from the books. Vaginia mentioned the more powerful lightning bolt, as well as a shield spell she could centre on herself. Another was a yet-to-be-mastered form of invisibility, maintainable as long as her concentration held.

Babs was particularly interested in one called the 'hands of hairdressing', twin ethereal hands adept in combing and braiding hair. They could actually perform many tasks, but Babs was most interested in their prime penchant for platting pony tails.

Vaginia talked excitedly about her new abilities. Insecurities had plagued her since feeling inept in the Zombie fight. In contrast, her companions seemed far more powerful. As a result, she desperately hoped her new knowledge would close the gap. It needed to. The 'majestic plan' relied on her.

Like most insecurities, she'd blown them out of proportion. Clamax was patient, knowing it would take time for her spell craft to develop. In Babs' eyes, Vaginia held the important title of 'the smart one'. The mere ability to add up any two single-digit numbers already making her 'Archmage' material.

Watching the two girls from a considerable distance, Clamax trudged through grassland with a warm wind at his back. He eventually saw them descend out of sight to lower ground, towards a forest of crispy dry pine trees. The canopy extended to the horizon.

The girls saw a squirrel at the forest's border. It simultaneously saw them, running thirty metres back to run up a tree and out onto a high branch. Now confident in its safety, the tiny creature looked down with unpanicked curiosity at the humanoids below.

Vaginia ran underneath it and immediately started channelling her new lightning bolt. This wouldn't be an ineffective spark though, now she could kill a creature rather than just injure it.

For all her intelligence, Vaginia had failed to consider two things.

The first was her target's body mass. Her standard spark had merely wounded the 40kg hunting dogs and 60kg zombies. A squirrel however, weighs 500 grams. When Vaginia fired off her newly emboldened bolt, a blinding light shot directly upwards. The crack of sound was painfully loud.

Clamax had just reached the edge of the plateau when he saw a burst of light and heard a thunder clap emanate from under the canopy. All that was visible *above*, was a small dot shooting into the clear sky. It came closer to him on its return to terra firma. The blackened, smoking husk of a rodent landed a short distance in front of him.

It didn't look appetising.

The second thing Vaginia failed to consider, was that lightning striking tinder-dry foliage, is a recipe for fire.

The fire did not last forever. Seven days later, a drought breaking rain put it out. However, the nine hundred and seventy-four thousand acres destroyed *before* said downpour, made it the largest collateral damage from a squirrel execution, ever.

They walked behind the conflagration for a day before saying goodbye as a wind change took it. Giving up hunting altogether, Vaginia and Clamax rationed their remaining food, much to Bab's disappointment. Their journey became easier on the second day as their path intersected a road heading to their next destination.

Vaginia tried out her 'hands of hairdressing spell' and was impressed that she only needed her to visualise the desired style. The hands would 'lock-on' to the desired head, even performing the complex work on a moving subject. Babs decided on asymmetrical braids running along one side of her head, with the rest of her auburn hair given a tasteful jshushing. When finished, it was a perfect fusion of warrior-beauty

For Clamax, she just patted his dagger-cut hair down. Her spell couldn't trim his hair. For herself, Vag tried something aristocratic, ornately drawn up in a towering structure above her head.

"Well, it looks impressive." Said Clamax "Are you not worried about it drawing too much attention to yourself though?"

Vaginia affected a pout "Urgh. Fine." She got the hands to de-escalate the dramatic styling into a more humble, approachable form of beauty. At least it wouldn't look incongruous above her plain face.

If life insurance had existed, two young women travelling overland with only one male escort wouldn't have lowered their premiums. Convoys were the common travel method because of the prevalence of brigands and monsters. To travel without a convoy meant one of three things: desperation, foolhardiness or lastly, that you could really handle yourself in a fight.

Therefore, other travellers eyed the odd trio (as many trios are) with suspicion. After all, a mysterious looking female, a heavily armoured Dwarf and a unique-to-the-world Six foot four Half Orc with a matt-black great sword clearly hadn't met at a Cup cake decorating convention.

It was safest to assume that the only thing they had in common was their ability to 'handle' themselves in a fight, (note: not 'handling themselves' in a fight. The latter dramatically lowers combat effectiveness and is therefore unwise).

As the ethereal future started coagulating into the present, Babs became more interested in it. She enquired where they were going next, would there be lots of food there and what they would do after eating said food.

Clamax informed her they were continuing their whirlwind real-estate tour of dead mage residences. Vaginia needed a rare spell component that hadn't been at the necromancer's place. Mages had been becoming increasingly rare over the last couple of decades, and Clamax knew of a second location where one used to live. Maygul's tower was their best shot. It was also on the way to their ultimate destination, the Citadel.

9

Heroism

Jackhammer was no behemoth, but he had been riding his mare for a considerable time and sensed its fatigue between his thighs. It had been a hard ride, but they would require one last charge of the horses before day's end.

There was a healthy nervousness amongst the men behind him. They awaited the signal from the second cavalry force that was encircling the far side of the High-mana barrier.

Brightspark, his third in command, sidled his horse beside Jackhammer's.

"Cautious or bold Colonel?"

Jackhammer raised an eyebrow, "What sort of question is that?"

A moment later he reflected it was actually a rather good question, but verbal bravado is like an uncovered erection. Once it's been 'whipped out', it tends to demand something be done with it.

And so, he kept up the pretence of conviction.

An ignominious bird call travelled from the opposite side of the temple, signalling little portent of the hell it would unleash.

Jackhammer spurred his steed forward. The men dutifully followed on a broad front. Hitting the barrier at pace, they made a soft cacophony of dull popping sounds as each man penetrated it. A thousand metres away, they immediately made out the temple.

-

Sylviana was a young Elven girl of 53, barely an adult, but she'd embraced the teachings of Orgasmodan with relish. She lay on her back moaning as her lover moved his tongue as expertly as a cunning linguist.

Suddenly the ground rumbled ominously. Confused, she looked up. The path from pleasure to confusion to terror took only three seconds. Clutching her dress in a trembling hand, she ran to the temple.

Hodgkins was the least fit soldier under Jackhammers command. He was immediately short of breath, even though his charger was the one carrying his fat frame. An angry, bitter blob of a man, he rode without a coat, excessive weight gain having made his own unwearable. Even his shirt buttons looked ready to burst, giving a tantalising peak at the portly flesh beneath (if that was what one was into).

Hodgkins was happy to fight for the side of chastity, since his underperforming manhood had enforced chastity on him. Unfortunately, his ex-wife had spread word of the once private dilemma of his privates to a fellow private in his regiment, leaving him the butt of a thousand jokes amongst the men.

Unwilling to stand up to the taunts of his fellow soldiers, today he would show his power, his force, and above all, his brutality. Running away from him was a young slip of a woman. An elf? She wore a white linen shirt but was comically stark naked from the waist down. He readied his sword, comforted to feel its hard steel in his grip. An unseen force blasted multiple riders beside him backwards but he did not notice, he was focused on his quarry.

Swinging the weapon back and high in the air, he busted every desperately clinging button on his shirt open as he prepared to bring the blade down on the elf's back.

Hodgkins started a rather weak battle cry, but was cut off by an invisible wall of wind that threw both he and his horse backwards, ripping his now-open shirt off his body.

Hitting the ground hard dazed the anthropomorphic blubber ball, but he collected himself and stood, shirtless in the surrounding madness. Soldiers everywhere were being pushed backwards by the same unnatural wind that had struck him. Only the lithe frame of Colonel Jackhammer seemed to make any progress, resisting the spell and inching his way forward. A powerful Elven Priestess of Orgasmodan stood at the temple gates, forcing the soldiers back while the remaining cultists ran inside the large front doorway.

A small haven from the wind grew into existence, centred on his person. It was a surreal pocket of calm in the midst of the Maelstrom. Not questioning his fortune, Hodgkins started forward like a heavy marble picking up speed on a decline. His white bouncing belly quickly went past the Colonel who looked at him in amazement through blinking eyes, and he rolled on, towards the Priestess. As he closed the distance, he noticed she looked tired. Then something terribly odd happened. She looked to him and smiled. It was perhaps the most serene smile Hodgkins had ever seen in his life.

Ovula, High Priestess of Orgasmodan was feeling all of her six hundred and fifty-two years. The Elven Matriarch of her church had used all her power to push back the encroaching soldiers, buying time for followers outside the temple to reach safety within its walls. Fortunately, most had got inside. Of those who had avoided slaughter, only one remaining acolyte remained outside the safety of the temple.

He was quite an overweight man, which explained why it had taken him longer to reach the gate. In truth, she did not even recognise him, but he must have been one of the new arrivals that had come yesterday. He was certainly not one of the attacking soldiers. His physical condition and half naked, shirtless body marked him clearly as an innocent.

The man ran with an odd crazed look on his face, almost like he'd been driven mad by fear. The poor thing, he was probably beside himself with panic. She turned her gaze to him in what she hoped was a comforting smile. But, instead of moving past her to the safety of the temple, she was hit full force by what amounted to a 120-kilogram ball of adipose tissue.

Ovula's head hit the ground and consciousness vanished, her limp body collapsing between where the double doors of the temple needed to close. The shocked acolytes inside worked frantically to kick the corpulent Hodgkins off their leader, drag her inside and close the gates. They managed the first two of these tasks, but Jackhammer and a countless stream of soldiers rushed the gates before they could place its crossbar.

What ensued was an Orgy. One of the bad ones, where no one has sex, and half the participants die. Jackhammer only took part until confident of victory before heading outside to destroy the Phallus of Felicity. His second in command, a brutish Major by the fitting name of "Longsword" continued the bloodbath, relishing the slaughter, even of those surrendering. The only worshipper kept alive was Ovula herself, bound and gagged, ready for execution in the citadel.

Outside, Fellatio Jackhammer attacked the phallus with gusto. He and several men destroyed the statuesque fountain that had stood periodically erect for centuries. They were about to head to the 'female' end of the lake, when he glimpsed a faint light underneath the destroyed phallus.

"Clear this rubble" he panted through laboured breath. The light was from something important, something very important.

Hodgkins got to his feet, the main contingent led by the hulking frame of Major Longsword, was already inside. Given his proximity to the high priestess, the portly private had helped bind and gag her. The Elf who looked to be about sixty in human years had been unconscious following his tackle. When he grabbed one of her hands, she woke up abruptly and stared directly into his eyes for a second.

Time seemed to slow. He felt momentarily like all his burdens had vanished. No, he realised, not vanished, shared, for he now saw them reflected in her eyes. Never had he felt someone empathise with him as she did in that instant. The Priestess knew of his broken marriage, the taunts of his peers, the trouble with his...

"I can help y..." she said inside his mind as he felt the faintest hint of warmth, of blood flow to his loins. It ended abruptly, however, as another soldier spun her, face-down to bind her hands.

He stepped into the temple backwards, away from Ovula. They made eye contact again as she stared back at him kindly whilst being dragged to their encampment. Eventually Hodgkins lost sight of her and turned around, immediately awestruck at the temple's interior.

Ornate murals depicting couples of the world's races in loving embraces covered the four storey walls. Like Hodgkins, most of the soldiers present had been raised on the conservative teachings of the CCL (Church of the Cross'ed legs). They jeered at the images, elbowing each other as they pointed out each lewd scene. Though loathed to admit it, many were secretly a little aroused.

Hodgkins though, saw something deeper as he stared upwards, mouth agape. In both quality and content, the artwork was stunning. It depicted a world free from judgment, it even displayed portly people as worthy of love. As a taunted, plus-sized soldier, this resonated strongly with him.

His reverie crashed to a halt as he slipped over, hitting the ground hard. The polished marble floor was slick with blood oozing from the dead. The men turned to laugh at his pitiful plight. Still shirtless and now covered in blood, Hodgkins had the urge to sob. Though he reflected, it didn't feel like it was just because his peers were laughing at him. There was another reason, one he couldn't quite put his finger on.

-

Captain Argile Brightspark may have had the armour and blonde hair of a storybook hero, but he did not feel like he'd taken part in a glorious victory today. He'd joined the army ten years ago, perhaps naively, to protect the innocent from invading armies or rampaging monsters. Today's 'enemy' fit neither of those descriptions. As he looked around the bodies inside the temple, he was ashamed of the action he'd participated in today. Even if it was just 'following orders'.

There was a sickening thud to his right, breaking his self-admonishing reverie. Looking down, he saw the Private who'd resisted the powerful spell cast by the priestess. Recalling his name, Brightspark took pity on him.

"That was amazing what you did today Hodgkins." He said, extending a hand. The man looked on the verge of tears.

"Thank you sir, it was nothing." A glimmer of pride returning to his face.

"Modest as well?" he replied, loud enough for the nearby soldiers to hear. "Tell me how on earth were you able to get under the High Priestess's defences so easily? Do you have some secret power? A secret weapon not wielded by us mortal men?"

Hodgkins, now on his feet, tried in vain to wipe the blood from his back. Major Longsword came up behind Brightspark and clapped him on the back with a force bordering between friendship and antagonism.

"Well, if there was a secret weapon involved, we can all be confident it was not-Hodgkin's-limp-boner!"

The stone walls echoed with uproarious laughter as Hodgkin's again looked crestfallen. Brightspark's shoulders slumped too, his attempt to lift the man's spirit undone by his superior officer.

"I have found Orgasmodan's God stones!" exclaimed the seemingly always back-lit Colonel Jackhammer from the Temple's Entryway. He held up a brilliant white ball in each hand. A cheer went up from the men (despite few knowing what 'god stones' were). They certainly looked fancy and important.

"What are God stones?" asked Hodgkins to Captain Brightspark.

"They are the physical manifestation of a God's power in the world. Their power flows through the stones to their followers."

"Will we destroy them?"

"I think god stones are indestructible, though I'm sure the church will try. If they succeed, they could banish Orgasmodan forever."

"Oh." Said Hodgkins. "That sounds way above my pay-grade."

"And mine." Said Brightspark.

The soldiers looted what they could and got ready to leave soon after. The Colonel ordered the tainted waters of the lake off limits to his men. However, no one thought to stop the thirsty horses. Heading back to the citadel proved arduous. There was a marked uptick in horseplay amongst the horses. Admittedly, horseplay is highly correlated with the condition of 'being a horse', but this was a new level of equine excitability. Even the geldings were so sexually aroused that the journey took four days instead of two.

Striking a deal

A blue-tinged dawn apathetically greeted the companions. With no food, they were soon on the sparsely populated road again, off to visit another dead mage's abode. Clamax taught a ravenous yet attentive Barbidon about the interchangeable words people have for sexual organs, and that Orgasmodan's followers typically found it more polite to use the proper word.

"You see Lass, euphemisms can be a way to make the topic sound taboo. For example; calling a vagina a "La La" to a child is to imply shame regarding the true word."

"What's a you-femanism?"

"It is when you call something, something else."

"Why would someone do that?"

"Exactly! Or at the other extreme, sometimes people bring an unbecoming crassness to the topic of sex with terms like 'Pulsing blade of penetration', or 'Custard swallowing almighty sarlacc pit'. Why, even the simple terms 'cock' or 'dick' are less polite words for penis".

Barbidon nodded "Say 'penis', not 'cock'. Got it."

She was so focused on embedding the lesson, that it took a moment for her to recognise that Clamax had doubled over beside her, dropping his hammer.

"Clamax, what's wrong?" asked Babs earnestly.

"So much... destruction." The cleric almost sobbed.

"Clamax, your hammer!" Vaginia said, pointing at the once golden love hammer.

It was now a simple steel Warhammer. The phallic end had morphed back to a more traditional shape.

He recovered over the next quarter of an hour. The ladies were confused, but Clamax suspected the cause.

"I believe they've attacked the temple and destroyed the Phallus of Felicity. Perhaps even removed Orgasmodan's god stones from their resting place."

Vaginia's face paled. Clamax had told her so much about the fluid feature. She'd been eager to see the magnificent structure for herself.

"What should we do now?" asked Vaginia.

Clamax rolled onto his back, wincing as he stared vacantly at the darkening sky above.

"I don't think it changes our plans. If they have Orgasmodan's god stones, they will probably take them to the citadel. Wagrum is close, let's just look for the spell components you need and continue on. Then with our 'majestic plan' we can hopefully prevent any attempts to damage them."

Babs and Vag nodded, though Babs was still not sure what the 'majestic plan' was.

Babs whimpered, belatedly dismayed.

"What is it?" asked Vag.

Babs had an ashen look of dawning realisation.

"The penis hammer." she said, pointing to the now nondescript weapon. "Does that mean no more gasms?"

Vaginia reached up putting her hand on the Half-Orc's shoulder, "Not so easily I'm afraid, but perhaps I can teach you how to do it yourself, or..." A new thought dawned on her. "I could reprogram the hands of hair dressing spell to do all the work!"

Clamax lifted his head with a hopeful expression, the faintest hint of a smile returning to his face.

Before they set off, they took stock of their capabilities. Vaginia was confident that hers were unaffected. She drew her energy from Arcane power, not Orgasmodan. Babs was still 100 kilos of muscle with a massive sword, so no change there. Clamax however, felt a slightly diminished connection to his Deity.

It reassured him to discover his clerical spells still worked. This meant her god stones were definitely intact for now. The Orgasms-on-*tap* hammer was perhaps the biggest loss. Fortunately, Clamax was trained both as fighter and priest, so he felt confident of still contributing to their little threesome.

It was a hungry day of walking through light but relentless rain on the road to Wagrum. The melancholic weather well matched their mood. By the next morn, the companions stared at the tower they'd sought. It was hard not to feel a little underwhelmed. At only three stories high, Maygul's tower failed to achieve a commanding prominence over the forest canopy. Like a micro-penis in macro-pubes.

It was only two kilometres from the town of Wagrum, yet given the foliage, they couldn't see the settlement yet. They did however spot, what looked like a town guard on the far side of the tower. He was urinating against a tree.

Clamax quickly pulled his platonic harem down behind brushes to survey the situation. By moving a little, they made out at least two more guards positioned on the far side of the tower. This was presumably where the front door was, as the side they'd approached from had no opening bar a narrow archery style slit.

From this slit, a small hand appeared, flapping frenetically. When a similarly small eye spotted it had got their attention, the hand withdrew, reappearing moments later with a strange piece of folded parchment. It was shaped like a dart and re-leased at speed, soaring through the air towards them, with a flight seemingly aided by magic.

Well, perhaps not the most *powerful* magic. It fell short of their position, but near enough to a shrub that could still afford some cover. The trio looked at each other. Clamax shrugged and the stealthier Vaginia moved forward.

Magic users used to be rare. Now they were rarer than Dragon's fur. The only publicly known magic user in the land was Electran, an arch mage who advised the Queen. Maygul, the occupant of this 'Tower', died of a mysterious illness a year ago, but perhaps, thought Vag, this parchment was given flight by an apprentice!

With trembling hands, Vaginia managed to cast the 'hands of hairdressing' spell. She sent one of them out to pick up the exposed parchment before bringing it back to her bush.

As she was about to unfold it from its flying form, three male voices in laconic conversation grew louder.

Shrinking into her cover, which now seemed horribly inadequate, Vag stayed as quiet as possible.

"Anyway, maybe you'll have an opportunity once she has an ale or two in her at the harvest festival."

"Perhaps, but even if I do, those acolytes Retentus has will probably watch us all like hawks."

"You'll be fine. There'll be so many people from the outlying farms, they won't be able to watch everyone, even with a full moon."

Vaginia braved a look through small gaps in her cover. There were three guards, all well-armed and armoured. The trailing guard looked more vigilant than the conversationalists. As they walked directly between her and the Tower he starting looking in her direction when an almost childlike voice emanated from the tower.

"Looking forward to the harvest festival gentlemen?"

All guards turned to the arrow slit.

"Go fuck a Dryad." Growled the trailing guard.

"Well I would love to but you have made it abundantly clear I'm to be arrested the moment I set foot outside this tower."

"Well you *did* fuck a Dryad." Countered one of the talkative soldiers. The remaining guards chuckled and continued their lap around the tower.

Vaginia rushed to read the parchment.

Dear adventurers(?)

I was the assistant to the late Mage Maygul. I've boarded myself in the tower since the passing of my master. This is because the chastity priest of Wagrum has issued a warrant for my arrest based on an 'unnatural union'. If you could get this warrant rescinded, I will repay you with valuables from the tower's inventory.

Your grateful servant, Fayzul.

Vaginia considered the letter, wrote an additional line of her own *'or just kill the guards?'* then got the hands of erstwhile hairdressing to carry it and her pencil to Clamax. He read it, scribbled on the note, frowned at her, shaking his head. Vag brought the note back. He'd crossed out her addendum. Typical Clamax, not wanting to harm innocents. She looked at him. He shrugged his shoulders and gave a thumbs up.

His facial expression was more aligned to his shoulder's gesture than his thumb's.

She pondered her next move. It would be a gamble, this apprentice may not even have the ingredient she needed. Vaginia scribbled a quick reply.

"If you have onyx and marble balls, you have a deal."

It was sent back through the arrow-slit window.

Five seconds later, a tiny thumb enthusiastically stuck back out, bouncing up and down in a manner that suggested its owner was also bouncing.

"Well, I guess that settles it." Whispered Vaginia to herself. With those spell components, she would have everything needed to cast the lynchpin spell of their 'majestic plan'.

"Fayzul has onyx and marble balls!" Announced an excited Vaginia to her companions once they'd regrouped away from the tower.

"Excellent news, assuming he's telling the truth. This would be a tremendous step forward for our plan."

"So cool!" Announced Barbidon, picking up on the enthusiasm. "What's our plan again?"

"To stop the church of the cross'ed legs oppressing you and everyone else. To stop them restricting you from loving whoever you choose."

"Right." said Barbidon with furrowed brows and thoughtful countenance.

"But how in the world are we going to get a large town's priest to rescind an arrest warrant? Particularly one for an unnatural coupling." asked Clamax.

"I think I have a fledgling idea, but first..." she turned to Barbidon "If we go into this town called Wagrum, do you think you could pretend that you don't like anything you've learnt about Orgasmodan?"

"Sure, I can pretend."

"Great. Now Clamax, could you take your tabard off? I need you to pretend as well, but to make it convincing I need to get the hands of hairdressing to stitch a pattern into the cloth."

"What will I be pretending to be exactly?"

"A Paladin," said Vag in a chirpy tone with a smile, whilst avoiding eye contact, "of Prudishia."

A Paladin and a metaphor walk into a bar

Two kilometres away, Father Annulus Retentus walked the Main Street of Wagrum. He too, sported a pair of furrowed brows. As a long-time devotee of the goddess Prudishia, harvest festivals made him nervous for three reasons.

Firstly, too much ale, too much revelry and entirely too much opportunity for his flock to turn to debauchery in a moment of weakness.

Secondly, the strength of his town watch was effectively only nine men. This was because of the rotating shifts required to monitor Fayzul, that pipsqueak of a gnome who'd steadfastly refused to come out of the magically protected tower. The cowardly sinner needed to accept his punishment and face his execution head on, then ultimately head off.

The whole affair had been terribly inconvenient and a huge drain on resources.

That alone would have been plenty for Wagrum's priest of the CCL to worry about. However, the third problem was that tomorrow night's festival would bring many outsiders to the normally tranquil town. Some of whom could prove difficult to handle if they got raucous.

It concerned father Retentus that the three adventurer types he had just now spotted from across the town square could fall into that category. They had weapons casually on display and walked with a swagger that at least suggested a willingness to use them. These three young men were already tipsy at noon. Like all drunken braggards, they classified anyone within the considerable radius of their body odour as 'audience'. To these unfortunate souls, they declared their adventuring exploits loudly.

"Urghh. It's going to be a long weekend." Retentus sighed to himself. Turning to walk down the main street. His gaze immediately fixed on *another* trio of outsiders. These were different though. Even outsiders would have classified these as outsiders, such was their level of outsiderishness.

One was a cloaked female. She would have looked mysterious by herself, but she was humdrum compared to her companions. A huge female... Orc? walked in the centre of the trio. No, she was too human, too... attractive, he was ashamed to acknowledge. She had on her back perhaps the largest sword Retentus had ever seen. Rounding out the trio was a dwarf, only the second one Retentus had seen in his life. This typically robust example was a heavily armoured male, with Warhammer at his side and a similarly aged face to his own.

Retentus slumped and started to sigh "Great." in ironic exasperation. The word 'great' turned literal halfway through utterance, as he made out the symbol on the dwarf's tabard. Could it be? Surely not, was that a pair of... cross'ed legs on his chest? Yes. Yes it was! Oh, virgins be praised!

He re-inflated his posture and boldly strode to the new arrivals.

"Greetings adventurers! My name is Analus Retuntus, a humble priest of Prudishia and head of the CCL in the town of Wagrum."

"Greetings Analus." said the Dwarf, matching his formal tone. "I am Clomax the Chaste, Paladin of Prudishia. This is the lady Virginia whom I am escorting to the citadel. And this," he paused "is Babs. I employ her as additional muscle, in case of trouble."

"Lady Virginia." He bowed deeply. Next, he acknowledged the Orcish looking lady's chest with a formal head dip.

"Boobs, it is a pleasure to make your acquaintance." he realised he wasn't looking her quite in the eyes, so lifted his gaze.

"It's Babs." She smiled back with charming innocence. "My name is Babs. It's short for Barbidon."

"Yes, yes of course." He stammered. That's what he'd said, wasn't it? Feeling a slight flush to his cheeks, Father Retentus continued the formalities. "And Ser Clomax! It is an honour to meet a Paladin of Prudishia. Tell me, I was not even aware that Prudishia had followers in the dwarven realm?"

For a moment he noticed the careworn lines on the dwarf's face just a little more.

"Alas that is true, I have been unsuccessful so far in converting the populace, though I will never tire of trying."

"Your desire to serve the church does you credit Ser Clomax. You could provide valuable service to Prudishia here, if I could persuade you to stay at least until tomorrow night's harvest festival?"

"Happy to be of service Father. What do you request of me?"

"You are too kind. My town watch is spread a little thin at the moment and I am concerned about the moral character of some visitors." He paused, inclining his head towards the less sober trio of adventurers behind him.

When he turned back his eyes paused on Barbidon. What a magnificent creature she was, and those thighs, so... so... thoroughly thick.

"I don't like organisms!" bleated Barbidon.

Rentutus's chin withdrew so rapidly into his neck, it was as if the fresh, befuddled look on his face had been imprinted by a maul strike. Okay, he thought, maybe she was intellectually thick as well. He looked to the dwarf who raised his hand and patted Barbidon's forearm in a gesture clearly designed to limit further outbursts.

"I would be happy to lend any assistance to such a high-ranking priest of Prudishia."

Gosh, what a delightful fellow this Dwarf was, thought Retentus as he tried to expand his modest ribcage a little further.

"I am in your debt Ser Clomax. Now, you must be exhausted from your travels. It was wonderful that you all have come to our little town. Please visit me in the church once you have secured lodgings."

Clomax bowed and took his leave to deposit their travel packs at the screaming eagle tavern. Rententus turned to watch them leave. Well, he watched Barbidon leave. Shaking himself out of a momentary revelry, he thought 'Prudishia give me strength' and adjusted his robes slightly.

Without turning her head Vag hissed, "Did you see the way he looked at Babs? Chastity Priest indeed. What a hypocrite!"

"He seemed awfully polite?" Remarked Babs

"Well-to-do men usually are when they want to sleep with you."

They crossed the town square. It bustled with hawkers hawking, peddlers peddling and farmers selling the selectively channelled proceeds of photosynthesis. As they approached the inn, their path took them past the drunk adventurers. "Greetings fellow warriors!" The skinniest one called out with a sneer.

After inadvertently giving them a few seconds of 'resting Dwarf face', Clamax returned a wary "Greetings."

"Tell me dwarf, have *you* ever fought a Jalux before?"

"Once, a long time ago though."

This response clearly interrupted the slender man's flow.

"It was a fearsome creature." Clamax added helpfully.

"Ah yes, right you are dwarf!" Concurred the braggart, finding his slurred tale on track again. "Well, it may shock you to learn that my partners and I defeated a whole den of them last night, six of the beasts! And one was even taller than you!"

"Only one was taller than me?" Clamax's face contorted in confusion whilst his brain struggled to put it back to normal. "Ah, you must have surprised the younglings whilst the adults were out hunting."

The man paused, realised he'd been belittled, and prepared a decisive comeback.

"Nah uh."

After another awkward pause, one of his companions (who looked like he ate the skinny one's rations), seemed to feel the need for a more expertly delivered verbal riposte.

"You suck!"

Touche, thought Vag.

It dawned on Clamax that he was winning what amounted to a dick swinging competition, one that he didn't realise he'd entered.

That was fine, but winning a dick swinging competition can be a pyrrhic victory when your opponent is insecure and possesses a sword.

Vag, who hadn't even heard of Jaluxes before, quickly spoke up. "I believe the sub-breed of Jalux near the dwarven lands are taller, but far less muscular and dangerous than those around these parts."

"Yeah that's right." Said fatty, before trying to match Vag's fancy way of speaking "I think I erd somfing to that effect."

"Indeed." she continued, "You and your companions must be both brave and capable warriors to take on so many of the terrifying beasts."

The drunkards beamed and turned their smug faces to Clamax.

"I think you need to listen to your learned colleague here. She seems more versed in the world despite her comparative youth."

Barbidon's hands clenched hard, she felt the pain of nails pressing into her palms. That tone. That face. It was exactly the same as the young bully Arque had used when taunting her back home.

"Right you are gentlemen." said Clamax, dipping his head in submission, as he moved towards the inn.

"Yeah, you just keep on walking stumpy."

It was hardly the most cutting insult to Clamax. Dwarves were generally proud of their stocky physique. He was also old and wise enough to have two criteria for starting a fight. a) Was it winnable and b) Was there something to be gained from it. This scenario only met the former.

Babs ground her teeth. As Vag and Clamax moved to go past the men, they turned their attention to the Half-Orc.

"Well hello! What have we here th..."

Babs cut the sentence short by hoisting the vocal, weasel-ish man into the air by his neck. His feet stretched out in a futile attempt to reattach to the ground.

His companions half drew their swords, Clamax and Vag whirled in alarm. Babs already had her forehead pressed against the dangling man's brow.

"Don't you ever talk to my friend like that again." Spat Babs up close. The man's eyes went wide in assent, staring down at her protruding lower canines. From two metres away they were an exotic novelty. At two centimetres, they looked disturbingly functional.

To everyone's relief, Barbidon dropped the man, who managed not to fall over. He tried various postural and facial expressions in quick succession, attempting to affect an air of nonchalance.

However, it was futile to pretend she had not shaken him like a rag doll. His friends knew it, these 'adventurers' knew it, and everyone in the entire town square knew it. What was worse, the smattering of stifled laughter made it clear they enjoyed it.

From a doorway a hundred metres away, Father Retentus observed his new allies. He struggled to make out the two groups interaction at first. But there was no mistaking it when the young Orcish woman picked the leader of the group up by his neck. Gosh, I wouldn't mind having her choke me like that, he thought absentmindedly.

A beaming smile grew on his face, born of ecstatic schadenfreude at the man's discomfort. He was sure the ruffian in question had made fun of him an hour earlier. Now Retentus bounced on his toes, delighted to have the Dwarven Paladin and this incredible creature in his 'corner'. Yes, no one would step out of line at the harvest festival with this well-timed addition to the town's guard.

Clamax reached out to Babs who was breathing heavily, still glaring broadswords at the man.

"Thank you for defending my honour lass. Now let's go get some grub."

Like a toddler distracted by a toy, the malice drained from Bab's face. She was *so* hungry. They entered the tavern. Despite being noon, the place was thrumming. The noise died down as many people eyed Barbidon with cautious curiosity. The townsfolk's wariness of her was elevated indoors.

Here the Orcish young woman with the brutal black sword threatened a potential for damage on par with a dancing minotaur in a potion shop. The noise eventually returned and when food came, Barbidon attacked it with little decorum. Enough hunger makes most meals delicious, but this food was already good.

"This tastes amazing." Said Vag.

"It's even better than amazing!" garbled Babs whilst chewing.

"It's...It's...." Babs paused, thinking of how to describe it properly with words. She thought back to Clamax teaching her about metaphors a few days ago. He had said you could sometimes call something, something else to describe it better. She creased her brow in thought, but not for long. Her brilliant intellect had found the perfect metaphor.

Relishing the moment, she picked up her second large mug of fermented goats' milk and skulled the lot. With drips of the white frothy liquid still dribbling down both sides of her lips - she declared at the top of her voice...

"It's like an orgasm inside my mouth!"

A plate dropped, someone spat out a mouthful of ale, and *everyone* in the establishment turned their dumbstruck faces towards her. Men with bulbous eyes, women had slack jaws.

Babs looked around at the sudden attention before realising their confusion. Apparently, even though she wasn't *really* smart, she was maybe more educated than many of these townsfolk. She giggled, amused at their confusion.

She stood up, emboldened by her virginal experience of alcohol. Vag reached out her arm, not sure what Babs was about, but if she extrapolated from the last comment....

Babs brushed it away affectionately, "It's fine, I've got this."

"Babs I don't thi..." Vag whisper-shouted

But it was to no avail. Babs confidently addressed the room.

"Good people of Waggle."

"Wagrum." Came a call from near the entrance.

"Sorry, Wagrum. Do not be confused. I do not mean that my mouth is actually a vagina and that it's having an orgasm." She giggled at the ludicrousness of the thought.

"It's a metaphor."

A room of blank stares continued. Perhaps saying it slower might help.

"MET-A-PHOR."

The silence grew awkward.

"Ha!" Exclaimed a well-dressed man nearby.

"Well said young lady!" He stood up and raised his glass. "To orgasms in mouths."

And with this bit of interplay, the moment went from singular strangeness to collective comedy. People started chuckling and the entire room raised their glasses in response.

"To orgasms in mouths!" They said in mis-timed chorus. More laughter followed, and lively conversation returned to the common room.

Clamax let out a breath, looking across at the man, raising a hand in thanks. He returned it with an amicable smile and went back to his meal.

"Well, now everyone knows about metaphors." said a satisfied Babs sitting down. Then in a moment of humility she realised that her education was still incomplete. Deciding this needed to be rectified, she looked to Clamax.

"Could you could teach me about all the other metas?"

Clamax looked at her in confusion.

"What do you mean?"

"Well, so far I only know about number four."

I 2

My enemy, my enemy's enemy

After paying an exorbitant fee for their lodgings (harvest festival and all), they unceremoniously dumped their kit in the small room. Clamax chivalrously insisted that the floorboards be his bed so that the ladies could sleep in comfort. They rested their well-travelled bodies for an hour before looking around the town.

"I'm worried about the Jalux." said Clamax, lying exhausted on the floor.

Vaginia and Babs lifted their heads to look at the dwarf. "The creatures those fools outside killed?" Vag asked, "What about them?"

"Not the younglings they killed. The adults they didn't."

"Oh." said Vag.

"Will they come to get even?" asked Babs

"Yes. Jalux are both intelligent hunters and known for the love with which they care for their young."

"What do they look like?" Said Babs.

"Seven feet tall and humanoid, but covered in wispy grey hair and almost canine features. They have a hungry look to them and are ferocious when hunting."

"Could they follow their tracks?" asked Vag.

"More than just follow tracks, they have a keen sense of smell."

"That could lead them to this very inn!"

"Will we have to fight them?" asked Babs, already reaching for her sword.

"Easy lass, they're night hunters. They won't come just yet."

"But you're certain they will?"

"I'm sure of it, they're not civilised, but they are intelligent enough to desire vengeance. Coming back to find their young slaughtered will not be something they'll just let slide."

"We need to get those idiots out of town so the beasts don't come here!" exclaimed Vag, now sitting up in bed.

"But how will we convince them to give up their soft beds and sleep outside?" asked Babs.

There was silence for a moment before Clamax spoke softly "Gold." He paused. "Retrievable gold."

The companions made their way to the church of the cross'ed legs. They walked on the westerly side of the street shading themselves from the baking afternoon sun. The wares in window displays fascinated Babs, be they trinkets, tools or food. There was one shop that caught Vag and Clamax's attention though: "Peter's potions and poultices." Declared an ornately designed sign. They decided it was worth a visit before they left town.

The church was the most impressive building in the main street. It had a clean white alabaster facade. Looking more closely, Vag noticed it was pock-marked in sections where the facade had fallen away and a dirty brown base material was visible underneath the false purity of white.

Above the entrance, two bent-at-the-knee crossed marble legs protruded from the building like an absurd proboscis. Unlike those decorative legs, the brown oak doors of the church were wide open.

'Clomax the chaste' entered first, feigning reverence as he stared upwards to the three storey ceiling. There were a few pious parishioners, praying at the pews, but the church felt empty, almost devoid of life. Austere, cold and without passion. Nothing like the interior of Orgasmodan's temple, he thought.

An Acolyte in off-white robes spotted them and floated over.

"Ser Clomax." She bowed deeply. "My Name is Fetishia. Analus told me of your arrival. It is an honour to meet a paladin of our order." Her eyes drifted to Babs and Vag. "Ladies." She said with less warmth and more wariness. She dipped her head almost imperceptibly. "This way please, honoured guests, his small rectory can be accessed through a rear passage."

It was almost a relief to enter a normal size room again, even if it was the private chambers of a chastity Priest. It exuded warmth, with red hued timber furnishings, polished enough to reflect a non-blinding sheen of light from the window. The silver haired Priest offset the warmth of the room.

Analus rose immediately upon seeing the Dwarf. "Ser Clomax. Welcome to my humble abode."

"Thank you, Father Retentus. An impressive church you have here in Wagrum."

Analus beamed and began talking excitedly of their 'shared' faith. Clomax knew enough of the CCL to fake interest. Barbidon's eyes were in danger of glazing over before the Priest veered onto the topic of mixed-race couplings. This was a sensitive topic given she was the product of one and Clomax's ex-wife was human.

"Anyway, we had the late Maygul's little Gnome Fayzul enter a heinous cross-race, out-of-wedlock relationship with a dryad. A dryad! Can you believe it?"

Clomax frowned.

"I note your concern ser Clomax, but rest assured, we caught the little woodland wench and burnt her at the stake.

Barbidon started clenching her fists hard.

In a moment of normally oxymoronic male intuition, Analus recognised Barbidon becoming unsettled and he finally realised who she was.

"Ah! But I apologise Lady Barbidon, I realise now, you must be the half-orc I heard had been born all those years ago! Do not be anxious young lady for the Cross'ed legs church does not blame a child for the sins of their parents." He gave Babs what could pass as a kindly smile.

Vag quickly interjected, placing a hand on Bab's leg.

"That is most benevolent of the church, and you to Father. You were saying about this Gnome Fayzul?

"Ah yes, Fayzul. He magically locked himself in the dead mage's tower and refuses to come out. I don't know how he is surviving in there without food."

Clamax saw his moment "As you have mentioned this must be a huge drain on your resources keeping him under guard. Perhaps the execution of his beloved and banishment from Wagrum is both a fitting and practical solution."

"You are wise Ser Clomax, but alas I cannot allow the Church to be seen as weak on this matter. He will surely run out of whatever food and water he has access to. Then we will make further example of the consequences of abandoning Prudishia's light."

Clamax paused just a moment before deciding it was probably prudent to not press the issue here. Maybe after wine at the harvest festival would be the moment.

"I understand." Said Clamax.

"There is another point I wanted to raise with you. I have received a credible report those brigands you met outside the inn raped a farmer's daughter on the outskirts of town yesterday."

This was common ground for both the CCL *and* Orgasmodan's followers, even if it was for different reasons. The CCL abhorred rape because sex was the sacred domain of sanctioned marriages. For Orgasmodan, consent was sacred.

Father Retentus continued. "I am not sure of their proficiency as warriors and so am fearful that using the watch to arrest them could lead to lives being lost. As a paladin, I wanted to ask your advice Ser Clomax."

"We may be able to solve two problems at once without the need for direct intervention."

"How so?"

"These men were bragging of killing Jalux younglings last night. I am certain that the adults will trace these warrior's tracks and scent tonight to seek vengeance for killing their young."

"Tonight! Are these Jalux dangerous creatures?"

"Yes. If they were to enter the town itself, they could cause tremendous collateral damage."

"The we must not let that happen!"

How wise of you thought Vag fighting to stop her eyeballs from doing a grand tour of her peripheral vision.

"Fortunately, I have a solution for you. If we could entice them with coin to sleep in a nearby paddock, this could protect the town from the Jalux and serve these ruffians a harsh punishment without the need for a confrontation."

Analus beamed "Oh, Ser Clomax, you are a wise man indeed! I will provide you with some funds from the church to act as bait."

He went over quickly to a lockbox and the unmistakeably sound of coin filled the room.

"Would 20 Silvers do it?" Analus asked.

"Twenty five might be safer Father."

"Yes, yes of course" he responded, sounding absent minded.

Analus brought the coins over and paused, just as he was about to place them in Clamax's hand.

"Do you think we will get these back?"

"We may, but unfortunately Jalux are enamoured with shiny objects. Perhaps any equipment left behind could be sold to recoup losses by the church?"

"Right... yes, of course, you make a good point." Analus drew himself up (he did that a lot) and took on a posture fit for issuing a royal decree. "Ser Clomax the Chaste, I hereby authorise you to conduct this transaction on behalf of the Wagrum branch of the CCL. With this action in place, may we protect the town and dole out justice to those seeking to disobey Prudishia's sacred laws."

Clamax, who had been uncomfortable sitting through this oddly formal decree, stood up, giving himself more personal space in the process.

"I accept this charge" he said, affecting a grave tone that would pair well with the pompous dish of a decree Father Retentus had served up.

The three visitors departed, Babs was the last out the door. Her swaying hips mesmerised Retentus as she left. "Hate to see you go but love to watch you leave." He said under his breath as Fetishia entered the room from a side entrance.

"I didn't catch what you said father."

"Oh, nothing Fetishia, I merely said I want a reprieve. You know, from all this harvest festival shenanigans."

The companions left the church pleased with the Jalux plan. They were still no closer on releasing the Gnome though. Without freeing him, they wouldn't get her hands on the onyx and marble balls needed for Vag's spell that formed the lynchpin of their 'Majestic plan'.

They made their way back to the inn, passing the potion shop again.

As they reached the open doorway, a cheery hail came from within. "To orgasm's in mouths my friends!"

They looked inside and recognised the well-dressed man from the tavern. The one that had rescued Babs from her awkward comment.

"Oh hello!" called Babs with a wave.

Clamax smiled at the man. "Thanks for stepping in at the tavern."

"You're most welcome friends! If you ever have need of tonic's elixirs or potions, please stop by. I will give you an excellent price!"

"Thank you, we'll stop by tomorrow." said Clamax. They continued to the Tavern, keen to put their plan in place.

"When we get there, could you let me speak with the brigands?" Asked Vag as the dwarf broke into one of his occasional short jogs needed to keep pace with his longer striding companions.

"But did you not hear lady Virginia." said Clamax, impersonating Analus's mannerisms and tone. "Twas I, Ser Clomax the Chaste authorised to conduct this transaction."

Babs giggled.

Vag's lips parted, "Just, trust me." She said smiling at the uncanny rendition. "You know, you could have made a fine chastity priest."

"Hmpff." Replied Clamax.

The Screaming Eagle tavern was even busier at 5pm than it had been at lunch. The brigands were not in the large common room though. Clamax went to the bar, putting up with already sozzled patrons shouting things like "Oh look a fookin dwarf!" and "How's the weather down there?"

Clamax eventually got the ear of the barkeeper, and soon after, the room number of the brigands.

"First floor, second on the right." Relayed Clamax over the boisterous noise.

"Ok, maybe wait at the top of the stairs, in-case there's trouble." Said Vag, now nervous of convincing the men to give up their room.

She walked down the hallway and knocked on the door.

"What do you want?" Came the muffled reply.

"My name is Virginia, we met earlier. I was impressed by your exploits besting the muscular Jalux."

There was a groan, someone got off a bed and stepped to the door.

It swung open, revealing the half-naked weasel of a man Babs had lifted off the ground.

"Hello again. I came to ask a favour regarding lodgings."

"Lodgings?"

"Yes lodgings, you see the dwarf and brutish woman I am travelling with have taken the two beds and are insisting I sleep on the floor."

"Not surprising, I knew they weren't good people the moment I laid eyes on them."

"Brutish indeed. Anyway, I was wondering if you would be willing to give up your room for some silver."

"Ha! Not likely, we paid a pretty penny for this room, we're not about to give it up for a few silver."

"How about twenty five silver?" countered Vag.

This gave him pause.

"Twenty five you say?"

"Yes good sir, and if it sweetens the deal, it is with silver I stole from my horrible travelling companions."

"Ha! How about that boys, you wanna sleep under the stars for 25 silver taken from that fucking dwarf and the green bitch?"

"Twenty five?"

"Yeah, twenty five."

"Fuck yeah."

The Weasel looked like he was about to give his ascent but paused.

"Why us, and not someone else's room?"

"You are brave men, and strong enough to scare aware any monsters that might be around."

"You make a good point Lady Virginia." Said Weasel, holding out his hand. "Very well, I accept"

Vag produced the purse, placing it in his paw. He couldn't help but smile when he felt the weight of it.

"You are most kind gentlemen, could I trouble you to vacate your room after dinner?"

"Yeah yeah, no problem lady." He said, closing the door.

She walked down the hallway, giving two thumbs up to her companions. Behind her, she heard excited banter coming from the room.

Dinner and the drinking afterwards was a merry, social affair. The lowering of inhibitions combined with the overall novelty of Clamax and Babs (who was less intimidating without her sword) led to numerous conversations.

Babs thought several of the men were particularly friendly. They'd been there at lunch and were asking if they could give her an orgasm in her mouth.

This made no sense as she'd already eaten and they weren't offering any food. She just sighed and shook her head. It seemed some people just couldn't understand metafours.

After dinner, the Brigands brought their packs down. Vag worried they might stay late drinking, but they headed straight to the door. Avoiding strangulation by Babs could have been a factor in this decision. They seemed to be glowering and shaking their heads at Clamax as they left. Clamax stared at them in befuddlement.

"You really should give up your bed for a lady you jerk!" Said the fattest one.

"Yeah!" Said another.

Babs immediately stood up and raised her voice. "Jerk? Jerk?! Why I'll Jerk you!!!" She started moving towards them with teeth bared, but they were out the door in a flash and into the night.

Her face instantly reverted to its beautifully innocent smile and asked, "Who's up for another drink?"

Vag left quietly a moment later to check the direction they went to camp before returning to the lively din of the common room. Clamax, feeling like curmudgeonly father, encouraged both girls to bed. They were reluctant given the merriment at hand.

When upstairs, Clamax explained he wanted to wake early to confirm the Jalux had taken care of the men. He took the room of the arrogant brigands, paid for with 25 silver by his organisational nemesis, the church of the cross'ed legs, all so they could be murdered in their sleep.

The only thing that would make this night any more perfect was if Babs decided she wanted to experiment with an old dwarf and the Jalux left the silver behind.

-

The Jalux left the silver behind.

They also left the Brigands corpses, presumably not enjoying the taste of humans. They also cared nothing about shiny things. This was vengeance, nothing more. Clamax was pleased to feel the weight of silver in his hand as he surveyed the carnage of the brigands' camp. He spotted Father Retentus and the acolyte Fetishia through the early morning light and quickly pocketed it.

The companions waved them over, and they strode quickly to the scene.

"Wow, they made a mess" was Analus's statement of the literally bleeding obvious. "Did they leave the silver behind?

"Unfortunately not father, but they left weapons, armour and some other equipment which when sold will hopefully be able to recoup the Church's expenses."

Analus lifted his robe and waded through the remains noting the sword and some pieces of armour were serviceable "Yes you are right Ser Clomax, these will indeed help reimburse the church. you've done excellent work here. Wagrum owes you a huge debt of gratitude, I would like to make you my guest of honour at tonight's Harvest festival banquet."

"You are most kind Father, it would be my honour. I remain a little concerned for the moral security at this event though, as you stated yourself, the town watch is spread thin. Would it be best to let this Gnome Fayzul flee in exile and free up men for tonight's event?"

Analus listened to Clamax attentively before answering gravely. "Your concern does you credit Ser Clomax, but to speak plainly I am as worried about the town's watch being tempted by carnal pleasures as I am the rest of my flock. Besides, I have had Fayzul under guard for 4 months now, I can't throw the effort to capture him away because of one party."

To Clamax that sounded a lot like chasing after sunk costs. Resolving to find a different solution, he nodded. "Of course, you are wise Father."

"Well, let's hope the revelry remains sensible and our shared worries come to naught."

Analus turned to his young female acolyte, who looked in morbid fascination at the scene before them. "Fetishia. Take these weapons and leather armour up to town for sale." She went to unclasp the armour but paused.

"Oh come on Fetishia. Don't act like you've never handled sticky leather before."

Back in screaming Eagle's common room, the companions ate a hearty porridge, fretting.

"I've asked him twice." said a despondent Clamax. "Asking a third time will not change his mind. Have you got some magic spell that could somehow get Fayzul out?"

"Not without needlessly killing the guards." Said Vag. "If I only had a sleep spell."

Babs looked up after destroying her second bowl. "It would be good if people just stopped listening to what he told them to do."

Vag blinked before her face suddenly lit up. "Babs you're a genius" She declared without irony. "I've got an idea. But Clamax, you're going to have to pretend you have a problem, down... there." Vag gave a pointed looked to his crotch.

"What?"

"The potion shop. He might have an elixir of the glorious morning wood tree."

"Oh no you don't." Hissed Clamax leaning forward so his head was close to the table. "I'm not going into Pete's potions and poultices as an impotent paladin of Prudishia!"

"I think you're important" said Babs encouragingly.

"Come on Ser Clomax." Said Vag, unsuccessfully attempting an earnest expression. "You'd be doing it for Orgasmodan, not for me."

A little bell above the door trilled as the mighty Ser Clomax entered Pete's potion shop. Babs and Vag stayed near the entrance whilst Clamax coyly approached the proprietor.

"Hello again friend! What can I do for a sturdy adventurer like you and your merry band? A potion to aid sleep? Curing spider poison or... perhaps the most valuable item in my entire shop. An extraordinarily rare potion of strength?" He looked pointedly in Bab's direction. "Imagine what she could do with two minutes of giants strength."

"Er... nothing like that today," Clamax began, scratching the back of his neck. "you see... I have this friend, and he has just been married."

"You must be very happy for him." Smiled Pete.

"Yes, very happy for him, though he mentioned that often his... equipment, does not stand to strict parade attention. If you catch my meaning."

Clamax thought he heard Vag giggle from the front of the shop. Pete was all thoughtful professionalism.

"Your friend is fortunate to have someone with whom he can confide such personal matters with. He is doubly lucky that I have just the thing to help him with his troubles."

Pete went out back and returned a minute later. To Clamax it felt like an eternity. With a modest flourish he produced for Clamax a vial of red fluid. He leant forward and said in a hushed tone inaudible to the girls. "Behold the distilled sap of the glorious morning wood tree. Just a droplet of this and your friend will stand prouder than a newly promoted Sergeant".

"Excellent, he and his wife will be most grateful. The only thing is, my friend is also a dwarf and the hearty constitution might..."

"Of course, say no more." said Pete, producing a second vial, almost as if he knew Clamax's 'friend' was also a dwarf. For a moment Clamax thought he saw a hint of a smile on Pete's face. It disappeared quickly, leaving the dwarf wondering if he'd imagined it.

"For a Dwarf, I would recommend two droplets. This supply should last him at least 30..." Pete paused, thinking of the right word. "encounters. Please make sure he is careful not to exceed the dose. There can be such a thing as too much libido."

The bell on the shop rang again as a female customer entered immediately walking towards the counter.

"Of course." Stammered Clamax "How much for both?"

"Just 25 silver for you sir."

Clamax produced the coin and quickly buried the vials in his cloak as the woman came up to the counter.

"Is there anything else I can help you with?" asked Pete of the departing Dwarf.

"Actually yes. maybe I will take a look at that potion of giant strength."

13

Hard Liquor

"It doesn't get much better than this." Observed Clamax, staring at the idyllic late afternoon scene. The harvest festival banquet was getting started in a paddock on the outskirts of town. The same paddock in fact, where three recently deceased (and hastily buried) brigands had commenced their forever-careers improving soil fertility.

It was a lazy, summer evening. Tonight would be a full moon, though father Retentus added to the promised illumination. Dressed in his fanciest robe, he walked along rows of 6 foot stakes, casting a light spell atop each.

He saw the companions and came over with Fetishia in tow to greet them. "Lady Virginia, Lady Barbidon and Ser Clomax. I hope Prudishia will not mind me stating how lovely you look this evening ladies."

Babs giggled a thank you, Vag gave a curt nod to acknowledge the compliment and Fetishia cast a sidelong glance at the Priest. Retentus wasn't wrong. The hands of hairdressing had gone close to getting RSI working on their hair.

Vag's swirled upwards in an ornate tower that wouldn't have looked out of place on a princess. Babs had an asymmetrical version of her new style, with tight braids running one side. Vag had again asked Clamax if he wanted them to 'do' him (he assumed she meant his hair) but declined. "After all," he'd said, "I'm a middle-aged male dwarf, nobody cares what my hair looks like."

Fetishia ushered them over to the head table. Clamax was to be the right-hand man of Father Retentus. This seemed perfectly proper for a visiting Paladin of their order. What was odd, most odd indeed, was that he'd asked for the muscular Orcish girl to be immediately on his left. Fetishia thought it would have been more appropriate for Lady Virginia, the watch sergeant... or even, would it be too much to ask, herself to take that seat?

Almost four hundred people flocked to the festive paddock. The food was plentiful and they quickly set ale to work, bringing tomorrow's joy forward and pushing today's pain back.

Whilst most people sat on the gently sloping grass, the main table was at the flatter base of the hill with a dancing space in front. The effect was a natural amphitheatre where all eyes could watch the talented, (or drunk) revellers dancing, jugglers juggling and the important people importanting.

The grand table comprised a few well-to-do merchants, the sergeant of the watch, Fetishia and the companions. The half-orc warrior woman was still a novelty. The dwarf too, but the looks directed at him were only glances, given he was little more than a short, bearded man.

Barbidon, being more exotic in her appearance and was stared at for a myriad of reasons. The women, in prudishness or jealousy thought there was too much sensual flesh on display. To the men, there was almost enough. To the children she was an approachable monster.

After one brave child established her friendliness, the dam wall of cautiousness burst open, leaving her surrounded by curious youngsters.

Fetishia sat at an end of the grand table. It was not where she should be. To make matters worse, she observed Father Retentus, letting his hair down too much with the evening's festivities. He was even trying to keep up with Ser Clomax's ale consumption.

She did not judge the dwarf, everybody knew it took a lot to make the stocky fellows drunk. Father Retentus however, was not a big drinker and would need to slow down if he was to deliver his speech with the dignity his office deserved.

The potion merchant Peter Tylor sat next to Fetishia. Peter was not interested in talking to the Prudishian nun though. He was far more interested in observing the newcomers on his table.

They were such a curious bunch he thought. Barbidon was obviously an aberration, but there was also something about lady Virginia that went beyond her cover story. Then there was Ser Clomax, the aphrodisiac purchasing paladin. He may wear a tabard with the Cross'ed legs stitched front and back, but he didn't fit the mould of a devout CCL member.

Before the feast's second course, Peter observed lady Virginia do an absent minded movement with her hand.

He thought he saw a strange flicker above the Priest a slight blurring of the stars above his head. It vanished just as quickly, leaving him wondering if he'd seen it at all. Perhaps it was just the ale he'd drunk. He must have been subconsciously keeping up with the dwarf who definitely set the drinking pace.

Vag was relieved to get the second vial of glorious mornings into Father Retentus's third mug of ale. At one point her heart sunk when it seemed the potion merchant had seen her ethereal hands of hairdressing perform the deed, but the moment passed and he did not raise any alarm. Oh well, Vag thought, you're complicit now as it's your potion about to wreak havoc. The hands of hairdressing were definitely handy.

She watched Retentus for signs the elixir was working. It was. He looked unsettled, like he was fighting an urge. But, duty being duty, he tapped his glass with a spoon. Others followed suit, and the musicians stopped playing. Soon, the only noises in the paddock were from unquietable infants.

Oddly enough, Retentus did not stand, he began his speech seated.

"Good men, *and women* of Wagrum. We are gathered here in these undulating hills" He cast a side-long glance at Babs. "To celebrate the bountiful harvest," He looked for an awkwardly long moment at her chest. "That Prudishia has bestowed upon us. We have some honoured guests with us today.

Ser Clomax the Chaste, A paladin of the order sits today on my right. Could you stand for the crowd please?"

Clamax, who was taking little interest in the speech, was taken aback to find himself an active participant. He duly got off his chair and stood, though it was pointless given it made him no taller.

"Stand up!" Came a heckle on the hill. Many laughed at this, including Clamax, endearing him to the crowd.

"And to my left, I have the magnificent warrior Barbidon. Could you stand up please Lady Barbidon?" Barbidon stood up and gave a sheepish wave to the crowd.

"Barbidon" Father Retentus continued, "Is a stunning example of what Prudishia can create out of the ashes of sin." There were some murmurings at this oddly lascivious statement. Fetishia was particularly concerned at the tone of speech. Yes, by all means introduce Ser Clomax, but why all this attention on a Half-Orc girl? She put her chair back to go over to him before he made a fool of himself.

"Those muscular thighs..."

Barbidon smiled

"Proud buttocks..."

Barbidon frowned

"And magnificent breasts, that you just need to..."

The end of the sentence was inaudible to everyone, except Barbidon's sternum, as Retentus jumped up and buried his face in her cleavage.

A collective gasp of shock went up from everyone, and not just for the ridiculous display of a Chastity priest helping himself to a breast buffet. The other reason for shock was because, by standing up, Retentus had revealed to the world a monstrously thick ten inch erection. One which he now furiously pumped for release.

"What kind of messed up god puts a cock like that on a Chastity Priest?" Mumbled Vag in shock. "It's like putting wings on a Pumpkin."

After recovering from the shock, Babs uttered a loud "Ewwwww!" Grabbing his head with both hands, she extracted the crazed priest from her person, pushing him backwards. He was flung into the alarmed Fetishia who had rushed over to stop this outrageous display. After a split second, he recognised her and ripped off her robes in one inhumanly strong motion.

Barbidon was capable of defending herself, Fetishia was not, so Clamax and the watch-Sergeant crash tackled the crazed priest. Fetishia screamed in shock and embarrassment standing naked in front of the town.

"Might be the same god that put perfect perky c-cups on a chastity nun?" Said a voice in Vag's ear. She turned with alarm, having meant to internalise her last comment. The smile on Pete's face suggested the very public, and very *pubic* disgrace of the CCL priest also amused him.

After restraining Retentus, Clamax left him in the capable hands of the Watch Sergeant. Fetishia, shaken from the ordeal, was attended by an obliging female parishioner who covered her in their cloak.

It dawned on Clamax that as a senior member of the CCL, it was probably up to him to settle down proceedings. He had never been one to seek out the limelight and his right hand trembled at the prospect of speaking to so many people. Standing on his chair, he dinged his glass. It took noticeably longer to quieten the crowd down.

A third of the town were dismayed by what had just happened, but the majority clearly thought it was hilarious, and were still laughing at the spectacle.

"Good people of Wagrum." Clamax began with a booming tone that cut through the hubbub.

"I think we can all agree the unforgiveable and frankly odd behaviour of Father Retentus renders him unfit to lead you. I will have discussions with Sister Fetishia about the Church's leadership in Wagrum before I leave for the Citadel tomorrow. We will not let this unfortunate event put a dampener on tonight's proceedings though. I encourage you to continue celebrating your hard work with the Harvest. Drink and be merry! But remember one thing. The first law of the true church is consent. Always make sure both parties give consent."

Babs clapped loudly at the end of Clamax's Speech, leading a smattering of applause amongst the townsfolk.

"I liked what you said about consent." Said Babs. "What Father Anus did really grossed me out. I still have his spit all over my boobs!" Babs spotted a napkin on the table and began soaking up the saliva.

The companions did not drink heavily that evening. They wanted to complete the deal that had brought them into town in the first place; getting the onyx and marble balls Vag needed for their 'Majestic plan'.

14

Goods in exchange

The town was hungover the following morning, so most shops were still closed when the companions exited the screaming eagle. One shop doing some occasional trade was Pete's Potions. He had set up a table out front with a single product on it: Pete's hangover remedy.

As they approached on route to the Church, Pete looked up and beamed upon seeing the trio. "Welcome friends! Can I interest you in an affordable tonic for a sore head?"

"Er, thank you, but we are okay this morning." Replied Clamax

"The rumours of dwarven constitution must real. Tell me how did your friend go with his little problem?" Pete had an enormous I-know-what-you-did grin plastered on his face.

Clamax looked sheepish, and whilst not comfortable admitting too much, replied, "Yes, thank you. Perhaps a larger success than I imagined."

"Well said sir, well said. So, are you leaving our town now Ser Clomax?"

"Yes, off the Citadel."

"Well, safe travels then, I hope you all make as big an impression on Del, as you did on our humble town." He smiled and waved goodbye, before turning back to his wares, shaking his head with a grin that took a while to fade.

Clamax opened the doors to the church. Fetishia rushed to greet him, clothed in a replacement robe. "Ser Clomax, it is good to see you again. I apologise that I was too shocked to thank you for pulling Father Analus off my person last night."

"I'm only sorry to have not acted sooner sister."

"It was very embarrassing to be sure, but please do not blame yourself. The culpability lies with that hideous man, and with him alone. You know Ser Clomax, I did notice him acting a little peculiarly since your arrival."

"I too." Nodded Vag gravely.

"Tis a sad truth that the most sanctimonious are those externalising anger for their own sin." Said Clamax.

"Wise words, I feel I must call upon that wisdom to guide me for these days ahead ser Clomax. Especially as the church's standing was so damaged by last night's scandal."

"You are kind with your praise sister. I do have time to offer advice. First and foremost is the long-term expense of keeping this gnome Fayzul under guard. If, Prudishia forbid, there is unrest because of Father Retentus's behaviour, you would be wise to have all your watch on hand, not two kilometres out of town. Exile the gnome for his sin and let months of house arrest and the execution of his lover stand as his punishment."

"Thank you, I will action that immediately."

"Another thing, now may not the time to be too harsh on interatrial or same sex dalliances. It might come across as..." Clamax searched for the right word', "hypocritical, given the recent actions of the town's priest."

"I see." said Fetishia. "Yes I suppose that would be prudent." A frown suggested this went against her natural judgement.

Clamax stayed for a short time, generally trying to water down the church's more brutal policies. The most important thing, had been securing a sentence of exile for the gnome Fayzul. Fetishia affixed the decree with the wax seal imprint of Retentus's confiscated signet ring.

They offered to personally deliver the message to both Fayzul and his guards. Fetishia accepted the offer, and they said their farewells. When at the door to leave, Fetishia called across the empty church.

"It is actually the 7th law of Prudishia, not the 1st Ser Clomax."

"I'm sorry lass, what do you mean?"

"Last night in your Festival speech. You said the true church's first and most important law is that of consent."

"Oh, I didn't realise I said that." said Clamax. "I must have been a bit muddled and in shock. Though I do think consent could be elevated in importance, especially as it is women who often suffer when it is disregarded, even in marriage."

Fetishia looked thoughtful. The CCL's only exception on consent was when a husband took liberties with his wife. "Indeed." said Fetishia, looking like she'd been a perfectly watertight argument against an unquestioned belief. The companions turned again to leave the town, not waiting for her to resolve her cognitive dissonance.

The guards gladly finished their shift early upon seeing the letter. They'd partied well into the night and were desperate for sleep. The companions wished them a good rest before turning their attention back to the tower.

The only distinguishing feature at the front of the structure was its main entrance. The oak doors were obscured by a shimmering barrier, clearly magical in nature. So, they went to the rear arrow slit window and called out.

"Fayzul! It is Vaginia, I was here two days ago. We have secured your freedom!"

There was an audible commotion before an eye appeared in the second storey slit.

"Really?" Fayzul exclaimed. "Do you have a declaration from the Church?"

"We do, though I'm sorry to advise it's conditional on your exile from Wagrum." Vag used her hands of hairdressing to send the letter with the church's seal.

"Oh, that's okay." replied Fayzul, "Branchilla and I will probably decide to leave this place anyway once reunited." He grabbed the letter and read it.

"This is amazing!" Fayzul declared, just as Vag said;

"About that."

Fayzul didn't hear. "I cannot wait to see her again!"

"Fayzul, I have some terrible news." There was a pause. His eye went to the slit again, but it was downcast this time.

"Father Analus Retentus told us of a Dryad he captured and burnt at the stake because of your relationship. I'm so sorry Fayzul."

There was a long pause, then a longer one. Vag thought she heard silent anguish from the arrow slit, it was clearly the sort of grief that is so intense and private that almost no noise comes out.

"Fayzul?"

"It's okay," said Fayzul, followed by an audible sniff. "In my more honest moments of reflection I'd suspected as much. After all, she hasn't made contact for months." There was another pause. "I suppose you should enter then, come around to front and I'll lower the barrier for you."

The companions got to the front door in time to see the shimmering barrier dissipate. Babs took the honours, pulling both doors open in style. The sight of a small humanoid with eyes a little red from crying greeted her.

"Oh, he's adorable!" she cooed, scooping up the alarmed gnome and pulling him to her chest, inadvertently burying his head in her cleavage. "We need to talk to your daddy, is he home?"

A perplexed Fayzul looked in two minds whether he should clear up the confusion, or return to his unexpected deep dive into Bab's mammarian ocean.

In the end, Clamax cleared it up.

"Ahem. Babs, I believe this is Fayzul himself. Gnomes have a wee stature you see, but he's a fully grown adult."

"Oh." said Babs, holding out a blushing Fayzul and setting him down. "Sorry about that. You really are very cute though."

"Er, thank you miss..."

"Barbidon, but you can call me Babs."

"I'm Clamax." said the Dwarf, holding out his hand.

Vaginia held out her hand, but she couldn't hold back her excitement anymore. "Oh Fayzul, it is so exciting to meet another living magic user!"

Fayzul gently shook his head. "I was not his apprentice per se, more a helper. But I am honoured to meet another magic user myself." He backed this up with a slight bow.

"But... the flying note?"

"Oh that? Nothing really, I call them paper aerodragons. They're not magical though, just physics."

"Physics?" Enquired Vag.

"Physics. The laws governing the movement of objects in the absence of magic. For example, a dragon can glide downwards without arcane intervention, it is just a matter of the air catching under its wings."

"Very clever." Said Vag, genuinely impressed.

"Kind of you to say, though I confess I learnt it from my Master Maygul before he passed away. But please, where are my manners, come up the second floor, I can show you some items to show my gratitude."

Fayzul took them up stairs that hugged the inner circumference of the tower. The interior decor theme was 'decayed luxury'. Tapestries lined the walls, whilst a large circular worn-out carpet filled the floor. A heavily populated book case stood proudly against the opposing wall.

"How did you survive here for so long?" Asked Clamax.

"Oh, Maygul created an arcane food creator years ago, and a displacement latrine. I was fortunate I didn't need to live in my own filth. I really could have lived the rest of my life here, but I did get terribly bored."

"What's a displacement latrine?" asked Clamax

"It's a portal of sorts to make sure your waste ends up somewhere else."

"Where exactly?"

Fayzul shrugged, a little perplexed at her faecal fascination. "Don't know. Don't really want to know either."

"It sounds like something I've read about called a 'paired portal ring', do you mind if I take a look at it?"

"Sure, I won't need it anymore once I leave this place."

Fayzul took them to the top level of the three-storey tower. Two single beds, one of them Fayzul sized, took pride of place. A robe, clearly belonging to the Late Maygul, hung in the air beside the larger bed on a coat-hanger with no visible means of support. One side of the floor contained a tiny room that was the privy. Sure enough, the blue ring around a two foot wide black abyss looked exactly like the paired portal rings she had read about in one of the necromancers books. They could be placed in distant locations, 'if you needed the other one back, you could reach through one to retrieve the other.

Trying hard not to imagine the image that would greet her if she stuck her head through the portal, she reached just inside the blackness on the outer rim. Sure enough, Vag was able to feel the outer rim of a second portal. Grabbing it, she tugged hard, pulling it away from its resting place. A moment later it emerged in her hand from the blackness. She pulled the first one up from the floor, leaving her holding a floppy blue ring in each hand.

Everyone was impressed at the feat, Barbidon clapped with a broad smile on her face.

"It's such a shame Maygul didn't explain how these worked. You could have thrown one of these onto the ground, away from the guard's one night and been on your merry way."

"Oh." Said Fayzul's, realising that he had just suffered months of unnecessary incarceration. Eager to not reflect on this for too long, he remembered the marble and onyx balls promised in exchange for his freedom. He went to a small box on a desk and produced the two smooth balls, one inky black, the other a beautiful marble white. His tiny hands cupped one in each as he held them out reverently for Vag.

"Have you got a plan for your spell?" asked the gnome with a wry smile.

"I might have a plan." Said Vag, matching his expression.

"It's a majestic plan." Chimed in Babs with a knowing smile. An ironic 'knowing smile', given there was no knowledge backing it up.

"Well, it's not for me to know your business. As a further token of my gratitude there is a spare bag of holding here, I only need one, so you're welcome to it."

"What is the deal with this coat hanger." Asked Vag pointing towards the gravity defying rod holding up Maygul's robe.

Fayzul went over and took the robe off it. The coat hanger stayed suspended mid-air. It was a little rod with a dull metallic sheen and a button on it.

"I've always thought it a silly thing, you can have it if you want it?" He tossed it to Vag. She noted the coat hanger was magical by its Aura.

"What happens if you press the button?" she asked.

"Nothing." Said Fayzul

"Nothing?"

"When you press it, the hanger becomes completely immovable. I'd only ever used it to hang wet clothes on after washing them."

"Anyway, I've packed own my bag and I am keen to get going, you're free to take anything else you'd like from the tower. I certainly won't be coming back here ever again."

"Your bag of holding?" Said Vag, half question, half statement.

Fayzul's expression turned to distrust, and he put his body between his bag and the companions.

"Now I've given you the balls you asked for and I'll even let you have the portable portal potty, but this is bag is mine."

Seeing the fear on his face, Vag quickly sought to set him straight. "Oh Fayzul, I don't covet your belongings. It's just that that with a bag of holding, you could've positioned yourself on the parapets of the tower, put your body inside a bag, used an outstretched arm to push the bag off the edge, then crawled out of the bag once it landed outside and made your escape?"

"Oh." Replied Fayzul, looking even more downcast as the list of unrealised escape methods grew. "Well, take whatever you want that remains. Oh, do you want a meal before you leave?"

Babs head snapped up. "I like food."

Fayzul smiled, "Well come this way miss Babs, and stand before this device. Now, what food would you like to eat?"

"Roast pork!"

There was a gentle 'Ding' and a large plate of Roast pork appeared in front of Babs.

"Wow, that's amazing!" said Babs through a mouth of pork that was somehow already in her mouth.

Fayzul smiled and waved his goodbyes, eager to leave his prison cell.

"Fayzul!" Vag called out. "How would we reactivate the magical barrier on the front door?"

"Why would you want to lock yourself in here?"

"Oh, I'm just curious how the magic works."

"It's just a blue button at the top of the stairs we came up." Responded Fayzul from entrance.

"Thank you! And safe travels!" Shouted Vag.

And with that, the companions were alone, finding themselves rather abruptly the new custodians of Maygul's tower.

"Why do you actually need to lock the front door?" Asked Clamax.

"Two reasons. Firstly, I can keep Maygul's spell books safe here without transporting them. And secondly, with these portable portals, I can come back anytime to study them, or...." Vag moved over to the magical oven, "Come back for unlimited free food."

Babs looked over wide-eyed, "You mean?"

"Yes Babs." Said Vag with an impish smile. "We can travel far from this place but return in an instant if you're hungry."

Babs did a very un-orcish squeal, rushed over to Vag and hugged her off the ground.

"I love you." Said Babs, tears forming in her eyes. "You're so clever!"

"I love you too Babs." said Vag from the side of her mouth not buried in breast.

"Why didn't Fayzul want the portals himself so he could do something similar." Said Clamax, stroking his beard.

Vag's lips struggled to contain a fresh cream pie as she smiled "I don't think he thought of it."

After a feed, Clamax and Babs went outside with one of the portal rings. Vag turned on the magical barrier to bar the front door, set the second portal on the ground and climbed into it. The gravity reversal between portals was unnerving. She was grateful for Babs' strength, pulling her out of the ground outside the tower. They picked up the outside portal ring, stowed it, leaving the other ring in the tower ready to return whenever needed.

Full of food, the companions set a cracking pace for the Citadel, or 'Del', as the inhabitants called it. It was a sturdy, busy road. By afternoon tea, they could make out the spires of Del's keep. Traffic increased the closer they got, as outlying farms took produce into the Queendom's largest market.

Everyone was human. As a result, Clamax received many stares, and Babs more. The only kindred anomaly was a formally dressed Elf with two armoured guards who rode past late in the afternoon.

The rhythmic trotting first drew the attention of the companions, who turned to take their turn at staring. The noble-looking elf had a bored look on his face, eyes apathetically chewing on the countryside to his left. His foreground quickly filled with the 6'4 Half Orc, trailing a Dwarf. Both parties stared at each other, mutual novelties in a swarm of sameness. The Dwarf doffed a non-existent cap at the Elf.

He returned the gesture with a smile. "Greetings. It seems we both find ourselves a long way from home."

"I've come to accept roads are my home, haven't seen the Dwarven lands since I was a boy." Said Clamax, walking up to the mounted Elf. He reached up on his tippy toes for a handshake. "Names Clomax. This is lady Virginia, and this is Barbidon."

"Presley." Said the Elf, not bothering to introducing his guards. "Are you in Del for long? I do not expect the warmest of greetings during my stay. Might be nice to share a meal with some fellow outsiders whilst I'm in the Citadel?"

"Not sure, but at least a few days I should think?"

"Excellent. Always interested to hear tales from the well-travelled. Know where you are staying?"

"Not a clue Sir."

"Ha, never mind. We are an Elf and a Dwarf in a City of Humans. I'm sure our paths will cross. Good day ladies, Clomax." With that, Presley gave his horse a gentle spur and the three elves rode ahead.

"Who was he, do you think?" asked Babs.

"Probably an Ambassador, judging from the armour his guards wore."

15

⚜

117

Symbolism salad

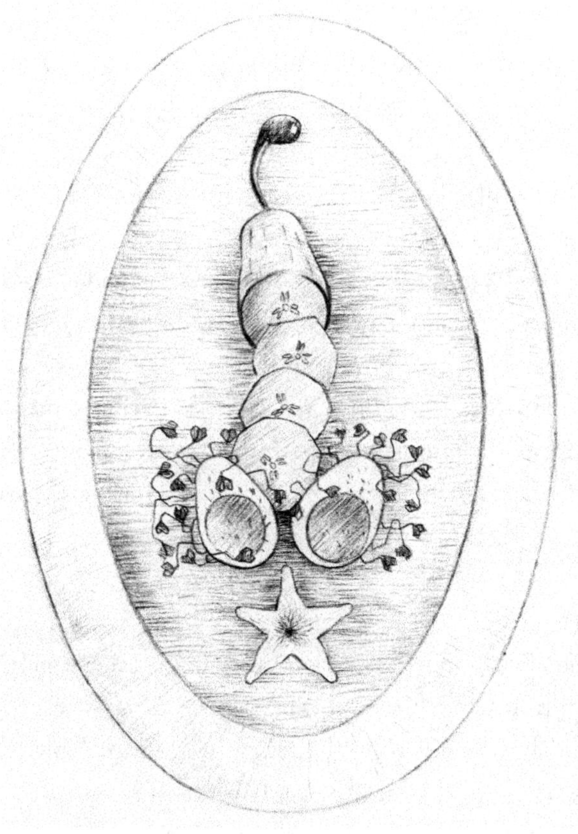

In the Centre of Del, High-Priest Virgun Blueballus of the CCL walked the halls of the keep. It was proper that he not just restrict his conversation to the elders at court. It was just as important he mingled with the young servants behind the scenes. After all, they were the pulsing lifeblood of the Castle.

Virgun soon found himself in the kitchens. Seeing a young apprentice chef he'd chatted with before, he waved a hello. Such a lively young lad, Virgun thought. Twink looked to be on the younger side of twenty, exuding youth and vigour. Clean shaven, a lithe supple figure and with an excellent set of clean white teeth. He wore a stained apron, but that didn't bother Virgun, for it was a sign of the lads willingness to get in and do things, whether bending over a hot oven to inspect a sausage pizza, or taking a turn at the pig on spit.

"Master Twink. It is very good to see you today young lad!"

"Your grace." said Twink, with a smile that brightened the entire room. "Is there anything I can get for you today?"

"Oh, you are very kind to ask lad. Perhaps just a salad would be nice. I'm trying to stay trim at the moment." He leaned forward with a wink to Twink and patted his stomach. A stomach tightly constrained in a hidden girdle beneath his robes.

"Wise choice your grace." Said Twink, winking back. "I have just the salad for you. A new style I've developed."

Virgun watched the young chef get to work, speedily sourcing the various ingredients from around the kitchen. In no time at all, he'd gently placed a plate in front of the priest.

"I give you..." Twink paused for dramatic effect, standing side-on and drawing his breath in, like an artist about to reveal a masterpiece. "Genitalia salad!"

One of the other Chef's snorted. Virgun focused on the beautifully arrayed salad before him.

Closest to him was a single slice of Star fruit. Two halves of a boiled egg were positioned centre left and centre right under a sizeable clump of Alfalfa. Extending to the opposite side of the plate was a sliced cucumber, still formed with a dollop of mayonnaise dressing at its zenith.

"It looks wonderful master Twink."

"Thank you." said the young culinary artist as he went to get a knife and fork for his guest. "The Baallllsamic mayonnaise helps the cucumber slide down the throat so smoothly"

Virgun licked his lips, "Fascinating, I can't wait to put it in my mouth."

Twink returned with the cutlery.

"Your grace, would you like your salad tossed first"

There was another snort from the same chef as before.

"No thank you. I am not so old to be incapable of tossing my own salad"

"Your grace must be very flexible."

"Well one need not be that flexible to toss one's own salad." Said Virgun, a little confused, as he preceded to toss with a flourish.

"Genitalia salad you say.. hmm I like it. I wish mine was larger."

"A bigger cucumber next time, my lord?"

"Yes, exactly, though I did find the star fruit a little puckery."

"Apologies your grace, yes it does tend to pucker."

The other chef let out yet another stifled snort.

Now a less observant highborn might have cared little for the welfare of lowly kitchen workers, but Virgun prided himself on picking up on subtle clues with people. He therefore went over to the older kitchen hand.

"Are you alright man, you seem to be snorting a lot?"

"Apologies your grace, tis nothing."

"I'm not sure about that." frowned Virgun, noting the man's eyes looked a little red and teary. "I will send a doctor down to look you over. We can't have our workers getting sick, especially those preparing meals for her majesty."

Virgun turned to leave, "Thank you master Twink excellent work."

Twink smiled that wonderful smile again and bowed deeply. "Your grace."

The high priest strode back down the hall to his quarters. He was rather pleased with himself, for not only had he been able to grace the honest workers of the keep with his presence, he'd also applied his superior powers of observation to spot the ill kitchen hand needed a doctor. Yes, not much gets past the attention of Virgun Blueballus he mused.

16

Four skinny cocks

Fellatio Jackhammer felt like banging his head against the approaching city wall. The return journey to Del had been frustratingly slow. A trip that should have taken two days, had instead taken four. His men weren't the problem. It was the horses.

He had been right to forbid his troops from drinking the powerful sin-inducing waters tainted by Orgasmodan's Phallus. His failing, was not ordering the horses kept away from it too.

The result had been days of unbridled equine passion. Well, this would not be *entirely* true, given the horses were, in fact bridled, but it captures their mood well enough. Even geldings were constantly mounting mares, whose startled riders felt the sort of crushing force a genitally located whale barnacle feels when not consulted about coitus.

It was late afternoon, so they competed with the exodus of the Citadel's daytime population. This was a regular event on Mondays, Wednesdays and Fridays after market trade quietened. Farmers that had travelled in to sell their wares would return home to their farms. Of course, the Queen's forces took precedent. Farmers made way for the column of soldiers, who by this stage were thoroughly tired of playing passive participants to the pony porno of the last four days.

There were some other exceptions to the outward flow of humanity from the city's main gate. Sir Richard Longsword, second in command below Fellatio spotted a noble with two guards in Elven style armour pass under the large arch from another merging road. The other oddity Sir Richard noticed was a trio of adventurers standing to the side to let the twice 'mounted' cavalrymen pass. There was a woman with a fancy hairdo beside a dwarf with a CCL tabard (which was peculiar enough). The oddest thing however was a huge Orcish looking girl, with a noteworthy physique.

Clamax watched the soldiers with disdain. He suspected these men were returning from an attack on Orgasmodan's temple. They looked a ragged bunch, even more pathetic for the slack-jaws many had as they passed Barbidon.

The most ragged of all was a bound and gagged elven woman, stumbling as she struggled to keep up with the horse she was tied to. His heart sank as he recognised her. It was Ovula, high priestess of Orgasmodan. She lifted her battered face to the words above the city gates. 'Redemption Through Purity'. Her face drifted right and her eyes rested directly on Clamax. Shock and excitement registered on her face for a moment before she collected herself.

Clamax was heartbroken to see his wonderful mentor in this state. The worst moment however, was when her gaze drifted downwards to the cross'ed legs embroidered on his chest. The look of confusion followed by pained disappointment that flowed over her face was difficult for him to bare. He realised how this must look, that he had abandoned Orgasmodan, or even worse, turned traitor and given away the location of their sacred temple.

He wished he could go to her, explain it was just a disguise, but it was impossible to communicate the sequence of events leading to that moment through two seconds of facial expressions. A moment later she was past him, past explanation, enveloped by the mass of humanity that was Del.

Eventually the last of the column, an overweight man with a ripped shirt, passed through the gate. The companions followed behind him. Clamax's CCL embroidered tabard aided their entry, which may have been difficult with an armed half-orc in their party. And so it was, on the 59th day of the 1st month of the year 8008, that Barbidon entered the bustling metropolis of Del.

She entered the city with wide-eyed awe, naïve of her future impact on the busy momentum of routine. Like a cow about to cross an eight-lane freeway.

"Do we look for lodgings or find somewhere secluded we can stick a portal for the night and go back to our tower?

"There are so many people around." said Vag. "I worry a two foot wide black portal would risk discovery no matter where we put it."

"Let's get the smallest room we can find with a lock." Said Clamax. Funds were tight, given most of his recent brigand inheritance had gone on the giant strength potion in Wagrum.

"And then we get food?"

"Yes Babs, then food."

From a distance, Del looked sleepy and at peace. Up close, a tremendous ecology of activity became evident, like inspecting a dead dog on an anthill.

Babs was in awe of the throng. She was *not*, in awe of the smell.

Del had a population of three hundred thousand people, almost twice as many armpits and a million anuses, once you included the vermin. None of those sphincters ever spoke to a flushable toilet. Then there were the hundreds of cooking spices wafting in the air. It was the nasal equivalent of standing between seventeen brass bands, all playing different songs.

The first Inn they found had an elaborate picture of four lean roosters above the name. It depicted them in the midst of a rooster battle royale.

'The Four Skinny Cocks' was a large, old but well-maintained establishment. The ground floor had a busy common room with beer garden out back. Clamax saw a sign to lodgings at the side of the room and made a B-Line for it. He was almost as hungry as Babs. Suddenly conscious of the religious symbol on chest he swung his pack around front, covering it up.

They captured enough attention as it was. Del was definitely more multi-racial than Wagrum, but it was hardly a cultural melting pot. As usual, Babs stood out. The old clerk at the accommodations/coat rack desk looked up from his reading glasses at the unlikely trio with a lazy eye and another, more wary one.

"Welcome to the Four skinny cocks, looking for lodgings?"

"Yes." said Clamax awkwardly. "Just your smallest room please."

"Our smallest room has only one bed, sir."

"Oh that's fine, I'm the only one sleeping here tonight, though, ah, the others might put their gear in my room."

"*Right.*" drawled the unconvinced clerk. "Well your business be your own, and I'm no chastity priest. Five copper a night. Third floor, room thirty two, common room is open till midnight.

The price seemed reasonable to Clamax and he immediately started fishing for coin.

"I suppose you're here for the Queen's guard contest tomorrow?" Observed the clerk to Babs while waiting for the coin to appear.

"No? But that sounds exciting! What is it?"

"As far as I know, it's when young men, well they've always been men before, waggle replica swords about. Those judged best get their recruitment fast tracked to the Guard. There's a poster by the stairs if you want to know more. Reckon some of those cocky bastards would shit 'emselves if they stepped out and saw you on the other side of the pit!"

"Thank you." Said Vag in a lilting tone, "We might look into that."

"No at all, have a pleasant night, wherever you end up sleeping that is."

Clamax and Vag moved to read the poster pointed out by the clerk. After already having taken a step away from the counter, Barbidon returned to it, leaning down thoughtfully to have a quiet word with the clerk.

"I don't mean this as a criticism, but you should really say the word penis."

"Penis?" Said the perplexed publican.

"Thank you, but I didn't mean you should say it right now. I meant earlier, when you named the inn. Ive been told that you should call penises by their proper names, not cocks or dicks. Those words can make something normal and natural sound rude and crude. So you should probably call the inn 'The four skinny penises'."

The man stared at Babs, dumbstruck at the bizarre impromptu lesson in nomenclature.

Babs continued. "Actually, I'll have to check, but I think all men have four skins, so you might not need to say that in the name at all. If that is so, you could probably just call the inn "The Penises."

"Um, I'll talk to my boss?"

"Thanks!" Said Babs, smiling in a beguiling way, placing her hand on his for a moment. "You're a nice man."

She turned to catch up with the others as they finished reading the poster, but she had another thought. Turning back again to the clerk. "I don't mean to go on about it too much, but you also called the sword waggling men in the competition 'cocky bastards'?"

"I should call them penisy bastards?" Proposed the clerk.

"Nice!" exclaimed Babs, holding up her hand for a high five. It hung awkwardly for a moment before the man realised what it was.

High five received, that beautiful smile appeared again, and she turned to follow Clamax and Vag up the stairs.

The Clerk and most of the common room paused to watch the only Half-Orc they would ever see in their lives walk up the narrow stairway.

Room thirty two wasn't tiny, it was miniscule. If you'd swung a cat in it, the poor creature would've received a fresh concussion every ninety degrees.

A single, short bed took up half the room. Having crowded inside and locked the door, Vag opened up her magical orifice on the bed and they all climbed inside. Soon they were back in Mayguls tower.

It felt bizarre to travel an entire day in one direction, only to instantly return back to where you started. This was the weirdness magic could bring to your world. Five coppers had effectively rented them a three-storey tower and unlimited food for the evening.

"So," said Vag eating a beef stew "Do you present me to the castle first thing or do we enter Babs in the Queen's guard contest tomorrow?"

"I would love to go in the contest!" Said Babs masticating on roast chicken and fresh bread.

"Are you sure?" asked Clamax. "The poster said it is only for contestants highly experienced in swordplay."

"You could enter?" probed Vag.

"Hmpf, I'm no swordsman, besides, my plan is to free high priestess Ovula and repair the Phallus of Felicity with her. I can't do that serving in the Queen's guard."

"Well then, let's try Babs in the contest. She has the necromancers dexterity ring, and it won't be that dangerous with a healer present. Plus, I'd guess there'll be some influential people from court watching. Maybe you could introduce yourself, make connections? It'll be a better way to get an audience than us simply turning up to the keep uninvited."

Clamax, sitting with his back against the wall, looked at the ceiling in contemplation.

"Your right." He said after a moment, "Babs, if you're up for it we'll enter you in the competition tomorrow."

"Yay!" Shrieked Babs in delight.

Having sated the extremities of her hunger. She stood up, unclasped her sword and began practicing. This was far more feasible in the girthy tower than their officially rented room. Still, Vag and Clamax were a little on edge as the black blade danced around.

Vag looked at the luxurious blue cloth. An idea formed in her mind based on the success of Clamax's Tabard. She cast the hands of hairdressing and got them working on the material. Babs continued with her sword practice.

"Take that, you penisy bastard!" she shouted, thrusting out against an imaginary foe.

17

Politics

Fellatio Jackhammer would have preferred going straight to bed. But while most of his command was getting ready for some well-deserved R & R, he was getting ready to present the heretical priestess to Queen Chastidia, Archbishop Blueballus and the Arch mage Electran.

Although now the senior ranking officer of the army and an accomplished swordsman, as a boy he fancied he could have been a master of the theatre. Fate however, had thrust an alternate path for him.

At the age of ten, he had worked with a travelling group of thespians under the tutelage of a superficially kind Elven man. It had been a happy life right up until when his mentor started abusing him. Utterly disgusted by the act, he had fled, filled with a passion to do whatever he could to fight the disgusting diseases of homosexuality and inter-race sexuality wherever it lay.

His proudest moment was at the age of 20, when the then Sergeant Jackhammer had tracked down his abuser, and put him to the sword. He had turned out to be quite adept at state-sponsored murder, though his suppressed life path had still helped him rise in rank over the years. And it was with his knowledge of theatre, that he thought how best to control proceedings, to best highlight *his* success.

Frustratingly his second in command had declined an offer of rest and insisted on helping bring the Priestess before the court. Sir Richard Longsword, or 'Major Dick' as Fellatio thought of him, was 2nd son to the Duke of Tion. He was a noble whilst Fellatio had started in the gutter.

This conflict of social vs military rank was a sore point in their relationship. Sir Richard was always looking for ways to share and even grab political points for himself. Like his sword work, this was usually done with poorly hidden brute force rather than finesse.

If Longsword was going, Brightspark might as well come too. Now there was the man who *should* be his second in command. Smart as a cartload of cats and an excellent swordsman too. He possessed $9/10^{ths}$ of Fellatios finesse, and $9/10^{ths}$ of Longsword's strength. He was a committed man too, with a lovely wife named Nadia. This was in stark contrast to Longsword, whom he suspected had the sexual constancy of an alpha rat in a grain silo.

The other person he'd decided should be there was the fat private Hodgkins. He still couldn't fathom how the remarkably unremarkable man had overcome the Priestess's spell, but credit where credit was due. Hodgkins had performed above his rank, and above everyone's expectations.

Jackhammer turned to judge the sun's position and adjusted his uniform. Another ten minutes and the timing would be perfect.

~

Ten minutes later, the doors to the chamber of planning swung open and the dramatically back-lit figure of Fellatio Jackhammer strode confidently into the room. Longsword, Brightspark, Hodgkins and two sergeants with the heavily restrained Orgasmodanic priestess followed.

Virgun, Electran and the Queen were there as expected. The stiff figure of Erec of Tion was a surprise.

Erec was Major Richard Longsword's elder, more emotionally mature brother. He was also heir to the dukedom of Tion. The four sat in a semicircle array facing a slender elf before them. A dignitary, judging by his clothes. Ambassador perhaps? He was likely the escorted noble that entered the gates ahead of them yesterday.

Jackhammer gauged the room. The Elf looked flustered, but so did the Wizard Electran. There's a story there, Fellatio thought. He bowed to the queen and elf in apology. He had thought he would be interrupting minor noble at most, not a representative from another realm.

The Elf's eyes registered the smallest hint of alarm at the sudden entry of soldiers. He recovered with grace and reciprocated Jackhammer's bow. "Apologies your majesty, I may have come at an inopportune time, perhaps we could continue our discussion tomorrow?"

"Yes, of course, we will talk more in the morning, Ambassador Presley. Thank you for your visit" The Elf bowed again and withdrew, Electran staring daggers at him for some reason. The Ambassador noticed the Elven captive on his way out. He did a short double take when he spotted her kindred ears. It was unsubtle enough to be noticeable.

When the doors closed, the young queen turned to Jackhammer expectantly "Well, did you destroy it?"

To a lesser audience he would have dragged the moment out, but instead gave a broad smile. "We did your majesty. The heretical phallus is no more."

The Queen beamed "Well done Jackhammer!"

"And who is this bedraggled woman you've brought before us?" asked Electran, craning his neck to get a better look at her.

"This," declared Jackhammer, stepping to the side allowing a better look for the dignitaries, "is the High Priestess of Orgasmodan".

Virgun stood up abruptly. "Extraordinary." he said in a hushed tone, walking over to her.

"Ovula?"

She looked at him with recognition, and upon taking in his vestments, with sadness.

"Do you know this woman, High Priest?" asked Chastidia.

"Yes." He responded absentmindedly before continuing more coldly. "That is to say I did. Many years ago, when I served your father at the Elven court. She was of a noble family, but must have thrown it away to serve what she mistakenly took as a higher calling."

Ovula kept her eyes on Virgun. Fellatio thought the priest looked uncomfortable, he broke her gaze and returned to his seat.

"You have done exceedingly well Fellatio." Said the Queen. "We will make a public show of her execution, perhaps at the Festival of Prudishia's culmination next week. Until then, I want her tortured to see if she knows the location of Orgasmodan's god stones."

"On that front, I have even better news your majesty." Fellatio continued whilst turning to Sir Richard, who held a long black box. "I found the god stones of Orgasmodan buried at the same site."

The normally cold and quiet Chastidia was now ecstatic. Virgun too, though Fellatio thought he still looked unsettled from the Priestess's introduction.

"Can we destroy these stones High Priest?" Asked Chastidia. "It would be wonderful to free ourselves of Orgasmodan's influence once and for all."

"Not easily your majesty." Said Virgun, "God stones are impervious to damage, unless, as legend states, they are struck by the Hammer of Castra against the Anvil of Tion."

"Do we know the location of these items? Erec, you're from Tion." Stated the Queen unnecessarily. "Have you heard of this Anvil before?"

"I have not your majesty." He responded stiffly.

Virgun was more helpful. "I believe there are records in the library on these items. I will review them this evening and report back to you tomorrow morning."

"Good, then we must decide who will be tasked with retrieving them. Well done Fellatio, and to your men too, excellent work. Guards, take this prisoner to a secure cell." The queen paused as a thought occurred to her. "Is the recruiting contest for the Queens Guard tomorrow?"

"It is your Majesty." Said Fellatio.

"Are you in a position to fulfill your duties? I would understand if you and your men needed a day's rest to recover from your mission."

"Thank you, your majesty. I am sure I speak for both the Captain and Major here that we will be ready to perform our duties tomorrow as planned."

"Your tireless duty to the realm is noted gentlemen. Now is that the last of the issues today?" asked the Queen.

"It is your majesty." Said Virgun.

The Queen nodded and rose, anyone seated did likewise.

Brightspark realised he had taken in little of the conversation. Thinking about the Queen had distracted him. It seemed almost unimaginable that that there was an unbroken line of consequence between the young, beautiful woman before him and the blood-slick floor of the temple they had attacked.

Erec of Tion did not leave, he came over to the officers.

"Well brother," said Major Longsword with little warmth. "How go things back home?"

"Father is unwell and getting worse."

"I am sure you are anxious for him." Said Longsword with a bucket-load of sarcasm.

"You're projecting your own style of thinking onto me brother. I don't wish my father's demise for the sake of his title."

No love lost there, thought Brightspark.

"The Elf's visit had Electran all flustered. What was that about?" interjected Fellatio.

Erec turned to him, happy for the distraction. "The Elf came to warn us. Apparently the Orcs may have their sights on our lands. Electran has apparently used his divination powers to determine that the Orcs will *not* be invading. He treated the news like a direct challenge to his insight. For someone who supposedly about the big picture, he carries on like a spoilt four-year-old prince."

"A lack of wisdom stands out most on the intelligent." said Brightspark

"True." Said Erec, regarding the Captain, "Anyway, Electran ended up accusing the Elves of trying to trick us is opening up another front against the Orcs, to distract them from Elven lands."

"What do you think?" asked Fellatio.

"Don't know, but the Queen will probably ask you to be on your guard."

"What about Ambassador Presley, you think he knew the Priestess?" asked Fellatio of Erec.

"Definitely, we'll need to keep an eye on him I reckon. Virgun's reaction to her was stranger though. Could they have been lovers all those years ago, when he worked at the Elven court?"

Fellatio snorted. "Not likely, I've got plenty of concerns about Virgun, but they mostly centre around the fact that I have never even seen the wretched man him look at a woman that way. If you catch my meaning." he followed up the statement with a frown.

"No!" said Erec, dismissing it out of hand, but as Fellatio held his pose, he reconsidered. "Really?"

"Really." said Fellatio.

"Someone picked the wrong career then." noted Erec.

Only Brightspark laughed.

18

A new friend

The companions woke to the sounds of birds outside their tower near Wagrum. They ate a hearty breakfast whilst the lady's had their hair done. Babs tried on the outfit the hands of more-than-just-hairdressing had worked on last night. Vag had struggled to balance freedom of movement with modesty.

Given the fabric's clinginess, modesty hadn't won. She looked amazing though, with muscles in places most people didn't even have places, exotic hairstyle and the azure fighting garments made her look like something out of a storybook. Her sword finished the look nicely.

"Well, they'll definitely notice you." said Clamax reviewing the completed look.

"Do you think so? I feel pretty good. Thanks for the outfit Vag, it's amazing what you can do!"

"You're welcome." said Vag smiling. She oft reflected that to stand next to the Amazonian goddess was to feel as invisible as her newly learnt spell. It was hard for that to brew into petty jealous though, when Babs was just so orgasmo-damn adorable.

"She we ladies?" asked Clamax, hand pointing towards their portal, towards room thirty-two of the four skinny cocks.

"We shall." said Babs, bouncing on toes and clapping her hands with light rapidity.

The arena was easy enough to spot. It was the height of a four-storey building and situated only eight hundred metres from their 'lodgings'.

Regardless, it still seemed they were late for signing their champion into the competition.

"Well, you are two minutes after the cutoff time." Stated the uncertain clerk under a sign labelled 'Registration'. "I'll have to check with my boss."

"Sergeant Stickler?" called the man to his unseen superior.

"What is it?" Came a curt voice from around the corner

"We have someone else wanting to register for the contest."

"Well, tell them they're too late, we've had enough skinny bastards sign up today anyway."

"Sir, you may want to..."

"Corporal, I don't see what is so important about someone who can't even turn up for registration on-"

Sergeant Stickler paused physically and verbally as he came around the corner and spotted the spectacle that was Barbidon. First starting at eye height, his eye height, before moving up to her serenely smiling face.

"Ok, sign her up." He said with no follow-up questions, before turning back inside, clearly in a rush. "And pair her up against that hoighty toighty land owner from Tion." His voice now echoing down the stone corridor.

The corporal quickly took down Bab's details and explained the next steps.

"Each contender is allowed a plus one to attend them in the dugouts. There are two holding areas, with contenders split into each. You'll be going to the 2nd holding area down that corridor." He pointed down the same route taken by the Sergeant moments earlier.

"You can choose short or long swords, with or without shields, or a two-handed sword, but all blades are blunt. The longest part of the event will be one-on-one bouts between contenders. You'll be in the last of those since you came late. If they judge you one of the three most promising contenders, you'll get a follow-up bout with one of the army's most senior officers. These will be either a Captain, a Major and even Colonel Jackhammer himself, if last year's contest is any guide."

"That's exciting!" said Babs.

"Yes. quite." said the corporal, unsure of how to take her child-like enthusiasm. "Each of those officers will then have final say whether their respective opponent is worthy of consideration for the Queen's guard, pending a character check."

Babs, who'd been listening with the attentiveness of a grade-a student, smiled and said "Thanks for being so helpful!" The corporal smiled and wished her the best of luck before picking up the rest of his things and ushering Babs through.

"You go, I'll sit in the crowd." said Vag. "I've got no place in a fighter's pit. I'll be cheering for you though Babs!"

Babs and Clamax waved goodbye to Vag as she headed for the general admission section. They turned to the dark, cool, noisy corridor, soon finding 'holding area two'. It was attended by a Prudishian priest.

"Well you two are something different. Contestant?" He asked, pointing at Babs.

"Yes." said Babs, bouncing.

"And you sir." Turning to Clamax. "Tell me, are you a priest in armour or just a pious middle-aged squire?"

"Neither Father. I'm Ser Clomax the Chaste, Paladin of Prudishia at your service." Clamax punctuated this with quick and minimalist bow.

"A Paladin you say? And a Dwarf to boot?" The priest looked sceptical.

"As you see." Said Clamax, frustrated at needing to clarify his race.

"Well Ser Clomax, I have never met a Paladin before, though I've heard that powerful paladins can perform the healing acts of a priest. Can you perform such acts?"

"I can father."

The priest looked at Clamax, sizing him up, this time metaphorically. "Very well, perhaps you could assist with healing injured contestants today? I am a man, *short*, today."

The Priest had the kind of smirk that begged to be punched off his face. Clamax kept calm. "I would be honoured to assist in any capacity required of me. Though could I ask a favour perhaps?"

"And what would that be?" asked the Priest.

"I'm new to the Citadel, and was hoping to gain an audience with High Priest Blueballus?"

The Priest snorted. "Let's see if you channel Prudishia's grace and wield the powers of a paladin first. *Then* we can discuss meeting his grace."

"Of course Father, completely reasonable."

~

Ejac Ula of Tion looked confident. At least he hoped he did. Ejac was the second son of a landowning family in Tion. The type of family with a good name and woeful coffers.

As such, he sought the well-trodden path of second sons seeking an income in the military. Even Sir Richard Longsword had taken that step five years ago, albeit with a far easier path to its senior ranks. He could have tried the clergy, but found it's calling a discordant fanfare of self-right-eous claptrap.

Here, today, he would make a name for himself. And in doing so, help his family's honour, which had become brittle after three poor harvests.

If his opponent was anything like the men in holding area one, he should be able to impress. Most of these looked younger than him, barely twenty years of age.

As he sat in anticipation, he heard the crowd gradually grow in size and restlessness. Eventually a Priest came out of the darkness of holding area two to address them.

"Greetings good citizens of Del! My name is Father Vin-dictus, and I will officiate today's proceedings. By the end of this contest, we will, I am confident, identify more than one recruit of sufficient skill to serve in her majesty's personal guard."

It was not the speech of a professional fight promoter thought Ejac. It still got a decent cheer from the crowd, who were eager for the contest to begin.

~

Vag was anxious heading into the stands by herself. There was only one queue, and it was *overwhelmingly* male. She was uncertain if one needed to purchase a ticket first.

A well-dressed woman only a few years older than herself noticed her trepidation and reached a hand out invitingly. It was supported by a disarming smile, like Vag was a dear friend whose arrival had been eagerly expected.

"First time here?" She asked.

"Yes, I wasn't sure if this is where I should line up."

"It is. What brings you here today?" She leaned in conspiratorially. "Do you have a handsome gentleman competing?"

"No." Vag chuckled. "A friend though. And you?"

"My husband's a soldier. He's helping out today. They gave me two tickets but I'm here alone, we can sit together if you would like?"

Vag took a look at all the men around and hastily nodded, "Thank you, Mrs…"

"Brightspark, though it's such a pompous name. Call me Nadia."

"Virginia."

Vag chatted with Nadia as they shuffled forward inevitably to the gate. She showed a slip of paper to the attendant who ushered them through as promised, without having to buy tickets.

The circular arena only sat five hundred, though it was an impressive scene to a provincial girl like Vag. As she waited, she saw a handsome officer wave at Nadia, who didn't immediately notice. He made his way over anywy. Vag got her attention, and she waved back enthusiastically.

"Hello, you had no problems at the gate?"

"None at all, thank you, and I've made a new acquaintance! Oh gosh, that makes it sound a bit cold. A new friend, I've made a new friend. Argile, this is Virginia, she's new to the Citadel."

"Captain Brightspark at your service." he said with affected formality. A subtle grin revealed he wasn't serious.

"Captain?" Said Vag, momentarily turning back to Nadia. "It appears your wife undersells you Sir. She simply described you as a 'soldier'."

He smiled "I am a difficult man to undersell I assure you."

Ok, thought Vag, even Nadia's husband was adorable too. "Does the rank of captain mean you have a role in adjudicating today's contestants?"

"It does unfortunately, though it will hopefully prove an interesting day. I've just been told that a Half-Orc has entered the competition, and she's a young woman! Two firsts in one day!"

"Extraordinary." said Nadia.

"Actually, she's with me" said Vag, a little self-conscious. The couple looked at her with intrigue.

"Really? You're friends with a Half-Orc warrior woman?"

"Her name is Barbidon. She's been one of my travelling companions for the last few weeks."

"Well, I'll make sure she is treated fairly. Unfortunately duty calls and I must get back to my post. It was a pleasure to meet you Virginia."

With a respectful bow, he turned and made his way to a VIP section. Two other officers sat at a table along with other dignitaries, including an Elf. Vag thought it might be the elf that had spoken with Clamax yesterday.

"Sounds like you have some interesting stories to tell, how much can you tell me?"

"Um, about a quarter of it?" responded Vag truthfully.

Nadia laughed, "Then I suppose that will have to do. For now." She added with a smile and pointed finger.

Vag recounted what she could without giving away that she was a mage, or that her trio was actually on an ambitious scheme to subvert Prudishian law in the name of Orgasmodan. This meant leaving out a lot, but the tale still enraptured Nadia.

"Oh, she sounds adorable!"

"That she is. Though she can become fierce towards bullies though, I think she might have..."

Vag trailed off, going deathly pale as she saw the priest entering the arena.

"Are you alright Vaginia?" asked Nadia at the sudden turn in her demeanour.

"What is *he* doing here?"

Nadia followed her gaze towards the Priest.

"The Priest? His name is Vindictus Blueballus. He's the younger brother of High Priest Blueballus. I understand he recently returned from provincial duty. Do you know him?"

Before Vag could answer, the priest started some vacuous speech. Seething hatred for the man who arrested her brother distorted his words. All she heard him say was; "Greetings good citizens of Del! My name is Father Vindictus, and I enjoy burning young homosexual men at the stake simply because I disagree with whom they love."

Fruits

Ejac watched some early bouts before tiring of the jostle for viewing space. There were only two modest holes in the wall that faced the central arena, and he'd already determined the general standard of competition.

His opponent was going to be a young lad with less experience, less strength, a long sword and shield. They *all* chose long sword and shield. Not that he would be any different.

Gradually the holding area emptied, leaving him space to practice his manoeuvres. After waiting so long, Sergeant Stickler calling him over caught him off guard.

"You're up, fancy boy. You get to fight a girl today."

"You can't be serious?" Ejac responded with an indignant, disgusted look on his face. He stormed to the door and out into the arena. The Sergeant smirked at him as he looked around, he was the first one out.

"Ladies and Gentlemen! From the first gate we have Ejac Ula of Tion!"

Some modest applause started up. Ejac looked around the crowd and spotted the judging bench where three officers presided. His heart sunk when he locked gaze with Ser Richard Longsword.

His father's landholdings were behind on taxes owed to Ser Richard's father, the Duke of Tion. By the look of the scowl on Ser Richard's face, The Duke's second son was acutely aware they were in-arrears.

Shit, thought Ejac.

Oh well, let's just smash whatever waif walks out this door.

She stepped out.

She wasn't a waif.

Shit Fuck, thought Ejac.

He hadn't even considered that he could lose a bout against a girl. Perhaps, not for the first time in his life, Ejac Ula of Tion had been premature.

"Ladies and Gentlemen! From the second gate we have Barbidon of... the orchard?"

Awed silence filled the five hundred seat stadium as they took in the remarkable sight of Barbidon. Quite simply, it was a fuck-tonne of aesthetic, athletic awesomeness. Her height, her striated muscles, the stunning azure outfit, exotically braided hair and a two-handed sword resting casually on her shoulder.

The only noise was a sketch artist who started feverishly drawing the moment she'd step out of the gate.

Then two young women in the crowd both stood up. One wore a stylish lilac dress with plain hair, the other had an older dress, but hair like a courtier.

"Go Barbidon!" They shouted, before starting several un-ladylike rotations of their fists in the air to the side of their heads accompanied by an almost guttural "Whoo!, Whoo! Whoo! Whoo!"

The Half orc bizarrely lowered her guard and called out, "Oh hi Vag!" Smiling up and waving at the women. The scene was like that of an oversized, simple child in a school play waving at their mum instead of focusing on the production at hand.

The woman in the lilac dress bent over laughing at this, and Erec thought he heard her say "Oh she *IS* adorable!" to her friend.

Keen to take control of the bout before it turned into a complete farce. Erec banged his long sword against his shield and let out a bellow.

This seemed to have the desired effect, as the women stopped laughing. But then the lilac dressed woman started chanting. "Bar-bi-don! Bar-bi-don! Bar-bi-don!"

She was soon joined by her companion. Then her seating section. Then the entire five hundred seat arena.

"Bar-bi-don! Bar-bi-don! Bar-bi-don!"

Fuck. Thought Ejac, now I've lost the crowd. Oh well. He hadn't studied swordplay since boyhood to have his moment of honour taken away by this half-caste cunt of a girl.

He went from a completely relaxed posture, to charging the three metre gap between them in an instant. He enjoyed seeing her eyes go wide in alarm at his sudden closing of the distance. That was his best chance, to close the gap between them to longsword range. That would be closer than the ideal distance for her larger two-handed weapon. There, it would be unwieldy and unable to parry the blows of his smaller blade. Yes, he thought, Ejac Ula of Tion would need to be all up in her face.

The bitch was quick though. He might have enjoyed seeing her eyes go wide, but he didn't enjoy the speed with which she got her guard up.

The half-breed had time to raise her weapon and bring down a surprisingly quick blow on his shield. Bang!!! The force of the blow was more powerful than any sparring part-ner he had ever practiced against. It almost pushed him to the ground, but he kept his feet. Now inside her defences he saw her legs planted and exposed. He swung his longsword out in front of him, eager to see the pain even a blunt weapon could inflict against her naked ankles.

Impossibly, both legs lifted off the ground, starting to spin as they did. This left him trying desperately to bring his air-swing under control. He stood up quickly, but his momentum had left him facing towards his shield side.

Then he was on the dirt, an incredible pain spreading across the back of his ribs. He tried to take a breath of the dusty air his face was surrounded by, but couldn't. The priest came over to see if he needed healing. Breathing slowly returned, and with panic subsiding, his pride declined the priestly heal for his back.

"One touch to Barbidon!"

It would take more than one touch for Ejac Ula of Tion though, and he stood erect, ready to continue.

Ejac heard the crowd applaud as he pieced together what must have happened. She had not only had time to jump his low attack, but also completely spin her body. This would have momentarily exposed her back to him in the air, but he been too busy controlling his air swing. Her whirlwind must have brought the sword around on his exposed left with the tremendous force he now felt imprinted on his back.

The crowd, and Erec's own breathing calmed. Then the half-caste was on the offensive. She struck again from a high arc, this time on his sword side.

Wary of trying to parry her powerful blows with his one-handed weapon, Ejac opted for an unconventional defence. He started to spin. This put his back momentarily facing his opponent, bringing his shield over to the side of the incoming attack. Crucially though, it enabled him to bring his sword rapidly towards her exposed left torso a moment later.

"Touch to Ejac!"

A smattering of applause.

"You want to dance bitch?" Ejac spat the words "Well I can dance too!"

The stupid girl looked at him with a frown on her face. She didn't look angry, more, disappointed?

Whatever.

Ejac feinted a charge and Barbidon swung again. This time he stepped back deftly missing her strike. Momentum from the swing exposed her left side and he lunged forward at the opening.

"Two touches to Ejac!"

"Yeah, how do you like that, cow." He taunted.

That seemed to get a reaction. Her face dipped forward, eyes staring coldly at him.

Good Ejac convinced himself. That rattled her.

She lifted her sword. He did the same. They paused, evidently both deciding on defence. Ejac eventually got bored and came at her. It was time to shut this silly abomination of a girl down once and for all. Her swing came in on his shield side. It came at hip height and he braced for the impact.

She lowered her strike sharply at the last minute and hit the bottom of his inverted tear drop shield. With all his mass braced against the top of the shield, there was little to stop the full force of her blow transferring through his shield and directly onto his left leg.

Ejac had prepared his counterattack, but it was never executed. He had leant too heavily into his shield to rebuff the strike. This pushed him out to the left, just as his left foot was swept beneath him.

He went down, landing shield side on the ground. The first follow up strike to rain down disarmed him, his own sword hitting his head. The next came at his neck. He panicked in genuine fear of what her blade would do to his neck, blunted weapon or not. She slowed it however, and it landed as a light tap on the empty sword arm he'd raised to protect his head.

"Two points to Barbidon!"

The crowd cheered, and another chant of Bar-bi-don! Started up. As he got to his feet. He was furious, faced flushed with anger. The crowd settled in anticipation of the decider.

Ejac decided he needed a better taunt to get her to lose her cool.

"You know what you need cow? You probably just need a bull's cock inside you. I've got one here for you if you want."

Some of the crowd heard this, someone booed, but he didn't care. He could see this had got her properly angry now.

"You shouldn't say cock." She staccato growled.

What are we in kindergarten? Thought Ejac. He leant forward, grabbing his crotch with a smirk on his face.

"Cock." he happily repeated, turning it into a two syllable word.

She started at him, sword like a lance in front of her. Ejac moved forward with his shield, ready to deflect the sword. It did deflect it, but not as efficiently as he would have liked. The impact took enough momentum out of his advance that the longsword thrust he launched towards her chest was slow, too slow.

Barbidon had already intentionally dropped her sword, batted away his impotent thrust with her left hand, and suddenly closed the rest of the distance between them. *All* the distance. Her face right up against his.

"You-pe-ni-sy Ba-stard!!!" she yelled through clinched teeth.

At a distance, her Great sword had the advantage. Closer in, it had been with him. *This* close however, her strength, her ferocity was difficult to defend against.

Ejec felt her ferocity connect with an open palmed uppercut to his groin.

It got worse.

She crushed her palm closed, utterly pulverising the delicate, precious contents within her grasp. She pushed him back with her free hand and he heard cloth tear as he fell backwards to the ground. He was shocked to see his opponent standing there holding the crotch of his pants along with the crotch of his body in her hand.

Over the next two seconds, all 480 men in the audience crossed their legs.

Ejac was in shock, he started shaking, reaching out to Barbidon for his mangled toys back. He was vaguely aware of the priest rushing out to him. He leant over and intoned some words to Prudishia, but it seemed to have little effect. He looked worried, which made Ejac freak out even more.

"May I father?" Ejac heard a gruff, accented voice say.

"You can try. I'll handle the crowd."

Ejac saw a dwarf come into his view.

"Easy lad. There you go." He said with a gruff yet soothing voice.

Ejac felt his consciousness starting to slip from all the blood loss. The priest spoke to the crowd, making a comment about Barbidon scoring a "...Final touch". Just as he was about to black out, he heard the dwarf say "Almighty Orgasmodan..."

And just like that, he was awake again, pain gone from his crotch as a pleasant breeze blew into the hole in his pants. It was then that he realised that his unfortunately very modestly sized cock was on display for the entire arena. He quickly covered himself with both hands. Whilst the crowd laughed at his humiliation, he remembered the dwarf's prayer.

"You... You said!" Ejac stammered at the dwarf.

"Not a single word lad, you hear? Ever." Said the dwarf with whispered menace. He put his mouth right next to Ejac's ear. "Or I'll make it all shrivel back up again in an instant. Understand?"

Ejac readily nodded his head as the Priest returned from addressing the crowd.

"Well done Ser Clomax." he said, sounding genuinely impressed. "I can heal wounds, but I've never been able to replace missing flesh before. I think you've just earned yourself an audience with High priest Blueballus."

"Thank you." the dwarf responded humbly. "Just happy to have helped."

20

Worthy?

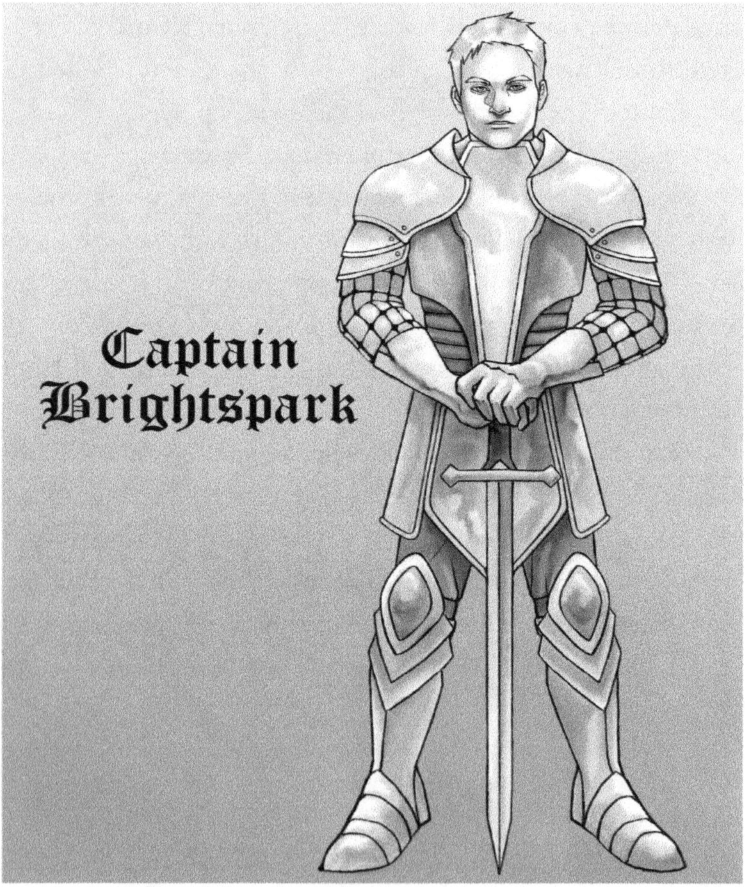

Vag sat in the stands, mouth agape. She looked across and Nadia, who looked at her, mouth agape.

"Wow." said Nadia flatly. "That wasn't in the brochure."

"I wish that happened to every man who talked to women like that." Responded Vag. "It would be a much better world."

"There would certainly be fewer penises in it." Responded Nadia out of the corner of her mouth.

Vag snort-laughed.

~

Ser Richard Longsword sat with Captain Brightspark and Colonel Jackhammer, deliberating on their final three. These contestants would get one-on-one bouts with an Officer. They were a foregone conclusion. It was simply an opportunity for the Army's best swordsmen to publicly display their flare. The victorious officer would invariably announce that the finalist was never-the-less, a worthy opponent, and showed promise for the Queen's guard.

"I don't disagree she was clearly the strongest fighter today." said Jackhammer. "I am just not sure we should go around hiring women with orcish blood to protect the queen's interests."

Richard countered. "It would show the elite guard as a progressive institution?" Whilst thinking *'It would be nice to those tits and that arse walking around the barracks'*.

"She is inexperienced, but the combination of power and dexterity has so much potential." Argued Brightspark. "If there are any lingering concerns over allegiances because of her Orcish blood, perhaps these could be tested following the contest?"

Richard suspected he could not have swayed Jackhammer alone, but of course, if *Golden* boy Brightspark thought it was a good idea...

"Very well Captain, you can take her bout then."

Richard smirked and nudged Brightspark. "Just watch your fruits lad."

Brightspark gulped to his amusement.

"What about the other two places?" Asked Jackhammer. "I thought Gagre Flexus fought well, so I would like to have my bout with him if you both agree?" Richard and the Captain nodded their ascent.

"Which leaves one more place. I thought Ejac Ula of Tion held off for a long time, especially under such a furious pounding?"

"Agreed." Said the Captain, "Though his language and crude taunting were unbecoming of a Queen's guard recruit."

Richard was about to side with the Captain's mention of conduct. It would be nice to send the whelp back to his tax dodging father where he could work hard to pay off the debt owed to his own family's Ducal estate.

An idea struck him. Both the captain's and Colonel's bouts were decided. Meaning he would duel with whoever they now chose. This would give him the opportunity to make justice for Ejac's family's tax evasion even more personal.

~

During the short recess, a visibly shaken Ejac was provided with some new, less breezy pants. The other fighters returned to the holding areas, most talked of the brutish bitch that had temporarily emasculated him.

They avoided him completely, though cast many glances ranging from pitying to amused. There was one exception. A strong lad came over and introduced himself.

"Gagre." he stated simply, extending his hand.

"Ejac."

"You fought well."

"She humiliated me."

Gagre sat down next to him, and together they stared at the wall opposite. "I wouldn't beat yourself up about it. That thing is a monster, not a human."

"I don't even know why they would allow her to enter." Ejac said, flicking a small stone away with his foot.

Gagre looked like he more to say, but the loud voice of Vindictus Blueballus addressing the crowd cut him short. It was time for the finalists to be announced.

~

Ser Richard watched from the first row, as Jackhammer donned some light armour with his sword and shield. He strode to the centre of the fighting area and saluted his opponent.

The brutish major hoped against hope that Fellatio would choke against Gagre Flexus, but alas, the Colonel was a consummate professional. He despatched the young man's attacks with elegance and grace, albeit without making him look a fool.

After declaring three touches, Vindictus formally asked the Colonel if his opponent had displayed sufficient skill for the Queens Guard. Jackhammer clasped the man's hand and held it high in the air with his, declaring to the crowd he was worthy of consideration.

Next up, Brightspark took to the centre with 'Boobidon'. Richard chuckled at his own witty word play. He heard a woman's voice call out.

"Babs!"

It was the waif of a thing with fancy hair that had been sitting next to Brightspark's wife. She made her way down the side of the fighting area, not three metres from his position.

"Hi Vag!" said Barbidon, coming to find out what her friend needed to say.

"I've been talking to Captain Brightspark's wife. I think they are both really lovey people, so could you please not try to do what you did to your last opponent?"

"You mean ripping his genitals off? Sure. Sorry, it's just that man was really mean. But I'm glad to hear this man is nice."

Richard listened to the conversation with amusement. The Half-Orc went back to the centre again as the crowd started chanting her name. Rather than take her guard, she walked right up to a confused Brightspark and wrapped him in a hug. The Captain eventually patted her lower back. That was as high as he could reach, given she'd pinned his upper arms to his side. It was a weird spectacle, and that was *before* the girl held the hug for another five seconds.

Richard didn't mind though, it gave him more time to stare. Now *there* was a notch he needed on his belt. Yes, bringing a muscular girl like that to heel would require a *real* man. With that determination made, he mentally added her onto his to-do list.

It was an interesting fight to watch. Her speed really was incredible in both attack and defence, however Brightspark's technique was far superior. When she attempted the same style of attack that had swept Ejac's feet from underneath him, the Captain had anchored the tip of his tall shield on the ground. This left the two-handed sword in a useless position and its wielder's defences open. Brightspark countered and got his first touch.

Soon after, another swing on his shield came in, but he must have spotted a tell, because he ducked this time, and used his shield to deflect Barbidon's sword above his head. This did not rob it of much momentum, leaving her the burden of stopping the fruitless swing. With the blade past him, and Barbidon temporarily off balance, he sprang, shield first and bashed into her, knocking her off her feet. His sword appeared for the briefest of moments, scoring a touch on her sternum, before sheathing it and offering her hand to get up.

"Thank you! You are amazing!" Barbidon said enthusiastically, like she was genuinely grateful for being knocked on her arse in front of five hundred people.

"I've just had excellent teachers and a lot of practice."

After dusting herself off, they touched swords and began again. This time Barbidon was more cautious, respecting her opponent's ability. They traded probing attacks, moving back and forth, awaiting an opportunity. Brightspark spotted one after the Half-orc awkwardly parried a fast strike at her abdomen.

He lunged forward, long sword out far in front, aimed directly at the base of her neck. However, somehow Barbidon had raised her weapon at the last moment, its point aimed at the base of *his* neck. Each sword connected.

Contact left both combatants choking, as the blunt weapons struck their respective tracheas with considerable force. Once Father Vindictus confirmed both could breathe, he spoke to the crowd. "A simultaneous touch! Final score 3-1 to Captain Brightspark."

It was a rare occurrence for a potential recruit to score a touch against a judge. Considering this, Richard conceded Barbidon might be more than just an exotic curiosity. With his exceptionally open mind, he recognised she might also have potential with a sword. Admittedly, scoring a touch against Brightspark was not the same as scoring one against him. But it was *something*.

The Captain and Barbidon both looked at each other, still clasping their throats, then burst out laughing at their shared predicament. *Get a room,* thought Longsword.

Vindictus took the arena centre again. "Do you, Captain Brightspark, find Barbidon of the Orchard worthy of consideration for the Queen's guard?"

Instead of troubling his voice, Brightspark raised his sword and smiled to Vindictus. She gave an unsoldierly squeal and a wave to the dwarf who had helped Vindictus then to the woman sitting with Brightspark's wife. What an odd group thought Richard, picking up his helmet, shield and sword.

A minute later, Major Richard Longsword, son of the Duke of Tion, strode confidently into the circle. It had been frustrating watching swordsmen less competent than himself stumble around all day. Now the audience would see what mastery looked like. He looked across at Ejac, ready to belittle him. The lad already looked defeated before the bout even began. "You know what's coming don't you boy." said Ser Richard in his deepest voice, affecting a mirthless grin.

Ejac didn't reply, just took his guard.

The first "touch" was a rattling blow to his helmet that sent him sprawling. The second hit his forearm hard making him drop his sword.

Deciding in advance to take out his knee, the impossible happened. Ejac scored a touch. The whelp smiled, but wisely dropped it when he saw Ser Richard Longsword's face. They took their position's again. Longsword immediately went on the offensive.

He punctuated every blow with a hate-filled sentence. "You little shit." Bang! "Your family dodges it's fucking taxes." Crash! "And you sully the name of my father's lands with your foul language." Bang! "Then grabbing your tiny little dick." Crash! "Before getting beaten by a fucking girl?!"

With that, he was through Ejac's defences and his sword struck the man's knee side on. There was a pleasing crunch, and a collective groan from the audience as it bent in a novel, unfacilitated direction. Ejac let out a cry of pain. It garnered no sympathy from Richard, who lent down and whispered. "You go back and till your soil like a fucking peasant until you pay what you owe."

Vindictus came out with the Dwarf who attended Ejac. Again.

"Three touches to one in favour of Major Longsword. Tell me Major, did you find your opponent worthy of consideration for the Queen's guard?"

"I found him lacking in both ability and character. He is unworthy."

The crowd started murmuring. This was highly unusual, but he didn't care. He made his way past Ejac, Vindictus and that bloody Dwarf on his way to the exit. The Dwarf had a look on his face, not malicious, but it looked like it was on the wrong side of neutrality. "What are you looking at stumpy?" He paused for the witty wordplay to strike home. "And stop healing that little shit."

~

Vag walked with Nadia out of the stands. The three hours of lively conversation had flown. She would have liked to spend more time with her, but Nadia's husband Captain Brightspark soon arrived and they bid their farewells, promising to see each other as soon as possible. Vag remained, waiting for Clamax and Babs to exit. Now alone, she noted the Elf from the VIP area also waited. He smiled and started moving over to say hello when Babs and Clamax emerged.

Babs was already beaming, and started her trademark bounces upon seeing Vag. Father Vindictus emerged as well. Looking to Clamax, he called out. "It was a pleasure to meet you Ser Clomax. Please bring your lady friend and Barbidon to the keep tomorrow morning." Vindictus turned to Vag who froze, waiting for him to recognise her. He didn't. He looked right at her and just gave a short, polite smile.

"Thank you Father." Clamax returned, and the Priest took his leave.

"That's the priest that arrested my brother!" Vag hissed to Clamax. His jaw dropped and was about to respond when he noted the Elf waiting to the side, albeit from a polite distance away.

"Apologies, I did not want to interrupt your celebrations. Ambassador Presley at your service." he stated before addressing Babs "May I congratulate you on your *crushing* victory."

To her credit, Babs got the joke and giggled. "Thank you, Mr Presley."

"I was hoping to dine with you as proposed this evening if you are not otherwise engaged."

Vag was about to politely decline, but Clamax jumped in. "Thank you for the kind offer, it would be our pleasure. We are staying at the Four Skinny's, it's just a short walk in that direction if you would like to meet us there for a meal?"

"Excellent, I will join you an hour before sunset. I won't keep you any longer. Ladies, Ser Clomax." He gave a slight bow before he and his attending guards were enveloped by the crowded city.

"It seems a bit weird." Declared Vag after watching him go.

"He probably just hopes we might have news from other regions."

"And what do we get out of it?" asked Vag as she folded her arms.

"He could be useful for distraction and misdirection."

~

True to his word, the Elf was on time. As Clamax suspected, they talked of Geo-politics. Presley was particularly interested in the intentions of the Orcs. Ser Clomax had some information from his travels, however Babs was not the fountain of Orcish knowledge the Elf had clearly hoped. She had not even met an Orc before.

The exercise was not fruitless for Clamax. After hearing about Ovula the Orgasmodanic priestess being captured, he planted the seed that she should really be released into Elven Custody for punishment by her own kind. Presley had mentioned she was an elf of minor nobility so it only seemed right. Clamax knew a formal request would fall on deaf ears, but it would benefit their plan if the ambassador at least tried.

Vag was impressed at how her dwarven friends' easy going conversational skills coaxed important information from the elf. Clamax learnt that Presley intended to leave at first light five days hence. He did this by burying the key question in amongst small talk.

Vag also found out that Presley had met Electran. The Wizard apparently had a strained relationship with High priest Blueballus and was very defensive of his divination skills. He'd argued vociferously against Presley's information suggesting the Orcs where readying to attack Chastidia's realm.

The dinner wrapped up after a couple of hours. The Ambassador had seemed to enjoy the company, even if it had not benefitted him professionally.

For the companions, the discussion had been invaluable.

21

Physics

"I'm a long way from the Orchard now." Said Babs the next morning, staring up at the keep in awe.

The ladies had dressed in new outfits for their visit to the keep. Vag's hands of hairdressing/sewing had been busy creating a second, more formal dress for Babs out of the Necromancer's Azure Fabric. For herself, she'd repurposed one of Maygul's robes into a respectable dress. When combined with their magically assisted hairstyles, the ladies looked fit for an introduction to the high priest of Prudishia.

Clamax just looked like Clamax. That is to say, Clamax looked like *Clomax*. He still wore the CCL embroidered tabard over chain mail. Of the four queen's guards at the gate, one recognised Vindictus and they were ushered through.

Another introduced himself to Babs, correctly assuming she was the Half-Orc who'd succeeded in yesterday's contest. The other guards looked less pleased at her presence. Vag found it difficult to determine if their frowns were due to racism, sexism or both.

The grand hall was cathedral-like and utterly enormous. Religious iconographic lined the walls, further cementing the religious comparison. Vindictus took them up many flights of stairs to a smaller, more intimate chamber. It was empty.

"If you would be kind enough to wait here." Said Vindictus with a head bow, closing the doors behind him as he left.

With nothing to do, the companions stared at the floor in amazement. It was the largest, most ornate map any of them had ever, *would* ever, see. It did not just encompass the Queendom, it covered the entire known world.

Clamax looked around at all the places he had visited as an adult, and the place he hadn't. Specifically, the dwarven realms near the door they had entered through. Vag looked at the map holistically. Babs walked around in awe.

"Vag?" said Babs said with a soft and sombre tone, uncharacteristic for the bubbly girl.

"Yes Babs?"

"Where did you find me?"

Vag thought for a second as she retraced their steps. She placed one hand on Bab's arm, pointing with the other at a forested area.

Bab's saw the forest. Then she noticed the small insignificant mark near the tree line. It was too insignificant to warrant a name, an initial, even on this enormous scale. Yet until three weeks ago, it had contained every person she'd ever known, hated or loved. Now, it was a dot.

She felt small.

The doors behind began creaking, breaking their reverie.

High priest Blueballus waited beside his brother, as two queen's guards opened the doors.

Virgin looked inside the Chamber of Planning. Inside was an odd looking trio. A dwarf took a knee, a barbarian half-orc girl bowed and a slender human woman curtsied so low, she was practically prostrate. Well, thought Virgun, at least they know how to show some proper respect. That's a good start.

"Ser Clomax I assume? My brother told me you are a favoured Paladin of our Order. A tremendous honour to meet you."

He came over to Clamax with hand extended and the dwarf kissed its dorsal side. Virgun thought he felt the bristly beard on his knuckles even after the gesture's completion.

"The honour is all mine your grace."

Virgun walked over to his seat. Wishing, not for the first time, that protocol allowed him to sit in the Queen's chair. Only because that would have better conveyed his importance.

"Tell me Ser Clomax, what would you like to discuss?"

"Not so much *what* your grace, as who." The dwarf stood aside and gestured to the young lady with him. "Your Grace, please allow me to introduce Lady Virginia. Devout follower of Prudishia and..." The dwarf smiled "A Magus." The phrase hung in the air as Virgun, his brother and even the guards all looked at her in shocked appraisal.

Virgun noted the young lady as she was suddenly elevated to 'most interesting person in the room'. It was no small feat given the room contained a Dwarven Paladin, a female Half-orc barbarian and of course, himself, High Priest Virgun Blueballus.

"Your grace, I would merely seek to offer my services to the church in whatever capacity you deem appropriate." Said the young woman.

Well at least you show some proper piety and humility, thought Virgun. Unlike that insufferable oaf Electran.

"Your desire to further the church's goals is admirable Lady Virginia. Could I request you perform a small demonstration of this arcane ability?"

"Certainly your Grace." Said Vaginia dutifully. The lady uttered some words softly, whilst contorting her fingers through various positions. Two ethereal hands appeared before her. They floated over to a small pitcher of water, picked it up, poured a cup and brought it to him without spilling a drop.

"Remarkable!" he uttered, amazed by the demonstration. "Do you have other spells of a more substantial nature?"

"Yes your grace. I am still learning though."

"What about divination?"

"Regrettably not, divination spells are powerful incantations, ones I am yet to master."

"I see." said Virgun, a little disappointed. He had already begun hoping they could replace the insufferable Electran with a mage whose loyalty better aligned with the church.

"Vindy?" he said, turning to his brother. "Could you be kind enough to advise the Queen and Electran that we have a young mage keen to serve the realm? I expect they will be interested to meet her."

"Yes your grace." Responded Vindictus before exiting the room. He turned back to the Dwarf. "Tell me Ser Clomax, what news from the Dwarven realm? I've been told to expect a permanent dwarven ambassador in the coming weeks, but perhaps you can get me up to speed on the Dwarven court before her arrival?"

"Regrettably, I have been travelling and do not have any news your Grace."

"I see" said Virgun a little disappointed. He proceeded to ask questions of the half orc girl, before Electran showed up.

Virginia was fidgety he noted. Probably nervous at meeting the famous mage. Electran looked, wary. Virgun had just finished the introductions when the Queen arrived. So he started again as everyone put their bodies into whatever shape they felt best conveyed submissive loyalty to royalty.

"Another mage?" said the Queen. "You are most welcome at court. We had thought Electran was the only magus left alive in the entire realm."

"Indeed," said Electran. "I am eager to see a display of your arcane talents if you would be happy to oblige us."

"The young lady has already proven her ability to me Electran. Let's not make her perform party tricks like a troubadour."

"If you please Virgun. I would like to witness her talents myself. As a mage."

Virgun's face flushed at the lack of respect from Electran, in front of so many people no less. His consolation was Electran's coming realisation that he was not the unique talent he'd thought himself five minutes ago.

"Thank you, High Priest." Said Lady Virginia with a respectful smile. "I do not mind."

She repeated the demonstration and Electran's expression went from cynicism, to incredulity as he scrutinised the magical hands as if testing for unseen wires or some non-magical mechanism.

"Are you impressed Electran?" Inquired Virgun, taking pleasure at how visibly rattled the arrogant blob looked. *Strangely* rattled, he thought.

"A nice cantrip, it is true, but tell me miss, do you have you any divination powers?"

"I am afraid they are beyond my current abilities."

"Ah, yes, they are challenging, but so rewarding." Said the wizard, his confidence returning. "That is why I have dedicated years of study to the discipline."

"Perhaps you could show her your divination chamber Electran?" Proposed the Queen.

"Of course, your majesty. If you could just give me a moment to prepare." Said Electran, bowing away from her presence.

The Queen looked to the half-Orc girl. "And you must Barbidon, the young lady who performed so well at the contest yesterday?"

"Yes. Your majesticnessicity." stammered the star-struck girl.

The Queen laughed. "Your Majesty will do. We've only ever had men, *human* men, in the guard before. I think it will be good to mix that up a bit, don't you?"

"I would be honoured to serve you your majesty."

"You certainly look strong. That's not to be argued with."

The mutual appreciation session was cut short by Electran, who returned, nearly breathless from his twenty metre expedition down the corridor.

"It is ready."

Virgun picked up an apple from a fruit bowl and followed them all to Electran's divination chamber.

Once inside, Virgun heard the familiar squeaky sound again, along with the crackling hum of his lighting orb.

He noted that it was now the young mage's turn to look sceptical. "What's that squeaky noise I hear?" asked Lady Virginia.

"Not now, I am divining your future." he exclaimed, hands on the orb as its energy channelled through his hands.

Virgun kept watching Virginia's reaction

"Why is there no magical aura?" she asked. Virgun was impressed that she'd not been awed into silence by the arch mage.

There was a look of frustration on Electran's face, he took his hands off the orb in a dramatic fashion, as if jolted. Both mages simultaneously pointed and shouted at each other.

"Physics!" shouted Virginia with what looked like gleeful realisation, just as Electran shouted "Assassin!" With a look of shock.

Well, this is an interesting day, thought Virgun, as he took a crunching bite of his apple in the moment of indecision that followed.

Three Queen's guards sprung to guard the Queen, whilst one moved towards Lady Virginia. She evidently had a guard of her own in the Orcish girl, who looked no pushover, even without a weapon.

"What do you mean Electran? Have you seen a vision?" Asked the Queen.

"Y..Yes your majesty. This mage plans to weasel her way into your court and assassinate you in a devilish plot to overthrow your dynasty."

Virgun didn't buy it. He'd discerned this girl's piety within a few moments of meeting her. She was certainly more pious than the snivelling snot ball of a wizard that was Electran, Arch Arsehole of the realm. Virgun also knew he was an excellent judge of character, able to pick up motives on even the subtlest of clues.

"Your majesty, if you would allow me?" Said Virgun, deciding to join in the maelstrom. "Lady Virginia, what do you mean by 'Physics'?"

"Physics is the study of natural phenomena. If someone has sufficient knowledge, as this man obviously does, they can create effects that *look* like magic. He is definitely no magician though, for I can sense magical auras. There was no aura around him whatsoever, even though he claims to be casting a powerful spell."

"Preposterous!" Spat Electran.

"A Proven Prudishian Paladin *has* vouched for Lady Virginia your Majesty." Said Virgun, excited at how this was developing.

"The squeaking noise that still continues." Said Virginia, continuing the attack that was also her defence.

Everyone stopped talking and listened, watching the young mage follow a ten by twenty centimetre raised portion of the floor that extended from the base of the orb's stand to a wall. She put her head against it in an unladylike crouch, then against the wall it extended to.

"What's on the other side of this wall?" She asked of the Arch mage.

"This is absurd. Those are my private chambers."

"I think you should show the queen and I what is on the other side, Electran." Said Virgun.

"Your majesty, surely you could not entertain this accusation by an imposter we have known for less than half an hour?"

Queen Chastidia looked down at her hands for a moment, before walking over to Electran with two of her guards by her side.

Virgun saw he now had an almost pleading, puppy dog look. After seeing the expression was falling on eyes void of empathy, Electran reluctantly handed over his keys. Virgun accompanied the queen to the door of the mage's private chambers. The key turned, the door opened...

It took Virgun a moment to take what he saw. The young, strong-thighed assistant of Electran's was sitting on a contraption driven by leg power. It spun a strange, long belt that extended from the machine, straight toward the Divination room wall. The assistant stopped pumping his legs, gob smacked at his high ranking audience. The light sparks in the 'divination orb' stopped as he did so.

"You treasonous fraud!" Said Virgun loudly, pleased at the level of righteous indignation he managed to compress into the declaration.

Without warning, Electran produced a dagger from his sleeve and let out an unmanly scream, rushing Lady Virginia. The half orc girl was on the wrong side to protect the female mage. For a second, Virgun feared for the girl's life. He tried casting a spell to protect her, but was too slow. Fortunately, her reflexes were quicker.

"Frigidimus!"

A solid ice wall a metre wide and 10cm thick appeared just in front of the young mage at the last moment. The newly demoted gamma male Electran, hit it head first with whatever momentum he'd accumulated over two metres. This knocked him unconscious. As his body was about to flop to the floor, Virgun's hold-person spell belatedly took effect. This left Electran looking like a loose-stringed, drooling puppet.

"Are you alright my dear?" Asked the queen, then her face went white "Oh Prudishia, what of all his false prophecies?" Asked Queen Chastidia.

"I think we may owe the Elven Ambassador an apology, for we must surely give greater credence to his warnings of..." Virgun hesitated as he considered Barbidon's orcish blood. "...invasion."

"Yes, yes you are right. Though I still don't want to grant his request to release the Orgasmodan Priestess."

"Agreed your majesty, perhaps just that we grant him permission to visit her this afternoon before she is executed."

"That seems reasonable, and we should rethink sending Jackhammer on the mission for the Anvil of Tion. I want him here in the city, bolstering the army. He should also be on our council, taking Electran's place."

Virgun smiled, it was about time Jackhammer was on the council of planning.

Turning to the young mage, she continued. "Lady Virginia, you have done the court a great service today, but you will forgive me if this experience has made me a little wary of newcomers to court. There may be a way you can prove your loyalty to the crown though."

"How may I prove myself?"

The Queen began walking back to the chamber of planning. Everyone followed.

"Have you ever heard of God stones?"

"No, your majesty". With a look from the Queen, Virgun took over the recruitment process.

"Each God has their power channelled through two identical glowing white God stones. They have been handed down through generations of high priests and priestesses. Our senior commander, returned from an expedition only yesterday with Orgasmodan's god stones. I am now the first high priest of Prudishia to control the stones of another God. They are actually indistinguishable to us mere mortals so we keep Orgasmodan's in a separate closed box to avoid confusion."

"Can they be destroyed?" asked Virginia.

"Not easily. It would require two unique relics; the Hammer of Castra and the Anvil of Tion. I've determined the Anvil's location. We need a small, capable party to retrieve it. I would propose that party be you, Barbidon, Ser Clomax and a Queen's representative, perhaps Captain Brightspark or Major Longsword. If you are successful, we'll grant you a position in court. As for you Barbidon, I could speak to Colonel Jackhammer about a fast-tracked promotion in the Queen's Guard."

Virginia and Barbidon accepted, Ser Clomax politely declined, stating he needed to return to the dwarven lands.

"I understand Ser Clomax. Perhaps Vindictus, you could take Ser Clomax's place as a healer?"

The trio were offered guest lodgings overnight in the keep, they gratefully accepted. As they left, Colonel Jackhammer and Ser Richard entered, the latter giving Ser Clomax a baleful stare.

Such a disagreeable brute thought Virgun, he can't even show a Paladin of Prudishia proper deference.

As Clomax was at the door, he turned and addressed Virgun.

"High Priest, would I be correct in assuming you'd rather lose your life, than see our goddess banished from this world?"

All eyes looked at the Dwarf, then to him. Virgun answered, with a hesitation, presumably to assure himself the question was purely hypothetical. "Without hesitation. Yes, Ser Clomax. Why do you ask?"

"Because I suspect a high priestess of Orgasmodan may feel the same. Perhaps the most fitting punishment would therefore not be *immediate* execution, but rather forcing her to witness the destruction of Orgasmodan's god stones. Assuming, Prudishia willing, that we retrieve the artifacts."

Virgun smiled. "Your majesty?"

The Queen nodded. "That sounds like an excellent punishment Ser Clomax. Your wise council is welcome."

22

A plan for the preistess

A well-dressed servant took the companions to a floor of guest rooms. Vag chatted with him, enquiring if the elven ambassador was staying on this floor.

"Why yes Mam, all visiting dignitaries stay in this wing"

She made a note of the door he pointed out.

"Thank you, I would like to introduce myself to him later."

They were shown their rooms and the servant left, meeting up in Clamax's room only moments later.

"Didn't the Queen look amazing!" said Babs.

"Exquisite, but don't forget that she wants to destroy Orgasmodan Babs, and execute Clamax's friend Ovula."

"What does 'execute' mean?" asked Babs

"It means kill Babs." responded Vag, then repeated in a more somber tone, "It means kill."

"Oh." Said Babs, looking down momentarily at her feet. "It's just that she was so nice to me, she didn't mind at all that I was half-orc."

One benefit of the portable portal was that they didn't need to go back to the Four Skinny Cocks. Everything they owned was at Maygul's tower, or already with them.

They got what they needed from the tower including spell books and quickly discussed plans. Things had moved faster than they'd planned, and their pace would need to match events. Clamax would leave in the morning, though first they needed to prepare High Priestess Ovula's escape. Clamax had done the setup, now it was Vag's time to shine. The Dwarf wrote a note for Ovula and handed it to Vag, she tucked it into a small pouch.

The pouch contained only one other thing.

Soon after, Vag was outside Presley's door. Waiting... then waiting some more. People came down the hall and almost walked in to her. Fortunately, she dodged them all. About an hour later, a guard came and knocked on the Elven Ambassador's door.

He advised Presley that permission had been granted for him to see the Orgasmodanic priestess Ovula. In addition, he could pass on the good news that, with deference to her nobility, her execution was no longer imminent.

The Ambassador quickly grabbed something from his room and followed the guard down the hallway. Neither of them heard the quiet footsteps behind them, nor saw the minimal disturbance of dust those additional footsteps caused on the clean floors.

Her invisibility spell was still a novelty. Vag had therefore doubted whether she could pull it off. The most surprising sensation was the isolation she felt. The loneliest people could sometimes describe themselves as feeling invisible in crowds. She better understood the analogy now. Despite walking within meters of several courtiers, servants and guards on the short walk to the dungeon, it was as if she didn't exist.

Vag managed to slip through the main jail door opened for Presley. Light was scarce here, but her senses still received the same net input, thanks to increased stimulus to her nose. She moved forward, enveloping herself in the foul air.

They soon reached Ovula's cell. A jailor opened the door for Presley to enter. Vag judged it too risky to try, so she watched from other side of the bars. The Elves knew each other, and had a long conversation about her living relatives.

Presley also mentioned his unsuccessful plea for her to be judged and sentenced by an Elven court. The composure she displayed impressed Vag, given her predicament. It was clear why Clamax held her in high regard.

It wasn't until after the interview that Vag found her chance. The Ambassador and guard had already begun walking back down the corridor when the invisible mage pulled out the pouch. She tossed it into the now visitor-less cell. It became visible the instant it left Vag's hand, and the mage saw Ovula startle when it landed beside her on the floor.

Vag dashed to catch up to the Ambassador, exiting with him as the door out of the dungeons opened. When she eventually got back to the guest quarters, Vag saw Nadia's husband, Captain Brightspark, knock at her door.

"Bugger." she said under her breath.

She froze as the ambassador turned around and looked in her direction. Seeing nothing, he shook his head and entered his room. Captain Brightspark meanwhile moved along to Barbidon's room and knocked. Looking behind her to check no-one else was around, Vag dispelled her invisibility.

"Captain!"

Barbidon opened the door at the same moment. This left the Captain uncertain which of the ladies he should address first.

"Ladies, good to see you both so soon! It seems the council of planning have chosen us for an expedition."

"You'll be coming with us to search for the Ant hill of Tion?" asked Babs.

"It's actually an *Anvil*, like a blacksmith's uses." Brightspark replied without condescension. "The Queen would like us to leave as soon as possible. Therefore, I wanted to invite you to a discussion with our fourth member, Father Vindictus about our plans this afternoon before we leave tomorrow at first light."

Vag thought frantically for an excuse to avoid being in the same room as Vindictus.

"Excellent idea." Said Vag.

As they walked, Brightspark looked at her in appraisal. "I recall you chastising my wife for underselling me, yet I hear you are a mage? You undersell yourself far more."

"Sorry. We wanted to do a surprise reveal."

Brightspark smiled. "Very theatrical, you might give Colonel Jackhammer some competition."

"I have a question." Sad Babs. "You said black smiths use Anvils?"

"Correct."

"What do white smiths use?"

The room they entered held little more than a map on a table and the man responsible for her brother's death. Vindictus smiled and gave her a polite bow as they entered. Vag still found it difficult to maintain a calm composure in his presence. She promised herself to never let that hatred fade.

"Lady Virginia, I find your face somehow familiar, have we crossed paths before I wonder?"

Vag felt sweat under her armpits. "I don't believe so, maybe it is just because I was in the crowd at the tournament yesterday?"

"Perhaps." said the Priest, sounding unconvinced. "The High Preist has discovered records of a Meritocracilian dungeon. 'Meritocracil' was an ancient god who rewarded power based on merit. He hid powerful artifacts inside dungeons of his creation. The Anvil of Tion was one of these."

"Thank you Vindictus." said Brightspark "The council has appointed me to lead the quest. I would request that you, lady

Virginia and Father Vindictus provide a complete list of your respective spell abilities."

Vindictus's strengths focused on healing, though he could also cast a light spell. Handy, in an underground environment.

Vag's listed all her spells, with the notable exception of invisibility and her yet-to-be-mastered spell involving the onyx and marble ball. This left:

The hands of hairdressing/dressmaking/aphrodisiac pouring/genital stimulation (she left off the last two), her electrical bolt, the defensive shield spell and the ice wall.

She brought out the bag of holding. Brightspark marvelled over this logistical boon. Travelling overland with an anvil would have been arduous without its weight reducing properties. As an afterthought, she also produced the immovable coat-hanger from Maygul's tower.

Brightspark chuckled, turning it on and off a few times. "Well. I guess it might come in handy if we need to hang up some clothes."

He went through a supply list, including horses. Two were to be large war horses for Babs and himself. Babs had never ridden a horse before, but in light of her overflowing eagerness, Brightspark declared they would forge ahead.

"Like a smith?" asked Babs.

"Like a smith." said the Captain.

Thirty minutes later, they were back in their rooms. Babs started getting ready for dinner, so Vag visited Clamax. He looked like he'd just woken up from a quick mid-afternoon grandpa nap. His hair would need fixing up, once Vag's hands of hairdressing were free.

"Did you get the pouch to Ovula?" He asked.

"I did." said Vag. "Then we met with Captain Brightspark. We leave tomorrow to retrieve the anvil."

"That's splendid news, that means none of us will be around when she escapes."

"Are you sure we should help them find the Hammer and Anvil? We are taking a colossal risk." Said Vag "I could just try to steal Orgasmodan's stones."

"You need to back yourself Lass, your arcane power puts you so much ahead of the people here. Use their resources to your needs."

"But I'll be doing it alone."

Clamax gave her a fatherly smile. "I'll be working to the same goal, just not right next to you. Besides, you'll still have Babs."

"You know what I mean. Someone who knows the plan, someone who can guide me."

"There aren't many of us left in a position to help the cause. It makes for lonely work. If there is one last bit of advice, I can give?"

"Anything." said Vag, eager for a pearl of advice that she could repeat to herself during coming the days or weeks as a replacement for Clamax's proximity.

"Don't share the burden. Quash any eagerness to confide your plan with others. Even if you think someone *could* be a potential ally."

Vag nodded, feeling guilty. She'd already been thinking whether Captain Brightspark and Nadia could be future confidants. Babs entered the room.

"Do you really have to go Clamax?"

"I am afraid so, but I have every hope of seeing you again once we complete the majestic plan." He said waving his hands theatrically, by dwarven standards anyway. Clamax reached into his pocket and produced a red vial. "In the meantime, I want you to have this."

"What is it?"

"It's a potion of giant strength. Just promise me you'll only use it when all seems lost."

"I promise. Thank you." Babs said, before wrapping him in a hug.

Once ready, the trio followed a servant to the large dining hall. Dinner was okay, but a significant step down from being able to imagine your perfect meal and have it appear in front of you. They didn't hang around drinking or making acquaintances, it would be an early start for the girls.

The next morning Babs awoke to a knock on her door followed by a gentle clinking sound. A large breakfast sat waiting. She shovelled the food into her mouth with slightly more grace than a dog, then got her azure combat outfit on. Thirty minutes later, she was outside Vag's door, greeting her as she emerged.

"Ready?"

"Ready." Smiled a bleary eyed Vag.

Captain Brightspark turned the corner as they were halfway down the corridor.

Babs jumped a step upon seeing him. "Hello Captain!"

"Morning Ladies." he replied, smiling at Babs' enthusiasm.

He walked with them to a courtyard where Vindictus waited with four horses.

It was an awkward start for Babs, who stared at her impressively sized charger with the same trepidation it felt staring back at her. Brightspark kept his steed beside Babs' to ensure it behaved. She looked pleased to receive his attention.

Vag didn't mind Babs giggling and flirting with all the subtlety one would expect from a girl who'd only orbited the sun sixteen times. Vag *did* mind the implications of this pairing, for it meant she was stuck beside Vindictus.

Making small talk with her brother's killer wasn't the biggest problem. It soon became apparent that he preferred 'big' talk. It was one thing to agree on the weather, it was another to sit smiling, *pretending* to agree on capital punishment for cross-racial or homosexual relationships.

As they made their way through the awakening streets of Del, it delighted Vag to see Nadia greet them near the gate. She spoke to her husband briefly, and he leant down for a kiss. She then looked at Vag mischievously, waggling a finger.

"You were right about only telling me a quarter of it. I wish we could have caught up again, but maybe after you've come back from this crazy quest."

"It's a date" said Vag.

"Good to see you again too Barbidon!" Said Nadia with a final goodbye wave "Look after my husband won't you!"

"I will Mrs Captain." said Babs.

They exited the gate against the flow of traffic and headed towards Tion. It would be a four day ride if they made good speed.

~

Clamax awoke at a more respectable hour. For the first time in weeks, he was not in a rush. The burden of responsibility was now firmly on Vag's shoulders and he felt almost guilty for it. He took a leisurely breakfast and said a short good bye to High Priest Blueballus. After leaving the keep, he explored the markets on his way towards the city gate. He made sure the guards observed him leaving the Citadel.

He spent the day walking back towards Wagrum. It was evening when he arrived and paid his respects to Sister Fetishia.

"Ser Clomax! What a pleasure to see you so soon." Said the chastity nun after opening her door to him.

"And you too, I am on my way back to the dwarven lands but wanted to stop by for a few days to offer my services in any capacity needed. I felt terrible for having to abandon you so soon after the unfortunate, incident."

"That is most kind of you, please come in."

And with that, Clamax settled in for 3 days of light duties in the picturesque town.

23

Compliments on the head job

Del the next morning:

Virgun almost skipped the halls of the keep, despite an annoyingly tight muscle in his shoulder. Electran and the heretical priestess Ovula were both in chains. He'd locked Orgasmodan's god stones in the vault of relics and four capable adventurers, including his own brother, were on the mission to find the required tools to destroy them. Finally, in five days', all eyes would be on him, hosting the Festival of Chastity.

He popped into the kitchen, to...discuss the menu for the royal feast held at the festival's conclusion. Yes, that was the reason. He might even get to say hello to the young lad Twink whose wellbeing he'd taken an interest in. As he entered the kitchen, the High Priest spotted Twinks' blond hair immediately and his already positive mood lifted even higher.

"Good morning your Grace!" said Twink "You look in a good mood today."

"Good morning!" Replied Virgun

"Did your Grace receive a headjob?"

Virgun's eyeballs unsuccessfully tried to examine his own scalp from within their eye sockets.

"What do you mean by headjob?"

There was some stifled laughter nearby, presumably part of a separate conversation in the kitchens.

"Apologies your grace, it is what the younger generation calls a haircut."

"Oh, why yes I did, it was just yesterday in fact. Thank you for noticing."

Such an observant young fellow, thought Virgun. "But that is not the reason for my chipper mood."

Virgun explained the events of the last few days, particularly how they were on the way to being able to destroy the god stones of Orgasmodan! Twink did not look as excited about the prospect as Virgun was, but then again, this was all very "big picture" stuff and well above the daily concerns of an assistant chef.

"You know what I found the most remarkable thing about them Twink? They look exactly the same as the god stones of Prudishia that we house in the same vault! Don't you think it's extraordinary that identical looking objects could channel the force of such diametrically opposed Deities?"

"Extraordinary your grace."

"Better not mix them up eh?" Said Virgun lightly elbowing Twink.

"Imagine that." Said Twink with a wink.

"Anyway, the reason I came, was to discuss the banquet dinner in five days time. Is the head chef available?"

"Of course, your Grace. I'll get him now for you."

~

Vag and Babs made good speed with their new companions. The bag of holding helped considerably by dramatically reducing both the size and weight of their bulkiest supplies. The first day had been on a major arterial road, followed by the comfort of an inn.

Babs monopolised the Captain's time, forcing Vag to listen to Vindictus's pious misogyny. She found the best way to deal with the priest was to nod politely, whilst thinking up scenarios in which she could avenge her brother.

Their subsequent three days took them off-road to the sparsely populated north of Tion. The countryside was an eclectic mix of cool-aired rocky high ground and plains covered with a coarse blanket of dry grass. Finally, as they neared their destination the party entered undulating forests with minimal undergrowth. Brightspark noted evidence of hill giants, so they kept their eye out, particularly at night.

~

In the Citadel, Virgun fidgeted alone in his room. Standing up abruptly, he exited, making his way to the dungeons. A jailor opened the door for him and he entered with his sleeve held to his nose. Ovula sat huddled in a corner, child-like. She raised her head, then her body, with as much dignity as possible, given her ankles and wrists were in short-chained manacles. A guard opened the door for Virgun and a humble chair was brought for him to sit on.

"Leave us." Said Virgun to the guard, who cast a wary eye at the elf before going back to his post.

"Hello Virgun." Said Ovula weakly. "It's been almost forty years, how have you been?"

"I'm very well as you can see. But I am not here to talk about me. I wanted to see if I could get you to renounce all this silliness. If you were to make a statement, a public statement that you have embraced Prudishia, I would be happy to commute your sentence to twenty years jail. It would still seem a sensibly strict punishment to human minds, but it would mean little to an elf."

"Twenty years is still twenty years Virgun. The Elven court has moved away from Prudishian law even as the humans have moved towards it. They will not take kindly to an Elf of noble blood, however minor, being executed for your religious crimes. They might even take steps to prevent it from occurring."

Virgun laughed. "Well the ambassador asked politely, but I'd hardly call that 'taking steps'. You must accept there's no way you are getting out of this."

Ovula lowered her head and Virgun's expression softened.

"Whatever made you leave the Elven court and follow Orgasmodan in the first place?"

"My son."

"Shavenish? What did he have to do with it?"

"He was homosexual Virgun, in a time when the Elven laws were as strict as yours are now. He was spending every moment of every day hiding who he was, increasingly hating who he was. It was tearing him apart. We both left to join Orgasmodan's followers for a wonderful life, free of judgement or inhibitions."

Ovula pulled out a simple pendant that hung around her neck. Virgun recognised it immediately. The gift he had given her son all those decades ago.

"Or rather, it was a beautiful life, before your soldiers butchered him."

"I'm sorry to hear that." Said Virgun fighting a lump in his throat. "Perhaps both of you could have been spared this fate if he'd had made different choices."

"Made different choices? Like you have? Virgun, you don't *choose* to be homosexual. You of all people should know that."

Virgun snorted. "Nonsense. I will not sit hear whilst you make up scandalous accusations, particularly after having gone out of my way to help you. Guard!" he called out. "I am finished here."

There was noise at the end of the hallway as the jailor got up.

"He loved you." said Ovula quietly.

Virgun frowned, "Then he wasted his love."

"Yes. I believe you are right."

The Guard returned, opening the door for Virgun, who left, shaking his head.

24

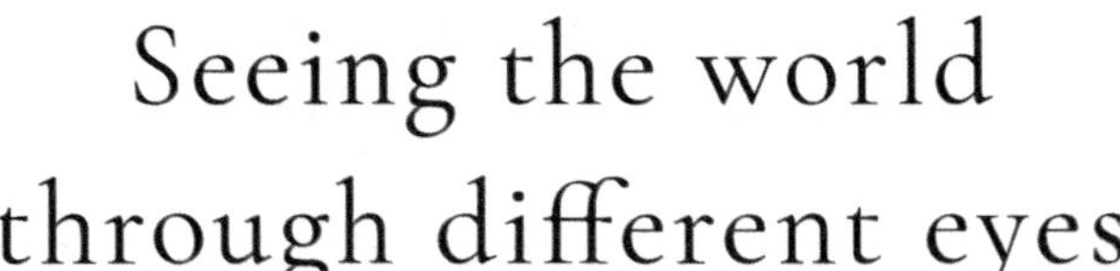

Seeing the world through different eyes

Brightspark was generous with his evenings, helping an attentive Babs with her swordplay. After each lesson, the pair would join the campfire conversation. On the last night, however, Vag thought she overheard Babs suggest a walk. Whilst Vindictus seemed oblivious, it worried her.

Babs' desires could not have clearer over the last few days and it posed risks given the way men looked at her. A risk that Vindictus would realise something was happening, a risk that Babs would have her heart broken by falling for a married man, or a risk that she could reveal their mission. Then Vag realised, to her surprise, that her biggest fear of all, was Nadia being hurt.

It was therefore with some relief that the two returned less than ten minutes later.

"Solved the problems of the world?" asked Brightspark.

"Not yet I'm afraid." replied Vag, focusing more on reading their countenance than providing a witty response.

Babs, heart on her sleeve as always, looked dejected. Vag felt for her, but it was for the best. Brightspark looked, circumspect. Her respect for him solidified.

"You haven't told us of your brave exploits defeating the cultists at the temple of Orgasmodan Captain." Said Vindictus.

"You were involved in the attack?" asked Vag, her tone starting aggressively before checking it mid-sentence.

"The temple was like nothing I'd ever seen before."

"Hmpf. Yes I'm sure it would have been quite hideous." Said the priest.

"When one of my superiors took his soldiers ahead and slaughtered the men and women inside, it... it didn't feel glorious. I'd signed up for the army to defend the realm from invaders, not to kill unarmed citizens."

Babs looked at her, clearly wanting to speak her mind. Vag subtly shook her head as Vindictus spoke up.

"It speaks well of a soldier, that he takes no pleasure in death Captain. But as you and I take on more senior roles, we must consider the broader good."

Brightspark nodded.

"Besides," The priest continued. "I assume many of them were homosexuals or hetero-racialists. It's the bigger picture you see Captain."

"Well I only hope this quest will avoid the need for any further bloodshed." said Brightspark.

"I couldn't agree more." Said Vag.

Brightspark gave her a tight, but not unkindly smile.

Babs awoke Vag for her turn on watch. The Half-Orc was soon asleep, leaving her alone with her spell books. It was perhaps not the most diligent of watches, but she couldn't help it. She was getting so close to figuring out the spell she needed.

As dawn approached, she saw a rabbit in the distance and a sleeping bird above it. Pulling out the onyx and marble balls she'd acquired from the gnome Fayzul, she started speaking arcane words in an inaudible voice comprising only breath and moving lips.

It took three minutes of intense concentration before she was rewarded with a shimmering cord of magic between the two animals. The rabbit startled and started flapping its arms, whilst the bird tried to hop along the branch using both its legs *and* wings before it teetered, losing its balance.

"What are doing?" Asked Brightspark.

It was Vag's turn to be startled now. She ended the spell. As she did, the rabbit brought its front paws to ground whilst the plummeting bird took flight to land on a different branch.

"Oh nothing, just a silly cantrip I'm learning that confuses creatures." said Vag.

"As far as anyone knows, you're the only person alive who can wield arcane magic. That requires incredible intelligence, I wouldn't call any spell you do a 'silly cantrip'."

Vag dismissed the flattery. She checked the others were asleep and turned to him earnestly. "Tell me more about Orgasmodan's temple."

"To be honest, it was like another world. The Phallus of Felicity wasn't the subtlest of water features, nor was the content of temples fresco's exactly child friendly, but there was a beauty to them. To cover the floors with the blood of worshippers was too much in my opinion."

Vag listened, drawing hope from his words. She wanted desperately to share the burden of her plans. To have someone wise to confide in. Instead, she heeded Clamax's parting advice. Turning to see if the others were stirring, Vag noted Barbidon was already awake, staring directly at her and Brightspark.

~

In Del, Ambassador Presley and his personal guards hoisted themselves into the saddle and left the courtyard of the keep, keen to make good time back to the Elven lands. They left on the main road, but soon diverted to a more northerly route. A precaution to avoid the Orcs he suspected were grouping at the border.

His mission had been a success. Queen Chastidia's Court now took the threat seriously and the more Orcs dying on human swords, the less Elves would die on Orcish Axes.

It had been fortunate indeed that the newly arrived mage, Lady Vaginia, had exposed the fraud Electran. She had kept her cards close to her chest during their casual dinner at the inn, but this did not annoy him. Presley was just relieved to hear the freshly promoted General Jackhammer was urgently bolstering their army's strength.

25

From jail to tower

In Wagrum, Clamax was also up early. He did not bother with breakfast or saying farewell to Fetishia. She had things well-in-hand. He'd been a little disturbed when she'd requested if she could show her torture techniques to him in a special dungeon room she'd set up, just, you know, for 'practice'.

He'd consoled the Chastity nun when she expressed her disappointment that the magical barrier remained on Maygul's tower. It appeared the contents of the mage's abode would remain a mystery to her.

Grabbing what little possessions he had on him, the Dwarf left the sleepy town as dawn broke to walk the two kilometres to Maygul's Tower.

~

In the Citadels' dungeon, High Priestess Ovula pulled out the small pouch kept hidden since it had materialised in her room. She'd eaten its note days ago, but not before committing every word to memory. She had feared the worst upon seeing Clamax at the Cities gate wearing the crossed legs symbol on his Tabard.

Ovula had cried in relief as Clamax's handwriting explained first that he had not betrayed her and second, that all was not lost. Since then, she had been counting down the days to follow the outlined steps he'd written for her.

Today was that day.

Ovula checked no jailors were in the hallway, then pulled out the mysterious inky black circle from the pouch. Laying it on the ground, she lowered herself into it and awkwardly pulled herself up out of the floor on the other side of the portal. It was difficult, as gravity pushed in an opposing direction on that side.

She found herself in a far more luxurious circular room. Kneeling, she reached back through the portal and found the edge of her original circle. With considerable effort, her bony arms pulled it through. Now both portals were in her new room. Ovula shimmied her manacled ankles down the stairs and pressed the big button next to a shimmering magical barrier. As it dissipated, the most wonderful sight she had ever seen greeted her.

Clamax beamed. "It worked!" Then, realising how weak she was, rushed to her aid.

"How did you do all this? Where am I?"

"I've got a lot to explain, but first things first. What would you like to eat?"

26

Meritocracil's dungeon

Brightspark's party took a few hours to find the entrance. It stood out like dragon's balls. That is to say, not at all. (Like lizards, dragons carry their testes in the lower abdominal cavity, directly attached to the kidney).

The entrance wasn't really an 'entrance' at all. It was a confusing wall of symbols and text behind foliage that had grown in front of it. For the first time on their four-day trip, Vag was happy to have Vindictus with them. He announced proudly that he could interpret the text. It was a language common to all religions: Hellvetica.

'Here-in lies the 4th Dungeon of Meritocracil, the god of Fairness. This dungeon is the home of the Anvil of Tion. He set these challenges to test and grant power to the worthiest individuals, helping them to further exert righteous rule over their populaces.'

"Shouldn't the Queen do this herself then?" asked Brightspark.

"Careful Captain." said Vindictus before continuing.

'The first test is one of intelligence. Press the symbols below in the correct order within three minutes and access will be granted to the dungeon. Start with number 1, then you will need to decide the remaining order. Fail to do this, and anyone who has heard or read these words will.... Die.'

"Sorry," said Vindictus "didn't realise what it said until I'd already said it."

"Nothing for it then, let's try to work it out." said Brightspark.

They stared at the symbols for a while. Vindictus talked through his theories as the others were trying to think. He seemed to have appointed himself 'person most likely to solve it', and, having done so, stood closer to the symbols than Vag or the Captain.

"Ah, I have it." Said the priest. "One, three, two, four, do you see it?"

"Why?" Asked Vag

Vindictus rolled his eyes before explaining the external and internal rotation of the shapes inside.

"Come now captain, we really need to be quick about this."

Brightspark looked thoughtful. "I am not sure Father, one of the shapes spins too far on the last one. What do you think Virginia?"

Vag abruptly held up her hand, not wanting to break concentration as the symbols started glowing an ominous red.

"But it does spins in the *right* direction." said the priest, moving towards the pressure pads on the rock wall. "We're running out of time. I'm entering the sequence."

"No!" Shouted Vag, trying to push Vindictus out of the way. He pushed back, leading to a short, undignified tussle. Brightspark was about to intervene, when Barbidon brought her own intellect to bare on the disagreement. She grabbed Vindictus, hurling him backwards with such force that he was momentarily airborne.

Vag lunged for the pressure plates, entering a different sequence one, three, four, two.

There was a moment of agonising silence. Then the symbols turned green. A vertical crack appeared in the rock face as large inward swinging doors revealed themselves, and a pathway into the dungeon.

Babs turned to look at her projectile, offering a hand to help him up. "Sorry Mr Vindictus. It's just that she's really, really smart. You read us the words though. That was an important job."

"Yes, well" said a red-faced Vindictus trying to restore his pride by brushing off leaves and dirt from his robe "No real harm done I guess."

"What was the logic Virginia?" Asked an intrigued Brightspark.

"It was the number of number of intersecting lines: This drawing has 1 intersection, this 2, this 3 then this one 4."

"Incredible. You saved our lives."

Babs and Vindictus returned to them.

"I would like to call you 'Vinpenis'." said Babs.

"What on earth are you talking about girl?"

"Well, it's just that Vin*dick*tus is a bit rude."

The party tied their horses up and carried all equipment except saddles in the bag of holding.

They had not travelled far into the stone tunnel before it became apparent the affair would be BYO lighting. Vindictus, (or 'Father Penis' as Babs had tried to call him before being discouraged), got them all to line up.

"Put your hands out in front of you, balled into fists. I will then cast two light spells at a time, turning your hands into lanterns"

Babs lined up first, her face squealing in anticipation as Vindictus intoned Prudishia's power. As the light was just about to leave his hands, Babs lost her nerve, dropping her hands to her side and asking.

"This won't hurt, will it?"

It was too late for Vindictus to hold back his accumulated religious load though, and the light shot out from his hands, directly to where her hands *had* been.

The twin light spells landed one a piece on Barbidon's breasts.

"Wow! Look at my boobs, their so pretty!"

Vindictus scowled, the others laughed.

"Let's do that again shall we?"

"Can I just keep them please?" Asked Babs, lighting up Vindictus, then Vag with her glowing breasts.

"Whatever." said the priest, who would normally have taken a more authoritarian style with such outrageous behaviour, but being rag-dolled by her had also thrown him figuratively. Soon, they were continuing down the well-built stone tunnel with six glowing hands and two high-beamed breasts.

They did not descend, but rather entered the hillside, which enveloped them in cool earth and stone as their distance below ground increased.

The two metre wide space opened to a large, square room with five metre ceilings and four colossal statues of scholarly figures. The detail was exquisite, Vag found it difficult to imagine a human artisan capable of creating them on such a scale. There was an age and grandeur to the room, it left her feeling small and unworthy. Each statue held a large tome and wore long robes. Their faces were contemplative. Vag was pleased to see equal representation of the genders.

Vindictus raised his left hand to point towards some script above the doorway out of the chamber.

"A wise man learns from his experiences, but a wiser man learns from the experiences of others. Reading affords us this opportunity."

"Well, I don't know about you Captain or Lady Virginia," Vindictus continued, "but I am a prodigious reader, so hopefully that will aid us in whatever challenge we face next." He started heading forward.

"There might be something we are supposed to do in this room?" asked Vaginia.

"The path forward is free, so unless want to pull out your spell book and read it some more, I fail to see what we are supposed to do here?"

"They're reading?" said Babs, pointing to the statues.

"That's it!" said Vag and Brightspark in unison.

"You're a genius Babs!" said Vag. "Come over here, so Father Vindictus can hop on your shoulders."

Babs looked down at the ground, clearly flushed cheeks illuminated by her breast-lights. "Aw thanks, but I wouldn't say I'm *that* smart. Not as smart as you. Maybe more mid-level genius."

Vindictus snorted, but came over anyway to suffer the indignity of sitting on her shoulders. This gave him the necessary height to read any potential script in the statues' books.

"Well how about." Said Vindictus, holding out a torch-hand. '1. *If an enemy can't chase you, do you really need to kill it?*'

"Barbidon, that one next." said her Jockey-Priest. The illuminated pair teetered over to another statue.

'2. *walk to the medallion and they will kill, wear it and they will fight for you.*'

They repeated the task two more times with the other statues.

'3. *ROYGBIV*'

And finally,

'4. *The same thing that bars your way could be half a bridge.*'

Vag wrote the advice down on the back page of her spell and looked up, smiling.

"Shall we?"

Thankfully, the dungeon was linear, and after fifty metres more stone tunnel, they reached an opaque barrier, obviously magical. Beyond it, Vag could make out many spectral looking figures.

"I'm going to test the barrier." said Brightspark

He attempted to put his arm through. It met no resistance, though immediately became the target of two ethereal creatures nearby. It was a shockingly fast transformation from semitransparent statue to horrific, rabid aggressor. As he withdrew his arm, the transition back to statue was almost as abrupt.

"They look scary!" said Babs, providing high level, strategic input.

"Can you make out an exit?"

Brightspark looked from many angles before spotting it.

"Yes. It's on the right-hand side. I propose Babs and I go first. Virginia, can your shield spell offer us any protection?"

"Only myself and one other person, and only if they stay very close."

"Ok, in that case you help protect Father Vindictus, and Father, can you prepare to heal if they wound us?"

"With Prudishia's grace I will heal you, though my ability it has its limits."

"Well, we'll just have to make sure we don't get hit too much. Maybe focus on Babs though, I at least have armour. Anyone have any concerns?"

He was met with silence.

Vag put one arm around the vile priest and cast the shield spell over them. The fighters burst through the barrier, with cleric and mage a pace behind.

It was complete mayhem. Sword strikes cleaved through the creatures, who reappeared behind Vag moments later as they surged forward. The creatures attacked her magical barrier with spectral blades. They connected with a shrieking sound that added to their hissing vocalisations.

The sheer number of opponents was overwhelming. Not willing to risk a lightning bolt, lest her shield spell falter, Vag just pushed forward. She could see an almost constant stream of blue light going from Vindictus to Barbidon, whose unarmoured body took multiple stabs and slashes.

Vag was the last to burst through the exit barrier. The violence stopped as abruptly as it had started. The onset of quietness was bizarre.

"Ow." said Babs, receiving a final heal from Vindictus.

Vag looked back at the instantly calm statues. They could've passed for sleeping angels.

The party caught their breaths and moved down the hallway.

Small mirrors adorned these walls. They fascinated Babs as she'd never seen her reflection before. She jumped in-front of each mirror with her breast bulbs illuminating a different pose each time. Even Vindictus smiled at her enthusiasm. A side path opened up and two towering stone guardians stood at the juncture, their eyes fixed to the party.

"They need pants." Observed Babs.

"This was the medallion one, right?" Asked Brightspark.

"Yes, I assume it's around the corner." said Vag, pointing to a kink in the path only ten metres behind them. "I could cast my ethereal hands to get it, but without a line of sight–"

"The mirrors!" Said Brightspark, going back to grab one off the wall.

Vag cast her spell and used them to carry a modestly sized mirror behind the guardians.

They did not move as it hovered past them.

Using one hand to direct the angle of the mirror, she spotted an oversized, ribboned, gold medallion on a pedestal, three metres around the corner. A few moments later she directed the second magical hand to it, bringing the huge disc of bling back to put around Brightspark's neck. The Captain looked like he'd just taken a one level dip into the 'Rapper Bard' sub-class.

The Stone constructs knelt to Brightspark then followed him as he made his way onwards. Vag and Babs walked behind the golem like creatures. It was a little hard not to look at their literally rock-hard buttocks wiggling as they walked. Babs couldn't help herself and gave one a playful tap on its rear. The creature stopped and looked at Babs, who, unperturbed, went on tippy toes and whispered "Nice butt" in its ear. It turned back to follow Brightspark, issuing no response.

"I think we should give them names." said Babs.

"Oh yes?" asked Brightspark "What did you have in mind?"

"I think I'll call this one Rocky, and this one..." she looked at the butt she had just spanked, "Buttwinkle."

Vag saw Vindictus look around, frowning, before continuing on.

Babs put her hands on her hips, doing an impressive impersonation of the priest's stern facial expression. Meanwhile Vag used her ethereal hands of butt cupping to cup the butt of Buttwinkle as it sauntered sexily down the stone segue to the next magical barrier fifty metres on.

When Vag got her turn to peer through to the other side, she saw seven larger, coloured versions of the spectres seen before. They stood, peaceful on the other side of a circular room.

"What was the clue to this room?" asked Vindictus

Vag open the page where she had scribbled it down.

"ROYGBIV"

"Hmm." mused Vindictus. "Could it be in some kind of code?"

"An Acronym?" said Brightspark.

"The colours! It's an acronym for them." Said Vag, looking back at the spectres in the room. "Red, Orange, Yellow, Green, Blue-"

"Indigo and Violet" completed Vindictus.

The party decided what the order signified, with the only guess being that the beings needed to be killed in that order, like destroying a rainbow.

After readying themselves, they surged though the barrier. Vag could not cast her shield spell again without recommitting it to memory, but Brightspark assigned 'Rocky' to protect her as the other party members and Buttwinkle went for 'Orange'. Before they got there, Vag unleashed her high-powered lightning bolt on the Red spectre, blasting it from existence.

"Orange down." called Brightspark a moment later.

Green, Indigo and Violet were all trying to attack Rocky, who focused on protecting Vag as per instructions. He was taking hit after hit to the face as his open arms formed two makeshift walls of a protective pen around Vag as they backed her into a corner. Hoping that 'Yellow' would be taken out soon, she prepared her last lightning bolt at green, who threatened to get over Rocky's arm.

"Yellow D-"

Crack! Was the sound of Vag's second lightning bolt as it obliterated the Green spectre. It had got within a foot of her face.

"Green down!" She said in a voice that sounded pitifully fragile in her ears compared to Brightspark's.

With little to offer now, Vag focused on survival. Rocky was getting pounded, so much so, that he went down on one knee.

"Blue down!" came another cry.

The Violet spectre shattered rocky's head, spraying loose rock and dust in Vag's face.

"Indigo down."

Vag blinked, making out 'Violet' as it jumped over her fallen protector. She ran along the wall's edge before tripping and hitting the ground. Vag swirled in time to see the final spectre about to tear her face off. Then a diving priest tackled it. Vindictus. It was enough to get its attention. As the creature moved to bite his face off instead, Babs got within Melee range. She decapitated it so clinically, an executioner with an unmoving target would have been proud.

Vindictus stood, extending a hand for Vag.

"Thank you."

"Not at all, Lady Virginia, we are all in this together. I'm sure you would have done the same for me if roles were reversed."

"Indeed." said Vag. "Indeed."

27

∞

Onward to the hammer

As Brightspark poured water on the dusty Vag, Vindictus spotted a hand size key dropped by the last spectre. They picked it up and moved to the room's only obvious exit, three-metre-high double doors with a monstrous cross beam and key hole.

The key turned. They lifted the crossbeam by positioning Buttwinkle on one side with Babs and the Captain on the other. The doors swung laboriously inwards with reverberant creaks.

In the room beyond, the sight of the Anvil overwhelmed Vag. Once in their possession, she would have one of the two required artifacts to destroy Prudishia's God stones. She just hoped the agents of the realm could uncover the whereabouts of the Hammer of Castra.

"What a sight. Would you agree, Lady Virginia?" Vindictus said. "Once in our possession, we will be a step closer to destroying Orgasmodan's God stones."

"Indeed." said Vag. "Indeed."

Unfortunately, they could not walk to it.

The room had no visible roof, only darkness. The walls extended beyond the reach of their light spells. There was also no floor, only three floating platforms that levitated the way hippos don't. They were on the first, a second hovered in the centre of the room, and on the far side, the anvil's platform resided.

"The same thing that bars your way could be half a bridge." said Vag, reading from her clues.

"That's probably referring to the beam." said Brightspark "But it's not long enough."

Vag thought on the problem. "We could get Buttwinkle. Sorry, the stone golem, to sit on one end to anchor the crossbeam. His weight should be able to hold Vindictus or I."

"There's an inscription on the opposing wall." Noted Vindictus. *"Upon reaching the Anvil, the platforms will connect."*

"Well, at least we don't *all* need to get across," said Brightspark.

After taking stock of their available tools, they spent half an hour brainstorming a solution. Unsurprisingly, it was Vag who figured it out.

Buttwinkle's butt sat on one end of the cross beam, with the impressive hard wood extending from his crotch. It reached a respectful distance towards the next platform. Brightspark and Babs stood on the golem's thighs to add to the already considerable counter weight. This would be necessary, leverage was not in their favour.

Vag stepped onto the plank, feeling like a mutineer sailor facing the abyss. In her hand she held the bag of holding, light despite its heavy contents.

Not wanting to delay the inevitable, she sprinted, leaping off the far end. For a split second, nothing was below her except the void. She landed with a thud on the central platform.

"Well done lady Virginia!" said Vindictus in a weak voice, nervous for his own jump. He sprinted but mistimed his leap, needing to do an awkward half-step before his final step. He landed with one foot just on the edge of the middle platform. His balance was precarious, he looked like he was about to topple backwards into the abyss. Vag's outstretched hand caught him.

"Thank you." he said. "See? We are already even."

Vag got out the bag of holding and Vindictus stepped into it as agreed, though not without trepidation.

Soon he was nothing more than a face and fingers holding to the bag's rim. Vag cast the hands of hairdressing. They picked up the bag. The weight was difficult to lift, but manageable. "You sure you want to go through with this?" asked Vag.

"I think it's our only choice. Besides, I trust you."

Vag floated the bagged priest over to the final platform. The spell was at the limit of both carrying capacity and range when it deposited him on the far platform. His relief was clear as he got out of the bag, cheered by Babs and Brightspark behind her. He went over to the Anvil, placing his hands on it, grinning.

Glowing beams of energy shot out to connect the platforms, and an exit appeared beyond the anvil. Regrettably Buttwinkle was still sitting with his legs dangling over the edge of his platform.

The materialising bridge cut his stone legs off at the chins. Vag tested the surface with a foot. Finding it firm, the party regrouped around the anvil.

"Excellent teamwork." said Vindictus smiling at Vag.

Vag returned it with a smile of her own.

Brightspark and Babs lifted the anvil into the bag of holding. As they did so, deep booming sounds resonated from within the dungeon. The booms quickened in pace.

The bag enveloped the heavy metal Anvil just as an enormous stone golem - probably ten times the weight of Rocky or Buttwinkle, rounded the corner to the rainbow Spectres' room.

"Run!" Came the unnecessary command from Brightspark.

Babs immediately scooped up the bag of holding. It had a heft to it now, even though the Anvil's weight was considerably lower inside the magical bag.

They ran down the large exit corridor, spotting light two hundred metres ahead. Vag risked a look behind her, seeing a valiant, crippled Buttwinkle attempting to tackle the larger Golem by grabbing on to one of its legs. The larger construct kicked it into the abyss, barely breaking stride as it continued towards them, across the bridges.

"Frigidimus!" Shouted Vag, but the animated rock giant smashed through the magical ice wall that appeared in front of it without breaking stride.

They wouldn't make it to the exit. It was too fast.

"Barbidon your strength potion!" called out Brightspark

"No!" Vag shouted. "Get the coat hanger!"

"What?"

"The coat hanger. Get it out of the bag!"

Babs put her hand in the bag and shouted: "Coat hanger!"

Her hand emerged from the bag, clutching the magical coat hanger.

"Now lift it up high and press the button!"

Babs pressed it. The metal coat hanger halted, nearly pulling her arm out of her shoulder. Babs was only two metres clear of it as the construct smashed into the immovable object. Tonnes upon tonnes of Rock golem instantly decelerated, with the entire momentum stopped by the small metal rod. Its torso shattered into several large boulders, filling the corridor with dust. The companions stumbled onwards, towards the light. Towards breathable air. Towards freedom.

They passed through another magical barrier, and found themselves in oppressively hot, yet very welcome afternoon air. All of them laid on their backs breathing it in.

"We did it. We actually did it." said Vindictus.

"I'm so sticky with sweat." said Vag. "The humidity doesn't help."

"Hmm," said a thoughtful Babs, adjusting her outfit. "I think I have a humidititty problem too."

28

An unexpected encounter

Vindictus dispelled their glowing hands and also Babs' 'boobs of bountiful brilliance'. The party made their way around the large hill to where their horses were hopefully still tethered.

"Lady Virginia." Vindictus began. "Whilst there probably isn't the need to discuss the specifics in *too* great a detail when we return to court, I will tell my brother that you accounted for yourself very well here today, very well indeed.

"Thank you, Father."

"I would like to apologise for not trusting you at the dungeon's entrance."

"The timing was urgent Father. We were both simply doing what we believed to in the interest of our Deity."

"Yes. Well said."

"And I'm sorry I threw you." added Babs.

"Yes, well, try to not do that again."

Brightspark held up a hand as a cooling breeze swept underneath the humid air, rustling the leaves loudly above.

There was movement ahead. A break in the trees revealed a rocky outcropping. A majestic, muscular white horse stepped onto it, surveying the forest. The cool incoming breeze blew its mane as if in slow motion. Vag realised what made this horse so unique. A foot long pearlescent swirling horn protruded from its forehead. This wasn't a horse at all. It was a –

"Stab Horse!!!" Shouted Brightspark as the creature turned its malevolent red eyes towards them.

The party turned to run for cover to avoid its charge. Vindictus was slowest to move, giving Vag an idea. She cast her hands of hairdressing/sewing/aphrodisiac pouring/butt cupping and now... ankle tapping.

As the beast bore down on them, the priest didn't notice the ethereal hand that tripped him. He went down hard, face first in the dirt. He scrambled to get up, but the beast impaled him in the rectum as he did.

The creature hoisted him into the air, the conjoined pair looking like a makeshift centaur. It flung Vindictus off. He whimpered in agony as the Stab horse, face covered in the priest's blood and colonic contents, turned its attention to Vag. She was just about to cast invisibility as a last resort when a stone struck it, then another, as Babs and Brightspark tried to attract its attention.

A heavy stone from Babs did the trick. The Stab horse whirled around and charged her. She'd set herself up by embedding the tip of her sword in a large tree on her right. Her right leg was also positioned against the tree, poised like a spring. Both hands held the hilt firmly out to her left. The blade crossing in front of her body horizontally at stomach height.

The Stab Horse picked up pace. It ran as fast as a thoroughbred with an ignited methane after-burner, yet the eyes remained steadily fixed on the Half-Orc before it. At the last moment, Babs used her magically enhanced dexterity and natural strength to push off from the tree.

The beast was travelling too fast to change direction. It tilted its head, attempting to follow Babs, but missed her by the breadth of a thousand hairs, (roughly five centimetres).

This left her great sword as an improvised trip wire between the tree and her leaping body. 'Trip wire' undersells the sharpness of her blade though. When the hurtling creature reached its eager edge, it sliced clean through bone like a battle axe cleaving cream.

The creature transformed from self-lanced stallion to flying bath tub. The four 'feet' of the tub sprayed blood as the pointy airborne barrel followed a sloping gradient behind Babs' position. It came to a violent, neck-cracking halt against a rock.

Babs crossed her legs and did a bow to the applause that she corrected assumed would be incoming.

The celebrations did not last though, as another whimpering cry from Vindictus Blueballus reminded them of his injury.

They gathered around him, with Vag working hard to feign the legitimate concern of her colleagues.

"I must... I must have stumbled on a rock." Said the impaled pale priest. He was already shivering from blood loss and or shock.

"Can you heal yourself?" asked Brightspark.

"This wound is too great and my powers are... too weakened by our earlier trials. Captain, I know you will do you sworn duty to the crown, but Lady V... Lady Virginia, could you please promise me you will not rest until Orgasmodan's God stones are destroyed?"

Vag paused, not wanting to make any such oath.

"I promise to end what you have started." She tried to say it solemnly, but her facial expressions failed to match her tone.

Vindictus's face contorted in confusion, fear and panic. Brightspark assumed it was because death was coming for him.

The real reason, was because in those last seconds of life, the priest saw the magus smile at him. She smiled in malicious victory.

As he drew his final breath, Vindictus finally recognised her. He recognised the dishevelled girl whose brother he'd had burnt at the stake, he recognised the hatred that burned within her. He understood her goal. Then... he understood nothing.

29

Expert hands

In the Citadel Keep, Virgun Blueballus and General Jackhammer listened, shocked by the blabbering dungeon Sergeant's report.

"What do you mean you 'lost' the High Priestess of Orgasmodan?" said Virgun. "You had her locked in a cell surrounded by three foot stone walls, did you not?"

"No one came or left this morning your grace, and there was no tunnelling."

"I want whoever was on duty this morning in the dungeons arrested." Said the normally laconic Jackhammer. "Guards." Two Queens guards stepped forward in their immaculate plate mail. "That includes the sergeant here. Lock him in the dungeons too. I will interrogate them all personally to get to the bottom of this."

After they left with the shocked Sergeant, Jackhammer turned to Virgun.

"When we attacked the temple, she channelled a powerful spell. It may have bested us if it wasn't for that unlikely private Hodgkins being immune to her attack. Do you think she could have channelled her god to escape our dungeon?"

"I doubt it. I know all the clerical spells and there is nothing that would have helped her escape a prison cell. Besides, I placed no less than three Prudishian holy relics outside the cell to dampen Orgasmodan's power."

"Then it is likely she had help." Concluded Jackhammer.

"The Elves!" said Virgun.

"Presley?" Jackhammer considered. "He was denied his request she be released into Elven custody."

"And there is more than that." Said Virgun. "I interviewed Ovula... that is to say, the Orgasmodanic priestess yesterday. She herself hinted to me that the elves may 'take steps' to prevent her execution!"

Virgun looked up to address a nearby Clerk. "Fetch me Ambassador Presley at once, he has some explaining to do."

"I'm afraid the Elvish Presley has left the building, the entire city your grace. I understand he left this morning."

"Dammit!" Said Jackhammer, smashing his glass against the other side of the room. "He must have bribed the guards and smuggled her out. Have you got a contact in the Elven court?"

"I have two." replied Virgun, feeling quite the spymaster.

"Good, I'll send riders to catch them. Prepare letters for your contacts in case they don't spot them on the road. And you'd best inform the Queen."

Military men, thought Virgun, so bold, so full of action.

Virgun realised, as the queen berated him, that messengers are tainted by the news they deliver. It also left him with the uncomfortable feeling that Jackhammer had feigned other duties deliberately to offload the task to him. After all, the offending dungeon sergeant did ultimately report to Jackhammer, not himself.

And so, Virgun walked the halls of the keep, feeling a little down. There was something especially emasculating about being scolded by a woman less than half your age, even if she was a queen. To add injury to insult, his tension headache had flared up again. As he rubbed his shoulder, he heard a welcome voice hale him.

"Your Grace, are you alright?" Asked master Twink. He looked like he'd just finished a shift in the kitchens.

"Oh, you're a good lad Twink. I seem to be unable to shake this tension headache. A terribly tight muscle right here on my shoulder."

"My father used to have a similar ailment, your grace. I learnt a herbal tea recipe that, when combined with a massage on the affected muscle, would relieve his headaches. If your grace would permit me, I could prepare the tonic and use my hands to relieve the pressure on your tight shoulder?"

What a considerate young man, thought Virgun. He was inclined to accept, though having a kitchen hand rub his shoulder in the middle of a busy hallway might seem a bit odd. Not untoward mind you, Twink was a man after all. It was just that it might look strange because of their difference in station.

"That is most kind of you Twink. I am returning to my chambers now. Perhaps you could bring me the tonic there and assist me with my headache?"

Fifteen minutes later, Virgun heard the knock on his door. Twink entered, his eyes taking in the room. As Virgun drunk the proffered tonic, he was proud to show off his many exquisite gowns. On Twinks request, he talked about his collection of keys, explaining that these opened doors to some of the most important places in the realm.

There was the one for the 'Chamber of planning' and the key to the 'vault of relics'. When that golden key caught Twinks attention, he explained to the attentive boy that the vault was where the god stones of Prudishia and Orgasmodan resided. Hopefully, it would not be long until they destroyed the latter.

Finally, the coup de gras of the tour was stepping onto the balcony. It provided a commanding view of the city and surrounding lands. The view was made even more beautiful by the setting sun's glow and a pleasant breeze that contained none of the city's odours.

"Well, now you've had the tour, should I sit on a chair? Asked Virgun.

"It may be best if your grace is lying down

"Oh? Yes. Yes of course."

Virgun lay down on his back, smiling up at Twink.

"Perhaps on your stomach, your grace."

"Right, good idea."

He rotated himself face down with the grace of a walrus. Twink sat beside him. Virgun reflected that no one else had ever sat on his bed before. Then he felt Twinks' hands on his shoulders.

Virgun's life was one of service. He spent so much time attending to the needs of the Queendom. Now, it felt nice to be vulnerable, to have someone attending to his needs for a change. The tension slowly melted from his shoulders and he felt his headache ease.

The relief from pain was so relaxing, in fact, that without realising it, he fell asleep.

Virgun slept so soundly that he did not awake until morn. Twink had seen himself out, but Virgun was a little embarrassed to have fallen asleep on his guest like that. The best thing however was the absence of pain. His mood lifted further when he saw a delicate handwritten note on his dresser.

'Hope you are feeling better your grace. I would like offer my services for further treatments over the future evenings during the next week, otherwise the headaches will probably return.'

Gosh, such a good lad, thought Virgun, feeling at the top of his game. This was timely, as tomorrow was the festival of Prudishia. Today would therefore be a busy one, overseeing preparations for the event. After a hearty breakfast that pulled double duty for yesterday's missed dinner, Virgun went to his first appointment.

It was a tradition of the festival, that the High Priest wash the feet of twelve beggars as a 'show of humility'. To Virgun, it felt like insisting a dragon show submission to a dozen rats.

But religious traditions were religious traditions, and you could no sooner change them than you could teach international diplomacy to a golem. One thing he insisted on, was to inspect and sign off on the chosen beggars before the ceremony.

He made his way to the back of Del's Cathedral with brisk authoritative steps, pleased with the crisp sound his shoes made on the marble floor.

Swallamina, the chastity nun in charge of sourcing the twelve candidates for podiatric cleansing, waited for him with twelve men behind her. It was like being expected to nod approvingly at the proceeds of a sewer dredge.

Virgun gave a quick inspection of the anthropomorphised refuse and took the nun for a quiet word.

"Is this the best you could find? They look filthy."

"Apologies your grace, they are beggars after all."

"Yes, but one can convey that through some ragged clothes, they need not *actually* be filthy. They are all to be clean for tomorrow's ceremony, do you understand? I don't want to have to wash any dirty feet."

"Yes your grace."

"Very well." He sighed, "I'll entrust you to see that it is done." He gave another quick glance at the beggars before heading to his next appointment. Virgun noted all of them had shaggy hair. He suspected none of them had ever lost a duel with a barber's scissors before.

"Oh, one more thing. I want you to give them all head jobs before tomorrow."

"Head jobs your grace?" The young woman looked mortified.

"Oh, don't look so alarmed sister, I know it's not part of your usual duties, they need not be of a professional standard. It is a part of the cleansing process."

She still looked shocked. *Honestly*, thought Virgun, some people got far too uptight about what was and wasn't their responsibility. If only more people were like Twink. Now there was a lad who *proactively* went above and beyond his official duties.

"Good day sister."

30

If at first you don't succeed...

Twink was tired and frustrated. The theocratic regime he lived under may have kept a facade of purity, but the underside was a dark, fetid place. Like a diamond encrusted princess with explosive diarrhoea. He had witnessed this dark side with the execution of his ex, three months ago. His 'grand' crime was being homosexual.

That their relationship had been a rocky one, was beside the point. As he had looked up the blue, hanging corpse, it reinforced his belief that he would have no chance of finding unparanoid love as long as the regime drew breath. And so, he had given up thievery to be an apprentice chef in the keep.

Last night had been his best chance yet of converting his proximity to power into action. He had failed. He'd thought he knew every guard in the castle. They stood like toy soldiers when under gaze, but offer them free food, and they'd toss it into their oesophagus with the velocity of a dog's breakfast.

The metal exoskeleton'd meat sticks were always seemingly unaware they were not starving.

The opportunity to sedate the High Priest in his room and steal the vault key with no witnesses, had been a golden one. Then it was back to the Vault of relics on the lower floor, near the kitchens. It should have been easy to distract the guard stationed there with the offer of left-over food and the promise to watch his post for five minutes.

He hadn't recognised the guard on duty. The big lump must have been a recruit, judging how he stood more erect than a masochist in a dungeon. He declined the offer of food, and so Twink had reluctantly returned to the High Priests' room. The golden key unwetted in its soul mate of a lock.

He looked across at the grand bed, which was far more attractive than its occupant. Virgun's skin had the uniformity of a half rotten banana, and the smell of a fully rotten one. Twink shuddered involuntarily. He resigned himself to repeating this exercise until his metaphorical stars aligned. And so, he picked up a quill from Virgun's desk and wrote a brief note, condemning himself to many future massages.

Virgun was pleased with how the festival of Prudishia went. There were sizeable crowds who seemed happy, most crowds are when you give them free food. The twelve beggars were suitably clean for his 'washing of the feet' ceremony, though he was disappointed their hair remained shaggy. Not one of them had received a head job from Swallamina.

What a stuck-up stubborn girl, thought Virgun. That would go as a black mark against her name for any future promotion.

The beggars seemed extraordinarily grateful for being chosen this year, thanking Virgun over and over for the opportunity to be involved. All requesting if they could 'do it again' next year.

Virgun again enjoyed his massage and tonic from Twink that evening in what became something of a little ritual.

-

Three days later Vag, Brightspark and Babs made it back to the inn on the arterial road from Del. The Captain had taken the fatal anal stabbing of the priest hard. Granted, Vindictus had taken it worse, but the man was the High Priests' brother, and he had failed to protect him.

Babs and the captain had continued sword practice each evening on the road. The speed of his student's progress impressed Brightspark. Her improved technique paired well with the strength and speed already possessed. Babs ate up his praise with the same enthusiasm of a baby bird machine gun swallowing the vomit of a parent.

Vag would have liked to leave it to Babs to console him on the loss of the priest. However, for conversation, Brightspark usually sought out the magus. She longed to tell Brightspark that Vindictus needed to die, that his death was righteous vengeance against a murderer. Clamax's warning still rung in her ears though, so she consoled him instead.

They heard of a rider about to leave for Del under moonlight, so the captain sent a message ahead with news that they'd secured the Anvil. After six nights and seven days in the wilds, it was a relief to be back to this tiny pylon of civilisation. Here they would get their fill of hot food, ale and music.

Babs predictably drew the eye of many a lonely traveller or romantically aspirational farmer. Vag noted that whilst polite to all, the Half Orc always returned to Brightsparks' side.

Vag did not get many looks, and those few were because she looked so unremarkable compared to her travelling companions. One man eventually fancied there might be some intrigue to uncover about her. He approached Babs with bulbous eyes that suggested his ancestral line evolved on a planet with vastly higher atmospheric pressure. He began a line of enquiry with her to determine Vag's 'story'.

"Oh that's Lady Virginia. She's a wizard."

This gossip spread faster than herpes in a brothel, and within the space of a minute, the entire establishment looked at her in feverish excitement, chanting "Magic, Magic, Magic."

Although exhausted from the travel, she didn't mind the attention. After an admittedly short lifetime of insignificance, it felt good to be extraordinary, to be above normality, to be above normal folk. She could become accustomed to the feeling.

She produced her two ethereal hands, sending them out into the crowd, skipping across the heads of patrons and across to the musicians, conducting them to play again.

The wonderment of the crowd was pierced by a slurred slur.

"That's pretty shit magic if you ask me."

The hands stopped conducting the musicians. The room froze, save for a reverse black hole that seemed to flash into existence. It centred on a tall, brutish looking man, and it pushed all nearby patrons away from him with a force proportionate to their proximity.

Babs stood up and turned to him. This gave the man pause.

Vag raised her non-ethereal hands as electricity arced between them.

"I thought firing off lightning indoors could hurt someone, though if you'd like to take a hit for the team?"

Masculinity is a funny thing. Once established, it is not "locked in". Instead, it has a fragility to it, threatening to shatter upon the failure of a single retest. At least it feels that way in the fight-or-flight lizard brain, which rarely consults the frontal cortex on such matters. So, it was striking that despite having an apothecary grade blood alcohol level and a large audience, the man apologised to Vag. A forty-five kilo twenty-year-old girl.

Vag decided she could get accustomed to this.

31

❧

Returning the anvil

It was with mixed feelings that Vag re-entered Del the following evening. The downside was returning to the smell. Three corpses hung near the gate had not improved this. A large sign below them read: *'For supporting an agent of Orgasmodan.'* Vag thought she recognised the skinniest of them. He was the Guard who'd opened the dungeon door for the Elven ambassador, and inadvertently, her.

The notification of their arrival meant a small clustered crowd greeted them. Unsurprisingly, not that many lay-people cared about the discovery of a magical anvil. The crowd comprised the lower members of the church, its most pious parishioners, and a few inquisitive blacksmiths. A bugler also hailed the keep to let the more important folks know of their return.

Babs got out the bag of holding and gave the assembled crowd a peak of the anvil. Her horse groaned asexually as the materialising anvil took on its normal weight.

Brightspark acknowledged the crowd with a few short words, and they made their way to the keep. The short journey was uneventful, save for a young lad of maybe sixteen, who rushed after them. He looked up at Babs in star-struck awe, producing a booklet.

"Excuse me, miss Barbidon, could I trouble you for a signature?" The lad asked.

"What's a signature?"

"What's the book? Asked Vag."

"It's a squiggle of your name," said the boy to Babs before turning the Vag. "and the book is 'The adventures of Barbidon'. It's pictures, mostly."

Barbidon picked up the book and the offered pencil.

"Hey look, it's me fighting lots of monsters!" Vag looked at some pages. The images got progressively lewder as the book progressed.

Vag leant down in her saddle and beckoned the boy towards her as Babs literally 'squiggled' on the back page.

"I wouldn't let a chastity Priest find that. Where did you get it?"

"Er, My brother bought it off an artist that saw miss Barbidon fight in the Queen's guard's contest. He's been selling lots of copies."

"Thank you, run along then." Said Vag, as Babs gave him back his treasure.

Brightspark, Vag and Babs were quickly ushered to the chamber of planning. It was busy filling up, even as they approached. Virgun was already there, looking alarmed as he noted the absence of his brother.

Erec of Tion was taking his seat. Jackhammer entered with them, putting a friendly firm hand on Brightspark's shoulder.

"Well done." He said before taking Electran's vacated place.

Last to arrive was the Queen. Anyone not already standing did so. Vag studied her, marvelling at the contrast between near flawless exterior and the ugliness presumably lying underneath. She sat, followed by everyone else with a chair. Babs went to sit on the floor, just to follow suit, but Vag stopped her by gently grabbing her arm.

"Captain, I understand your expedition met with splendid success? Is the anvil too heavy to bring up? I would like to see it."

"Your majesty." Brightspark bowed. He motioned for Babs to help with the bag of holding. "May I present to you, the Anvil of Tion."

There were gasps of amazement as Babs effortlessly produced the anvil which was the size of a medium dog, and the weight of eleven large ones, from the slim bag.

"Your grace." Said Brightspark with a sombre expression as he turned to the High Priest. Blueballus steadied himself.

"It is with great sadness that I have to inform you of your brother's passing."

The High Priest looked down, patting his robes. "How did he die, Captain?"

"A large Stab horse, your grace. It attacked us after we emerged exhausted from the Dungeon. He tripped as we rushed to a defensible position."

"I see."

"He died.... honourably" said Brightspark.

Vag successfully turned tiny explosive laugh into a sob. This received a kindly look from Virgun, whose own tear ducts were tiny dams trying desperately to hold the pressure behind at bay.

"I would also like to report for the council, that lady Virginia and Barbidon proved exceptionally capable in the quest. Without them, we would not have succeeded. One of the last things your brother said High Priest, was that he intended to vouch personally for Lady Virginia's ability and character."

High priest Blueballus stood up, eyes wet with a public vanguard of tears. He walked over to Vag, putting a hand on her shoulder, as she maintained the pretence of restrained grief.

"It is clear you gained each other's respect in a short period. I understand highly stressful situations can reveal more of a person's character than a lifetime of ease."

"He saved my life." Vag said.

"Then it is clear he thought it worth saving. Your majesty, I would like to request that we take father Vindictus' recommendation regarding lady Virginia."

"Certainly. Lady Virginia, you will be a welcome addition at court, and may I offer my personal condolences to you Virgun. May Prudishia light your brother's path. Barbidon, for your exceptional service, the Colonel and I would like to offer you a role in the Queen's Guard."

"Thank you, your majesty!" said Babs, doing her trademarked bounce.

32

Easy to swallow

Babs thought it a shame that they couldn't bring Father Vindictus's body back for the funeral, but it would have made all the other stuff in the bag pretty gross, so Vag had said no. The evening was going to be a big party held for the 'Heroes of the Anvil'. Babs fidgeted excitedly in expectation. She and Vag were given payment for their service to date. It was far more than her mother would have received for a season's worth of apples. Vag spent most of this sum on dress materials. The hands of just-about-everything went to work creating their outfits, and redoing their hair.

They both arrived 'fashionably late' as Vag had dictated. Courtiers, officers and senior clergy packed the grand hall. These were all mood-lit with sconces illuminated by light spells. When all eyes turned towards them, Babs decided it was best to wave.

"Hi everyone." She called out, but didn't get the response she'd hoped for.

A liveried attendant came to show them their places. Not being seated beside Vag disappointed Babs. To make matters worse, everybody seemed either too intimidated, snobbish, or racist to talk to a Half-Orc.

Lots of men *looked* at her, the way they always did, though if they got close, hands invariably covered their genitals like they needed protecting. Wives looked at her like she was a dangerous beast, dressed in the scarcely civilising veneer that was; 'evening wear'. Babs looked downcast at her wine, downing another glass. Maybe fancy people could be just as racist as the unfancy people back home. It made her even more glad that at least the Queen was nice to her.

In a contrast starker than a caffeinated squirrel blind dating a sloth, Vag was having a great time. On the other side of the hall, everyone wanted to meet 'The magus'. When not being introduced to someone, she chatted and laughed with Nadia; Captain Brightsparks' wife. Babs became paranoid that they were laughing about her. Maybe the Captain had told his wife about what she'd said to him. Now his wife had told Vag, and *that's* why they were cackling so much.

She was so deep into this negative train of thought, that when a deep muscular voice addressed her ear from short range, she startled, spilling half her wine.

"Lady Barbidon."

Babs turned around and saw an officer.

"Major Richard Longsword, at your service."

"Oh, Mr Richard! Yes, I remember you from the contest."

"Please..." He paused, raising an eyebrow. "Call me, *Dick*."

Babs frowned. "I try to use the proper word when I can. Is it okay if I call you Mr Penis instead?"

This time his other eyebrow broke free of gravity. "As you please." He smiled. She smiled back, admiring his physique. He was the strongest man Babs had ever seen, with a well-matched jawline and rich, dark hair.

She looked over to the Captain, who was talking with his wife and Vag. A thought occurred to her.

"Did you say you were a Major, Mr Penis?"

"That is correct."

"Is that more important than a Captain?"

He followed her gaze to Brightspark. "Why, yes it is. I am also a son of the Duke of Tion."

They chatted for a while, and Babs thought he was amazing. As her 7th glass of wine was downed, she wondered why she had seen anything at all in Captain Brightspark. Some lively music started up, and a polarised selection of the best and most drunk dancers braved the limelight. Babs met the criteria for the second group, so was keen to get up. Ser Richard instead put his hand on her forearm and leant over.

"I was thinking it was a little busy in here, maybe we could go somewhere more... private." He drove the point home with a look so unsubtle a blindfolded earthworm would have understood his intent.

"Oh." said Babs, understanding the intent one second after the hypothetical worm.

"I am going to go out that door, down the corridor to the left. There is a garden there. Follow me a few minutes after I go out."

"Um, are you sure this is okay?"

"Totally, It can be our little secret."

And with that, he stood up, exiting the hall.

It was a long two minutes. She ate her dessert, but was still left hungry from the human size portions. Her drunk eyes looked around the room, struggling to focus on individuals. She stood up and heard Vag call out her name. Babs couldn't go over to them now. Instead she smiled and tried to emote a gesture that said: 'Thanks for the invite, but I have something I have to do'.

A moment later she was in the hallway, walking towards the promised garden.

She spotted his robust physique, silhouetted by a single tiny light on the other side of the courtyard. It was quiet here. They were alone except for eight unjudging manicured conifers.

"Well, if it isn't the most beautiful girl in the world."

Babs giggled. "Well, if it isn't the most handsome man in the world."

It was fortunate both of them already wanted to 'get it on', because their mutually abysmal ability at seductive wordplay wouldn't have wooed a hesitant lover.

And so, 'get it on' they did. Although 'getting it on' wasn't quite what Babs expected. After kissing briefly, Ser Richard told her how pretty she looked again. That was nice. Then he asked her to get on her knees.

"Put it in your mouth." He confidently directed.

She needed to pee, badly. But Babs did as instructed, not wanting to seem inexperienced. Vag hadn't mentioned this activity, and it felt increasingly uncomfortable as he got harder in her mouth. She fought the urge to vomit. She had felt like doing so anyway, even before his prick started making her gag.

His speech and tone changed. He stopped professing her beauty, and started telling her, "You just needed taming by a real man" and "Yeah, you like that don't you bitch." She didn't know much about love, but she knew this wasn't it.

He grabbed her head with both hands, forcing it deep into his crotch. Her muscles tensed as she resisted this indignity. He kept on doing it. Her muscles tightened more, and in a reflexive action, she clenched her jaw.

Hard.

If a fortune teller had told Sir Richard that Babs would go down on him and swallow, he would have grinned. If, however, the fortune teller had told him *what* she would swallow, he might have stayed home.

Babs hadn't meant to gulp down the severed penis, but the truth was she was still starving from the miniscule dinner. What was worse, she kept on sucking, drawing the blood. Longsword looked in down in uncomprehending shock.

"Stop sucking my cock!"

It was the only time in history that the phrase 'Stop sucking my cock' had *ever* been said.

She pulled back and Longsword looked down in horror at his remaining stumpy blood fountain.

"Aaaarrrrggghhhh!!!" came the articulate baritone bellow of the Majorly Disarmed Major. Or rather, Dis-penised Major.

"Give it back!"

"I can't, I swallowed it."

"What?! You crazy fucking bitch!"

33

I'm not a man, not yet a woman

Vag heard the Major's scream from the banquet hall. She rushed out with everyone else. Several guards attended the Queen and High Priest.

They were all greeted with the sight of a kneeling, bewildered Babs looking around with blood dripping down from her mouth and neck. On the ground was a panicked, whitening Major, desperately trying to stem heavy bleeding from his crotch.

"Vampire!" Came the speculative cry from an uninformed observer.

Virgun, to his credit, was quick to act. He rushed over to the Major, asking to inspect the wound. When Longsword removed his hands, he bestowed the High Priest with a bloody facial.

"Aahh!" said Virgun, shielding his eyes. "Where is the, er, appendage?"

"The vicious bitch swallowed it!" said the Major, starting to lose consciousness.

Priests have difficulty replacing missing flesh. It was much easier to simply repair it. The only reason Clamax had been able to regrow the missing genitalia of Ejac Ula of Tion in the arena, was because Orgasmodan granted her priest's additional powers in genital healing.

Vag could see the indecision in Virgun's eyes. To heal the wound now would stop the bleeding, but leave Longsword without his manhood. The solution was obvious to her, induce vomiting in Babs. But she'd formed an opinion of the Major from Brightspark's campfire chats. So, she kept her smiling mouth shut.

Light emanated from Virgun's hands, illuminating Longsword's crotch as his penis stump healed. Colour returned to his cheeks, and he covered himself quickly getting to his feet, pointing an accusatory finger at Babs.

"That... thing attacked me!"

All eyes looked at the Babs who looked ready to burst into tears.

"Really, and how did your penis get out of your pants and into her mouth?" asked general General Jackhammer. His nose scrunched up disgust.

"I... was urinating."

"In the Queen's private garden? You know very well the privy is in the other direction Major."

"If I could speak in defence of Barbidon your majesty." Said Vag, appealing to the highest authority. "Barbidon is very inexperienced with alcohol and completely inexperienced with men."

"I've long suspected you of being a philanderer Major." Said Jackhammer. "But this time you bit off more than you could chew. Unlike Barbidon." A few sniggering laughs came from the crowd. "She isn't even human!"

The crowd quietened when the Queen took a step forward.

"Major, we do not accept your protestations of innocence. Barbidon may look like a fierce warrior when sober, but she is very young. You, however, are a High-ranking officer and man of the world. I would punish you for this, but frankly, our new 'hero of the Anvil' has delivered a swifter and more appropriate form of justice than I could have ever imagined."

Verdict issued, the Queen turned to leave.

"You are not going to punish her?" Asked an indignant Longsword.

The Queen paused, not turning around.

"Mind your tongue, Brother. You've brought enough shame to our Father's good name this evening." Said Erec, hitherto silent beside the Queen. He glared at his brother.

The Queen resumed her departure from the undignified scene.

Richard stared at his brother, looking like he was about to say something, but spoke to Barbidon instead.

"I demand satisfaction!" He shouted at her.

"Good luck without a cock! Came an anonymous wise-crack from the back.

"That is your right to request." Said the general. "Though I would not force Barbidon to accept, given the threat of war is looming over us."

"A war against *its* kind!" shouted Longsword, pointing at Babs.

Barbidon stood to her full height and turned her vampiric face towards him. "Don't call me an 'it'."

Longsword smiled. "Wanna make me? Then accept the duel you -"

"I accept."

Longsword smiled. Vag wanted to blast the smug bastard with lightning.

"Very well." Said Jackhammer. "The day after tomorrow. Two hours after dawn. Be ready." He turned to the fifty strong throng. "Well everyone, that should be enough gossip to last you all a month. Back to the banquet hall if you please."

The crowd reluctantly dispersed, a wide armed Captain Brightspark helping to herd them. This left Jackhammer, Vag, Babs, Virgun, and Longsword. The Major seethed in anger when he heard the same anonymous wisecrack in the departing crowd imitating his voice; "Major Shortsword, at your service." The crowd laughed uproariously and Vag smiled again.

"What do you find so funny woman? You're probably just another fake mage like the last one."

"Try me." Vag said with an even, calm voice.

"Don't you think one injury tonight is enough Major?" said Virgun. "I never trusted Electran either, but I can assure you lady Virginia is a real magus. I think it is time we all got to bed."

Longsword stormed away after a quick glare at the ladies. The general left, following him at an observational distance.

Babs looked like she was about to be sick.

Then she was.

Virgun looked at her, more in pity than disgust. He frowned and walked over to her. "Prudishia, forgive this child her sins and cleanse all toxins from her body." A blue glow extended from his hand to her shoulder and her posture immediately changed. She stood, shaking her head.

"I can think normally again. How did you do that?"

"Prudishia." Virgun smiled. "I do not judge you for what happened tonight Barbidon, you were taken advantage of by a terrible man. But you gave him a lesson he will never forget, and I have no doubt, it has been a learning experience for you too."

"Thank you Mr Priest. I have learnt a lot from this, and I'm very embarrassed for what I did."

"Well, best of luck for the duel, come and see me before it starts, he will be a formidable opponent. I can assist."

"With another Priesty spell?" asked Babs.

"Maybe." said Virgun with a non-creepy wink at them both. "But it's past my bedtime, so I must be off. There is a water feature over there if you want to clean yourself Barbidon. Goodnight ladies."

Vag watched him leave. She'd been observing him a lot, waiting to see him stare at Babs' body. She'd hoped to see the same lecherous hypocrisy Father Retentus in Wagrum had shown. Instead, he had displayed nothing but gentlemanly behaviour. In fact, she hadn't seen him stare at any woman all night.

"Is there going to be a war against the Orcs?" asked Babs, now alone with her friend.

"The army is prepping. It is looking like they are going to attack us."

"Is that why people didn't want to sit next to me at the banquet."

"People might feel conflicted about you. I'm sorry I didn't keep you better company."

"It's okay. I know how much you get along with Mrs Brightspark."

Babs washed the blood off her face and neck and they made their way back to Vag's room. Vag made a quick detour to say goodnight to Nadia, who, like everyone else, was gob smacked by the event.

"Longsword is *such* a Dick. He had it coming." said Brightspark's wife.

"He *was* a dick, and it's not coming any longer."

Nadia feigned shock. "You. Are. Terrible! Ok, take Babs back to bed, but we are talking more about this tomorrow. Promise?"

"Promise."

She wished she could have spent more time with Nadia, but it wouldn't have been right to bring Babs back in there for everyone to gawk at, and she couldn't leave her alone. Giving Nadia a kiss goodbye and waving to the Captain, she heard the bard start singing again with his lute. She recognised his voice as the wisecrack in the crowd. He introduced himself as 'Brandon Spears'. After quickly surveying who was in the room, he announced his next song was dedicated to 'Major Shortsword'. He started strumming amongst uproarious laughter and sung:

I'm not a man,

Not yet a woman

Vag left the room, shaking her head.

34

The duel

The next morning there were two notes delivered under her door.

The first was from the Queens secretary, requesting 'the attendance of magus Virginia as non-voting member of the council of planning, 10am'. The Second was for Babs. Brightspark was overseeing the training of new army recruits. She and the other Queens guard recruit, Gagre Flexus, were to attend in the main quadrangle nine o'clock. He also mentioned that there would be time after proceedings to give Babs some pointers for her duel with the Major.

Being thrust into the council of planning raised Vag's heart rate. The ability to tap the arcane arts seemed a poor qualifier for political power. As the day progressed, she decided it wasn't the worst qualifier either. At least it ensured the possessor was intelligent. The 120 year hereditary 'legitimacy' held by the Queen ensured nothing. Neither did the unhealthy dose of theocracy brought in by her.

Most of the sessions centred on preparations for an Orcish invasion. General Jackhammer led discussions on troop numbers, supplies, and the latest information from scouts. Her heart rate lowered as she realised she could take on more of an observer role than active participant. She used the time to watch the interpersonal dynamics, particularly the speech and mannerisms of the queen. Her concentration had thoroughly waned by mid-afternoon when the council closed, and went immediately to find how Barbidon had gone with her day.

Barbidon and Brightspark were easy to spot. They sparred in front of a lot of exhausted recruits. She had the impression they'd been dismissed, but voluntarily lingered to watch the spectacle. Babs did not have her black sword. They'd soon realised it was too sharp for sparring, even against an armoured opponent.

Everyone loves an underdog, and so the young men cheered every strike the half orc landed. She landed a lot of them too. The improvement under nine days of Brightspark's tutelage was remarkable. They had a short, early dinner with Brightspark and Nadia at their house. It was a sombre affair as all were nervous for Babs' duel tomorrow.

Vag awoke the next morning and enjoyed the blissful seconds before the dread of the duel hit her. They got some breakfast and went to see High priest Blueballus in his chambers. He opened his door, looking well rested, and ushered them inside.

"I best be quick about this. I can't be seen taking favourites. Could you stand before me please Barbidon?"

Barbidon did as asked. Virgun placed a hand on her forehead.

"Oh mighty Prudishia, may your power guide thy humble servant Barbidon."

A blue light similar to the one that had cleansed her of alcohol two nights ago emanated from his hand to her head.

"Do you feel different Babs?" asked Vag.

"Yes. I'm so awake, it feels amazing!"

Virgun smiled. "It will only last a few hours, but you'll have an edge in the duel."

Five minutes later, the assembled crowd parted for the Half-orc and magus. They entered the dueling courtyard with purposeful strides. Arched hallways supporting open air ramparts surrounded the ten by ten metre square. Spectators crowded both floors, eager to witness mortality. Ten minutes later and five minutes late, Major Longsword arrived.

The contrast between the duelists was stark. Plate male covered the Major, the gleaming weapon that was his namesake held in one hand and a huge tower shield in the other. He looked like he could walk through the kill zone of a Castle's entrance and come out yawning.

Babs, had the same azure outfit she'd worn in the Queens guard contest. It was designed for defence through mobility, useless against archers, but sensible against a single swordsman. Then there was her sword. The crowd was transfixed by the inky black blade that could destroy light and life itself.

The General officiated, laying down the only ground rule.

"No-one leaves the circle until someone has yielded or died."

Jackhammer withdrew, leaving the combatants facing each other. The crowd fell into eery silence, with courtiers unwilling to throw their support behind orc nor arsehole. They *were* fascinated though.

Longsword stepped forward confidently. He raised his sword to strike, but instead shield barged her. Babs was pushed back by his armoured weight yet was strong enough to stay upright. She gave ground, danced around him, and moved back towards the centre.

He came at her again, and again. She parried or dodged it all, but without her launching a counterstrike, he looked the more convincing opponent. With no armour, it would only take one successful strike to end the matter.

"Fight back coward!" Shouted Longswords as she danced around him once again.

Babs kept her cool.

After three minutes, Longsword's sword arm moved a little slower. He raised it high and wide. This time, Babs blocked it with her sword upright, then flattened her blade, bringing it pommel first into Longswords helmeted face. It struck with brutal efficiency, stunning him and crumpling the face guard. This gave time for her to bring her weapon to the other side of her body and swing down at his ankle. There was some armour there, but it went straight through anyway, leaving him without only one foot.

The Major toppled over, his helmet falling off as he struck the ground. Babs walked up to him.

"Call me an 'It' again!" Said Babs.

Longsword looked up with a stunned, crumpled face and said nothing. It was a similar response from the crowd. They looked uncomprehendingly at how this barbarian of a girl, a recruit with no armour, had taken down the Major so clinically, so professionally.

Satisfied, she turned around. As it happened, the major *did* call her an 'it' as she turned from him, but his sword clattered to the ground at the same time, obscuring his weakened voice.

This fortunate coincidence of noise was to bring him only another thirty-one hours of life.

35

The threat

Clamax and Ovula arrived at the Highmana barrier, tired, but not exhausted from their road-avoiding travel. The portable portals, one on their person and one in Maygul's tower, had enabled travelling light and fast. They facilitated regular rests and hot meals, not to mention sleeping in comfortable, safe beds each evening.

There'd been one major challenge, a Spriggan. The territorial humanoid tree had attacked them on their second day of travel. Even then, the portal had been useful. Quickly dropping it on the ground, they'd jumped through to the tower. This gave them a blind choke point, perfect for defence. When the confused creature stuck its head through, Clamax king hit it in the face with his hammer.

Ovula had forewarned him what to expect at the temple site, but it was confronting to see the devastation. The Phallus of felicity was a pile of rubble, the temple, an open tomb of rotting corpses.

"There is a reason the dead are buried or burnt." said Climax. "It helps us avoid the humiliation of in store for own bodies."

"Much as I would like to bury the dead and clean the temple, repairing the Phallus needs to be our focus." said Ovula.

Back in Del, Virgun sat in the chamber of planning with the Queen, Jackhammer and the two non-voting members: Erec of Tion, and the Magus Virginia. Numerous scribes and guards also lined the room. First up on the agenda was a newly arrived scout the General had invited in. He was greyhound lean and looked too tired to be nervous.

"I'd been watching them for about a week General. I left to report to you when they started packing up camp and heading toward Jaldur."

"What sort of numbers?"

"Three Thousand."

"Does that include women and children?" asked Virgun

"There are women in the group your grace, but it is entirely a fighting force. The women are armed just as the men."

"If they head straight to Jaldur, how many days would you estimate before they get there." asked the Queen.

"About four your majesty."

"Have they been told of the threat?" Asked Vag.

"Yes, your..." The scout paused, unsure how to address her.

"Magus will do." Said Vag.

"Yes Magus. I quickly told the priest of the town on my way back to Del."

"Three thousand doesn't sound *so* bad." Observed Virgun. "We've already raised a force of Ten Thousand."

"It's not comparable your Grace." Said the general, sounding frustrated. "You saw Barbidon defeat Major Longsword this morning?"

"Well yes, but she is something extraordinary though. A hero of the anvil."

"*She* is a female, and only *half*-orc. I can guarantee you a recruit will falter when they see a full-blooded male on the field."

"What are our advantages, General?" Asked Vag.

"Four hundred cavalry, better bows and our tactics. They are not the smartest race."

"I have heard from the Duke this morning." said Erec. "He hopes to have another six thousand to Del within the week."

The council discussed options. Jackhammer and the Queen settled on an immediate defence of Jaldur at first light tomorrow. The Duke of Tion's forces would have to arrive later to decide victory.

The second visitor to present to the council was a rider sent after the Elven ambassador and Orgasmodanic Priestess.

"We spotted neither on the main road." Said the man. "However, both of your Grace's contacts in the Elven court reported that the ambassador didn't return with the priestess. He also discussed with members of court, the feasibility of making an offer for her release."

"Well, if the Elves didn't rescue her, who did?" Asked the Queen.

Virgun tapped his chin. "Maybe she did it by herself after all? Charmed the guards using her demonic powers and escaped to-"

"Repair the Phallus of Felicity!" finished Jackhammer. Virgun looked at the general with a frown. *'Sorry for interrupting the start of your sentence with the middle of mine.'* Thought the High Priest.

"Surely your men utterly destroyed the Phallus General?" Said Vag in a nonchalant tone.

"They built it from scratch once, presumably they can do it again." He tensed. "Has anyone checked if Orgasmodan's god stones are still secure in the vault of relics?"

"I was in the vault yesterday." said Virgun "Both Prudishia's and Orgasmodan's god stones remain safely behind a locked door. It is guarded at all times."

The Queen visibly relaxed. "We should send a force to investigate the temple site."

"Your majesty." said Vag. "I am new here and also alarmed by this turn of events. However, with the Orcs at our doorstep, should we be diverting any of the army's strength at this critical juncture?"

The Queen contemplated.

"I could send Major Longsword." Said Jackhammer before turning to Virgun. "Your Grace, were you able heal Major Longsword's leg?"

"I was. Barbidon had the good sense not to eat the severed body part this time." There was a smattering of laughter. Virgun allowed himself a congratulatory smirk at his wit.

"Good." said Jackhammer. "He has lost the respect of the common soldier after the events of the last two days anyway. He'll go with just a few men, including Hodgkins, the private immune the priestess's spells. With all her followers dead, I'm confident they'll defeat her."

Vag looked about to interject. Perhaps worried about the diversion of men from the Orcish division.

The General looked at her. "The army will be stronger for it."

The rider did a subtle cough. The cough of one who needs to say something but isn't important enough to directly interrupt. His superiors took the hint and turned to him.

"I have another piece of important information. Apparently a noble on the Elves' southern border owned the Hammer of Castra. An Orc raiding party ransacked his estate five years ago. The hammer was stolen. The Elves believe it remains in the family of the Orcish leader, Karak."

36

Long live the Queen

To have the young Magus sitting with the council members for dinner pleased Virgun. It was nice to have another real intellectual around. Lady Virginia was young, but he harboured little doubt she would thrive under his mentorship. They chatted of palace protocols in detail, which she seemed eager to understand in a single evening.

He was sad to not be able to fully satiate her appetite for learning, but he had his regular appointment with Twink to keep. It was such a pleasant way to finish each day, having the tension kneaded out of his shoulders. The lad had such a positive disposition too, it was hard to feel unhappy in the presence of such a smile.

He bid the Queen and others good night, before heading up to his chambers, looking forward to his massage and another good night's sleep.

A scream stirred Virgun from his slumber.

The volume rivalled a teenage girl discovering the brotherly theft of a personal diary. The Tonic Twink prepared for him each night normally made him sleep through without fail, so it was with considerable grogginess that he awoke. Triple thumps sounded against his door. He opened it abruptly to see a guard.

"The Queen your Grace."

"Was that her screaming?"

"Yes. There has been an attempt on her life."

Virgun was groggy no more.

Many guards crowded around her doorway.

"Make way, make way!" He said.

He was unprepared for the sight that greeted him. The Queen's bedchamber embodied her purity with white sheers hanging around a four-poster bed. On the far side the Queen sat sobbing, covered in blood and holding one of the banquet hall knives.

"Your majesty! Are you alright?"

As he rounded the bed, he realised it was the blood of lady Virginia. The magus lay lifeless with multiple stab wounds to her torso. A more ornate, bloody knife resting near her hand.

Quickly examining the Queen's royal personage. He channelled Prudishia's grace to heal three ghastly gashes on her arms. None had been life threatening.

She stoically steadied her breathing and looked at Virgun. The Queen's hands were shaking.

"I was awoken, but not by a noise. It was as if.... It was as if Prudishia herself was alerting me to a threat. I grabbed a knife I'd take from the banquet hall and hidden under my pillow long ago. I used to think I was a paranoid for keeping it there. I looked into my empty room, seeing nothing, then... " she held out a trembling hand to point at the corpse of the magus. "Seeing her." Queen Chastidia jerked her head around to face him again. "She'd been invisible, but as she attacked, the spell broke and I defended myself."

"Oh, your majesty. I am so sorry I could not protect you, to see her evil."

"Do not blame yourself, High Priest, for we were all fooled. Her duplicity duped your brother, Captain Brightspark, myself and even the Dwarven paladin Ser Clomax. The person who inadvertently got closest to the truth was Electran, and that was a self-serving stab in the dark."

The Queen did a half-mad chuckle. "Ha! Stab in the dark!" as she looked down at the blood soaked knife in her hand.

Erec of Tion and Jackhammer burst into the room with belated energy. Virgun brought them up to speed.

"Any thoughts to motive? Asked Jackhammer.

"As she lay dying, she said she would have made a better Queen than me."

He gave a supportive, mirthless chuckle.

"Could there be a link behind this assassination attempt and the Orgasmodanic Priestess's escape?" probed the General again.

"Unlikely. Virginia was a hundred kilometres away from the capital when Ovula escaped." Said Virgun. "I suspect she was simply hungry for power, and her arcane talents alone did not satiate that greed."

Jackhammer looked unconvinced. "So, she expected we would all bow down before her because she'd snuck in and stabbed the rightful ruler? Seems like the plan of a simpleton, not a magus."

"Well, whatever her goal, it is thwarted now." Said the Queen. She looked to Jackhammer. "I don't want this attempt on my life to be a distraction from the Orcish invasion. I think even the investigation of the Orgasmodanic temple should wait until that threat is over. Besides, once we retrieve the Hammer of Castra from the Orcs, we can destroy Orgasmodan's god stones. That will solve the problem of the priestess once and for all."

Jackhammer gave her a look. It was not unkindly, but definitely had the patronising tone some use when counselling a victim of shock.

"You are wise your majesty, but I have already despatched the Major, Hodgkins and four other men with all haste to her temple. As mentioned, the Major would have only been a distraction to the men, and Hodgkins has few talents, bar his immunity to the priestess's spells."

"I see." Said the queen, sounding a little distracted. Understandable given the events.

"I have an early start leaving with the troops so I'll leave you to rest." Said Jackhammer. "I'll have Barbidon brought to the dungeon. It is a proper precaution given her relationship with the attempted murderer."

"Do not treat her improperly though General. I would like to interview her personally, and may even allow her to re-join the army as it marches out tomorrow if I am satisfied."

Virgun thought this an unusual request. So did the General judging by his face. His bow was respectful though.

"Yes, your majesty."

"May Prudishia guide you on the battlefield general."

"Thank you, your majesty."

The General left. Ser Erec looked like he wanted to stay, but also bid the Queen goodnight. Virgun assisted with practicalities. The Queen would sleep tonight in Electran's newly cleaned and vacated quarters with a double guard at the door. Leaving her in the capable hands of fussing maids, Virgun excused himself to go back to bed. His eyes felt heavy, despite the adrenaline inducing event. As he reached his chamber door, a door he'd forgot to close, Twink almost bowled him over.

"Twink, what are you doing up here at this hour?"

"I heard the call for guards, I worried that I might not have locked the door behind me when I left. I worried... I worried that something might have happened to you."

Virgun was speechless for a moment.

Being in a position of power meant people always said nice things to him. Being an excellent judge of character, he could discern simple sycophancy from 1.609 kilometres away. This, however, was the most honest, raw concern anyone had ever shown towards him. The lad was almost beside himself, taking short rapid breaths. Virgun felt his eyes involuntarily misting up.

"Oh Twink, sometimes I feel you are an angel watching out for me." He smiled and, on a whim, gave Twink what he clearly needed, a long tight hug, rubbing his back. Virgun realised it was highly unusual for someone of his station to take such care of a lowly kitchen hand, but it felt like the right thing to do in that moment. "Thank you Twink. I am fine. The commotion was around the Queen. There was an unsuccessful attempt on her life this evening."

37

Success for Twink

Thirty minutes earlier.

Twink walked down the hall, past the 'Vault of Relics' as he'd done every evening for the last week. Again, he saw the stubbornly dutiful guard who'd been on vault duty every night of late.

"Sure I can't tempt you to choose a left-over dessert in the kitchen? It's just around the corner." Twink kept his tone light and smile bright, trying to convey impartiality whether or not the lunk took up the offer.

"You are such a feeder master Twink." Said the guard, smiling back. "I can't when I'm on duty though."

"I'm only a feeder because you're practically wasting away." Twink held his smile as he turned away from him, continuing his stroll down the hall. As soon as he had his back to the guard, his smile turned to a silent scream of exasperation. How the hell was he going to get access to the relic room!

Five minutes later, there was a scream on an upper floor. Shortly afterwards a male voice called out

"Guards!"

Twink heard a metallic clunking sound getting softer. It was coming from the vault of relics hallway. Daring a look, he saw the guard at the other end, leaving his post to attend the raised alarm.

He bolted, reaching the locked door in an instant, his shaking hands almost dropping the key. He forcibly calmed himself and eased it in. There was a satisfying clink. He looked left and right, and went inside.

The room's only illumination came from two brilliant white balls on a pedestal at the room's centre.

"Ok, so they're Prudishia's god stones." He said to himself, looking frantically around the room. He lifted lid after lid on different boxes, all to no avail. Then at the back, he spotted the only plain looking black wooden box in the vault. The smallest hint of light emanated from its joins. On inspection he saw another two balls, identical to the ones on the white pedestal.

"There you are, my pretties" he said, bringing them over and swapping them with Prudishia's Stones. Soon he was back in the hallway, door locked behind him.

Twink may have been a lowly Chef's apprentice, but he had the notion that his actions tonight would have a ripple effect, forever changing the course of the world. Like a planetary-sized butterfly flapping its wings.

He took 3 steps at a time up to Virgun's chambers on the fourth floor, nervous that whatever had alarmed the guards would have also awoken the High Priest.

Virgun's door was open.

His heart was racing and breathing heavy. There seemed to be no activity on this floor, though there was noise directly above, on the floor of the Queen's chambers. *What the hell was going on?* He was relieved to find the High Priest's room empty, but anxiety still jittered inside him. Had the old man noticed the missing key? Quickly putting it back and exiting the room, he ran directly into Virgun.

"Twink, what are you doing up here at this hour?"

His synapses fired in a panicked frenzy, desperately trying to come up with some plausible reason. Why *had* he gone back to the High Preist's chambers in the middle of the night?

"I heard the call for guards, I worried that I might not have locked the door behind me when I left. I worried..." Twink paused, catching his breath. "I worried that something might have happened to you."

Virgun's befuddlement, which, in hindsight, had never bordered on accusation, melted into gratitude. It even looked like the old man's eyes were glistening.

"Oh Twink, sometimes I feel you are an angel watching out for me." Virgun smiled and wrapped him in an embrace that Twink feared would never end. He managed not to flinch at the creepy hold as the priest proceeded to rub his back.

"Thank you." Said Virgun, "I am fine. The commotion was around the Queen. There was an unsuccessful attempt on her life this evening."

Virgun relayed the events. The brutality shocked Twink, but ultimately he decided it was way above his pay grade.

"I've been told by the head chef that I need to pull some extra shifts in the kitchen."

"Oh?"

"Yes. One of the lads was drafted for the army. Unfortunately, it means I may not have time to help with your tension headaches each evening."

"Oh, I understand. Well, we will still see each other around the keep, I dare say?"

"Yes, of course your Grace."

"Please. When it is just the two of us, I would like you to call me Virgun."

38

Terrible news

A cough woke Barbidon. She opened her eyes to candle-light. General Jackhammer loomed above her, accompanied by three soldiers.

"What's going on?"

"The Magus Virginia tried to kill the Queen. Fortunately, her majesty defended herself, killing the Magus."

This would have been difficult news to process wide awake. It was incomprehensible a second out of sleep.

"Tried to kill the Queen?"

"Yes, you are being detained because of your close connection to the Magus."

Guards manacled Barbidon. Between shock and sleepiness, she did not even resist. On the way to a cell, she halted, addressing the general. "Did you say Vaginia is dead?"

"Her name was Virgina, and yes. The Queen showed impressive alertness and courage in fighting her assailant."

Babs started crying. She had the vague notion it wasn't appropriate for a champion warrior, but she felt child-like, alone and out of her depth. Was this the 'Majestic Plan' Vag and Clamax were always mentioning? Killing a Queen didn't seem right, it was too '*big*' and the queen seemed nice too. Now, Vag was dead, and Clamax wasn't here to help her.

"Could I talk to Captain Brightspark?"

"Captain Brightspark is sleeping, ready for the army to leave in the morning."

"I didn't know she wanted to kill the Queen." said Babs between undignified sobs.

"Tell that to her, she has asked to see you personally before deciding your fate."

Five minutes later, Babs was alone in a dark cell, in a dirty dungeon, in a strange castle, in a strange city. She'd not been there long before voices and the jangle of keys reverberated down the hallway.

"Leave us." said a delicate but authoritative female voice.

Her majesty, Queen Chastidia came into view, illuminated by torchlight. She looked out of place here, like a diamond, elegantly set in a dog turd.

Babs went to her knees. "I'm so sorry your majesty. I didn't know she was going to do that. I didn't know she was going to try to kill you. She was smarter than me, so I just, I just-"

"Relax Babs, it's ok. Everything is fine." Said the Queen.

Babs hadn't expected the Queen to talk like that. She sounded too casual. Why would the Queen call her 'Babs'?

39

❧

Deep cuts

Four hours earlier.

Vag was distracted at dinner. Things were moving too quickly. She and Clamax had not anticipated the efficiency of the realm's spy network, and that the council would already know Ovula was not with the elves. Vag would have to move fast to stop Longsword's expedition. If she failed, they would discover the efforts of Clamax and the High priestess to rebuild the Phallus of Felicity. Trying to get as much information about courtly life as possible from the High Priest, Vag then left the banquet hall before the Queen, palming a serrated knife and returning to her chambers.

In her room, she grabbed a second ornate knife sourced from the necromancer's abode and placed the marble and onyx balls from Maygul's tower in her pocket. Taking one last look around, she checked the hallway was clear, cast invisibility on herself and closed the door.

Finding her way to the Queen's Room was easy. It was on the highest floor, barred by tall oak doors behind two guards standing to an attention almost as steadfast. It was a twenty-minute wait before she heard four heavy and two delicate footsteps ascend the stairs. She had to awkwardly dodge in between the v shaped formation the Queen and her two accompanying guards formed. In contrast, entering the double doors as they opened for her was a breeze. With no shoes on, an imperceptible breeze was the only trace she left.

Once the doors were closed, she was alone with the Queen. Vag was more conscious of sound now, given the guards clanking armour could no longer cover her steps. A corridor extended to another set of doors. The queen opened only one of the double doors, making it difficult for Vag to slip through behind her.

The Queen undressed immediately.

They say beauty is in the eye of the beholder. Unfortunately, beholders of beauty seldom differ. Few would have said Vag possessed more of it than the Queen. She was around the same age and also slight of build, however, The Queen's blond hair was lustrous, her waistline thinner and her face more symmetrical. Royal inbreeding had apparently not caused issues for Chastidia.

She used a basin and cloth to give herself a quick Queen clean. It was a remarkably humble affair, Vag had expected a lavish bath attended by servants. Strangely the Queen put perfume on before going to bed. She sat reading a book by candlelight whilst Vag waited for her to sleep.

She was startled when the wall she'd been leaning against suddenly shoved her forward. She moved forward, spinning to understand the cause. She had happened to lean against a secret entrance. The door swung forward far more easily now she'd moved and almost slammed open, revealing Erec of Tion, Major Longsword's elder brother. The first, *and married* son of the Duke of Tion.

"Sorry darling." He said. "The door got stuck."

She got out of bed and leapt into his arms. "It's fine, I'm sure the guards wouldn't have heard."

They started kissing with Vag two feet away, head tilted, invisible face contorted in a 'What. The. Fuck?' expression. Here was the Queen, heading a Prudishia-worshipping regime, having an affair with a married man. She might not have found hypocrisy in the High Priest, but the Queen had it in spades.

They soon progressed to foreplay and sex, with the Duke presumptive 'getting off the coach outside the city walls.' (a euphemism for withdrawal). All said, none of the evenings' activities would have made it past page three of 'Orgasmodan's love making guide'.

Then came the post coital banter.

Without segue Chastidia spoke first, turning her head somewhat abruptly towards him. "Do you think this war will last?"

Erec sighed. "The Orcs are always at war. We've just been lucky they've pointed their axes towards the elves for the last decade."

She turned her gaze back to the ceiling. "I just wish we had all the remnants of Orgasmodan's followers taken care of so we could focus on one problem at a time."

"Why are you so obsessed with defeating Orgasmodan?" Said Erec, half turning, placing his hand on her upper arm.

"What difference does it matter to you if a man sleeps with an elf, another man, or even takes two partners?"

"My mother was a follower of Prudishia. People assumed her marriage to my father was the completion of the ultimate business transaction. She loved him though. It wasn't politics or money. It was love. I think the feeling was mutual. For a while at least, until she fell pregnant with me. With the access to women afforded by his rank, he strayed widely and frequently. It sucked the love out of their relationship and they never recovered. I don't want to live in a world like that, I want marriage to mean something more."

"I'm married." Said Erec.

"Yes, but you and your wife both know it's a political union. I am more worried about the people out there." She waved her hand vaguely. "In the city and beyond its walls."

Erec seemed to ponder her words, stroking her hair as her head rested on his chest. "Well, I should be off, I'll see you tomorrow no doubt."

"Good bye Darling." Chastidia said, kissing her lover.

A minute later, Vag was alone with her.

As the Queen snuffed her bedside candle and closed her eyes, the enormity of Vag's plan hit home. She'd felt detached when devising it with Clamax, like a chess player holding their pawn ready to move.

Now, she *was* the pawn. She'd moved past all the defensive pieces, be they bishops or knights. First by changing sides, then by disappearing. Now she looked at the Queen, with no squares beyond.

Thirty excruciating minutes into the queen's sleep, Vag silently retrieved the serrated eating knife and placed it on the bed within the queen's reach.

Her own ornate dagger was placed on the ground beside her. She grabbed the onyx ball with her left hand, the white marble ball with her right, and begun mouthing the words to her ultimate spell. Her arms traced the patterns she'd learnt from the necromancers spell book. Blue particles bridged between her and the Queen. It was the strangest sensation. She felt her consciousness travel along the bridge.

Then she was on the bed, in the Queen's body. Her old body fell to the floor as the sleeping Queen's consciousness, or rather *unconsciousness*, transferred it.

Vag was fast. Her hand grabbed the serrated knife. She was out of bed, lunging at her old body. The crude blade sank into her previously precious flesh, before the Groggy queen had time to comprehend what was happening. Vag's second stab penetrated her windpipe, and a third went to her heart. The Queen looked at her own face in utter, panicked confusion as she died.

Vag retrieved the Onyx ball, now below the right hand of her corpse, and marble ball, now below the left.

The black pawn had taken the white queen, ascending to royalty itself in the same move.

She picked up the ornate blade and cut her new arms until a convincing amount of blood flowed.

Looking around the room to make sure everything was in order, she screamed as loud as her regally upgraded lungs could muster.

Soon her new bedchamber filled with fretting guards, flustering maids and council of planning members.

She was glad to be healed by Virgun, displeased to be seen by 'her lover', Lord Erec, and devastated to hear the news from general Jackhammer. Major Longsword was already heading to the Phallus. That was the whole reason she had accelerated her plan. Now it would be up to Clamax and Ovula to fight off the Major's squad.

She washed and redressed before her guard escorted her to the dungeons to interview Barbidon. The poor girl looked pitiful, Vag rushed to put her at ease.

"Relax Babs. It's ok. Everything is fine."

Barbidon looked confused and said nothing.

"I want you to tell absolutely no-one of what I am about to tell you. I am Vag, but in the Queen's body."

"What? Where is the Queen then?"

"We fought, and she died."

"You killed the Queen?"

"Shhh.... Not so loud. Yes, I killed the Queen."

Babs looked at the ground. "But she was really nice? She was nice to me at least." Lifting her head, she glared up at Vag. "Was this the 'majestic plan' that you always talked about? It doesn't seem like the plan of a nice person."

"Sometimes you need to step out of the light to do the most good in this world Babs. It's only some of the plan, the plan has... grown. Tonight was one death to save the lives of many more."

Babs frown did not soften.

"Look Babs. You, are a Half-orc. Probably the only Half-Orc in the world, and the Cross'd legs church bans interracial couplings. So, it doesn't matter who you fall in love with, they could execute you and your partner. It is the same for men who love men, and women who love women."

Babs looked up, her scowl finally softening.

"Every year across the Queendom, there are hundreds of people executed, and thousands more forced to live a lie because of the church's oppression. Now I have the power to change that, for them, for me... and for you Babs, for you."

Babs, opened her mouth, shut it, then looked at her feet.

"I never told you why I had to leave my village." Said Babs, looking sideways. "I killed a boy that was bullying me. I'm not even sure it was an accident."

Vag reached through the bars to grab Babs's hand. "You see then Babs? We both seek justice. You seek it in the moment, I can take longer, but both of us want a better world."

"But, why didn't you tell me. I thought we were friends."

"We are Babs. You are the most loyal friend I've ever had. I didn't tell you because I wanted you to be innocent of my plan if you were ever interrogated. I wanted to protect you in case anything went wrong. Can you forgive me?"

Babs looked at her again. "I understand. You do not need me to forgive you."

"Thank you Babs." Said Virginia. "I'll get you released now so you can leave with the Army tomorrow. I need you to help them get the Hammer of Castra. Then can we destroy Prudishia's God stones."

40

Sergeant? Hodgkins

At first light, General Jackhammer sent Major Shortsword (as he was now ubiquitously known), on the mission to find Orgasmodan's Priestess. He felt no guilt at having lied to the Queen last night. The attempt on her life had obviously clouded her judgement. It was clearer than ever that all steps needed to be taken to kill the high priestess, even if the Queen momentarily lacked that insight.

The army really was better off without the ridiculed Major, corpulent Hodgkins and the four trouble makers sent with them. Meanwhile, he had promoted the deserving Brightspark to Major and felt confident he would do a better job than Shortsword ever could.

His ramshackle army wound its way out of the city's streets like the world's longest turd. Make that the world's longest *constipated* turd, for crowds of well-wishers had narrowed the streets, despite the early hour.

He rode at the front of the faecal snake. Behind him rode the newly promoted Major Brightspark, Barbidon at his side.

The Queen had reportedly been confident the half-orc was innocent of any involvement in the murder plot. He'd reluctantly agreed. The girl's emotions were easily readable, it was clear enough she had been in complete, uncomprehending shock at the news.

Barbidon had become both champion and mascot of the army. By ripping the disliked Ser Richard's wandering cock off with her bare teeth, she'd elevated herself to a favourite with the men. He wished her outfit was less revealing though.

A faint dust cloud coming towards them caught his attention as the last troops exited the main gates. It was another scout. A few minutes later, the young corporal pulled his steed up next to the general.

"Update on the enemy movements Sir."

"Go on."

"They are travelling quickly. I would expect them to reach Jaldur in two days."

"Still three thousand strong?"

"Yes sir."

He motioned for Brightspark to move up beside him.

"At that pace we won't be able to defend Jaldur." He said to the Major.

"Should we wait to join forces with the Duke's men General?"

"They could be a week away. The Orc's might be at the Citadels Gates in that time."

"Those walls *would* be really hard to climb." observed Barbidon, the military strategist.

"They have apparently never used siege weapons, Sir. In their campaigns against the elves, they repeatedly hit softer targets. I suspect they are likely to spend the time ransacking the towns between here and Jaldur."

There was sense in waiting for reinforcements, however the City had only just finished shitting out the army. The act of trying to shove it back in after all those well-wishes just didn't seem right, from a theatrical perspective.

Jackhammer paused, pretending to ponder. "I won't have any more towns decimated, we'll keep on moving."

—

Vag waved the army goodbye from her balcony and went back to bed. Fortunately, her private secretary had cleared her morning schedule in light of the tumultuous night. She desperately needed the sleep.

Erec of Tion jolted her awake late morning, caressing her hair. He clearly meant it as a loving gesture, but to a twenty-year-old girl who usually slept alone, waking up with a forty-year-old married man hovering over her was *super* creepy. She startled, moving away from him like an overweight child recoiling from a salad bar.

"Oh, I'm so sorry, that was thoughtless of me, given last night's events."

Vag struggled unsuccessfully to say something coherent, her heart thumping in an adrenalised attempt to force wakefulness.

"I obviously couldn't talk to you last night, I wanted to make sure you are alright."

"I am alright, I just need sleep."

"Which I've now interrupted. I'm so sorry."

Vag looked at him. He had a pitiful look, in sharp contrast to his typically austere '*I'm the next Duke of Tion*' persona.

"It's okay, thank for checking on me Erec. I just need rest."

"Ok, I'll see you at two in the chamber of planning, our first *ever* Dwarven ambassador has arrived. I'm curious to meet her." Before he quickly added, "But don't worry, I am sure her beauty will not compare to yours." He chuckled, then realised he was doing it alone. "I love you Chasti." He said in a more sombre tone, blowing her a kiss.

His unwanted words moved across the room and stuck into her skin, like headlights caught in a deer. Instead of responding verbally, she settled on a meek smile and wave before closing her eyes, pretending she had a chance of sleeping again.

The secret door closed behind his departure.

"Ew." Whispered Vag into her pillow.

Erec, Virgun and herself were to meet the Dwarven ambassador. Vag should have been thinking of trade, defence and diplomacy, but news of a dwarven ambassador made her fret about Clamax. Ser Richard, Hodgkins and the others would be surely be confronting Ovula and her Dwarven friend soon.

A more positive consideration was that Clamax claimed to have never seen a female dwarf in all his adult years. Vag found her curiosity piqued. If this Ambassador possessed personality and prettiness, maybe Vag could try her hand at match-making.

Ambassador Airola Clevage was a breath of fresh air to the normally stuffy council of planning. As charismatic as a bard, with the wisdom of a diplomat.

The guild leaders invited to the meeting all were enthused by the trading opportunities discussed. Afterwards, she invited Airola to dine with her council. Vag would have dearly loved to dine with Nadia, but in the absence of true friendship, Airola's Neutrality was more appealing than Virgun's misplaced loyalty or Erec's misplaced love.

After Dinner, Vag looked through her inherited valuables, finding three large keys.

"Escort me to the Vault of Relics." Vag said to the guards posted outside her room.

"Yes, your majesty."

Since her ascendancy, Vag went everywhere with two guards in front, and two guards behind her, all ironically willing to lay down their lives to protect their monarch's murderer.

Two additional guards stood in front of the vault, located deep within the keep. They parted for her.

"Now I need to remember which key it is." Said Vag to one of men.

The first key was a fail, the second gave a satisfying click.

She went in alone.

Prudishia's god stones were easy to spot. They sat on a white pedestal in the centre of the room. Locating Orgasmodan's stones was far harder, they were at the back, in a nondescript black box. The faintest hint of light escaping from its imperfect joins.

She swapped them over, placing Orgasmodan's stones on the pedestal. Prudishia's in the box, ready for destruction should the Hammer of Castra be retrieved.

Vag waited in the room to sell the notion that she was 'communing with Prudishia'. Instead, she contemplated that a few weeks ago she was an inconsequential nobody. Now as a Queen, she had potentially altered the world forever.

Outside the Highmana barrier, Orgasmodan's temple.

Hodgkins' arse was sore, but he still had plenty of compassion for the poor horse that had carried it for the last two days.

Major Longsword turned his charger around to face his small troop. Like the contents of his underbriefs, the Major had a lot less under his command than he used to. Hodgkins had found a certain poetic justice in Longsword losing half his cock after mocking his impotence. Ser Richard's de-knobification had not formed a genitally disabled bond between them though. Afterall, insecurity is the parasite that hijacks the bully's brain. As the major spoke facing the other men, he ignored Hodgkins as usual.

"Right, so this might have been a wild goose chase, or on the other side of this barrier, the high priestess of Orgasmodan may be rebuilding the Phallus we destroyed two weeks ago. If she is alone, we attack as one. If there are others, you keep them off Hodgkins and I. Clear?"

"Yes sir." Came the response with all the enthusiasm of a gigolo's cock meeting an unattractive client.

"And you." Ser Richard looked at Hodgkins. "You're with me. You take her down like you did last time and I'll see you make Sergeant."

"Yes Sir." Said Hodgkins, a little stunned. A Sergeant's pay was double that of a Private.

They punctured the Highmana barrier with the same popping sounds Hodgkins remembered. He immediately made out the temple, the enormous lake and a glowing light coming from a figure. It was the Priestess, her light flowing to the 'Phallus of Felicity'.

It was being repaired. The current status looked like a giant version of Lonsword's own stump.

Hodgkin's saw a light to his right as an ethereal hammer spun in the air. It collided with one of the men, knocking him off his horse.

"Oh you're fucking kidding me! It's that Dwarf!" Shouted Longsword before pointing "Cover us."

The others peeled off to charge him.

"He's a Paladin for the wrong fucking God!" shouted the Major. "That mage and the Orc bitch were probably agents of Orgasmodan too!"

They continued charging towards the phallus. Hodgkins saw the high priestess look at them wide-eyed, raising her hands.

An incredible wind stopped the horses in their tracks, the beasts involuntarily rearing up, throwing he and longsword from their saddles. He got to his feet, struggling to move forward as the deafening wind roared at them.

Then there was silence.

The wind still roared at Longsword to his right, the muscular man making no ground, but Hodgkins was suddenly protected from it.

He looked from Longsword to the Priestess. She smiled at him, not in malice, but serenely, that same kind, understanding smile he had only ever received from her.

Hodgkins looked to the Major, who looked back at him.

"I knew there was a reason we brought you." He shouted. "Go take her down... Sergeant." The Major attempted something like a beguiling smile, though with the wind battering his face it was like posing for a beauty shot mid skydive.

Private Hodgkins drew his sword, looked at the priestess, then swung the blade in a wide arc, slashing Longsword's neck open. For a second, the Major looked at him stunned, his blood flew sideways like a waterfall in a strong wind. After that blood failed to report for duty in his brain, his body flew backwards too.

The wind died down. Hodgkins spun around, keeping his sword out, ready to fight the remaining soldiers who'd gone to fight the Dwarf. He was shocked to see the Dwarf instead returning from a distance with a smile on his face.

"What is your name, good sir?" Asked the Priestess.

"Hodgkins Mam."

"I am Ovula, High Priestess of Orgasmodan, and this, is Clamax."

Hodgkins turned to address the Dwarf "How did you defeat four men on horseback?"

"Clamax has recently been granted the power and rank of Paladin." Ovula said as if that explained everything.

"Good to meet you lad. Clamax at your service. Thank you for switching sides."

"I felt like I had to."

"That speaks well of your character."

"The Major thought you were a Paladin of Prudishia I think."

"It's a long story, but since you've shown your allegiance, I think can bring you in on our little plan. Now tell me, was an attempt made on the Queen's life before you left?"

"Yes, I heard the young mage Virginia attempted to kill her, but died herself in the attempt."

"That may not entirely be the case. We're going to have to send you back the Del. Request an audience with the council of planning, including the Queen. Tell her you are the sole survivor of a *successful* mission to kill the Priestess."

The priestess stepped forward, handing Hodgkins a pendant that had been around her neck. "I can't supply you with my head, but this can act as a proof of my death. I believe High Priest Blueballus will recognise it."

"Lad." Said Clamax. "There is something very particular that I need you to say to the Queen after you report your success. Then I need you privately pass something else to her..."

Hodgkins was on his horse half an hour later, ready to leave the Temple, the Phallus, the lake, and the serene smile of High Priestess Ovula. It was difficult for two reasons. Firstly; his horse, and dead soldier's horses, had *again* drunk the aphrodisiacal waters. Secondly; He didn't want to leave Ovula's presence. His consolation was a request he return to her once all this was over.

41

Rapid penetration of the rear

Two days later near Jaldur, in the centre of the Queen's army camp, Brightspark emerged from Jackhammer's tent. The newly minted Major strode with purpose. "Calvary with me on the right flank!" He shouted to his officers nearby.

"Where are we going?" Asked Barbidon, adjusting her pace to keep up with him.

"There is forest cover over there. We are to circle around the Orcish forces and try to catch their leadership by surprise." He looked at her, stopping for a second, "Remember what I said. Don't try to fight with that enormous blade on horseback." He said, pointing to the black greatsword. "When we attack, I want you to dismount. Understood?"

"Major!"

They both turned to see the army's only Priest hailing them. Brightspark had seen the young man attempting to preach earlier in the morn.

His message of pious love and romantic constancy delivered in a shrill voice had seemed ill fitted to the bloodshed to come.

"I need to bestow a blessing on you before the battle."

"Give it to her instead." Said Brightspark.

He looked confused. "Major, the General said it should go to you."

"Sorry, but I refuse. I would like you to give her the blessing. You can tell the General you gave it to me if you fear his displeasure."

"Very well, Major." The priest placed his hand on Barbidon's forehead. "Oh mighty Prudishia, may your power guide thy humble servant Barbidon."

Blue light emanated from his hand. Babs felt the same hyper alertness she'd felt for her duel with Ser Richard.

"Thank you." She said, not sure if she was addressing the priest or Brightspark.

They rode hard through the forest. The vegetation was perfect for the task, sparse enough to not impede their movement, but with enough canopy to conceal it. They saw no scouts.

Soon they'd completely circled around the Orcs position on the large Hill. The invaders had stationed reserves to their rear, but it was far less intimidating there, like the underside of an echidna.

She heard drums start. They were not the crisp prepubescent snare drums of the humans. These were primal, visceral booms. A distant roar grew, then grew more.

The battle had begun on the other side. At the hill's zenith, they could make out two tents.

"We have two goals." Announced Brightspark as he stood in his saddle addressing all his men. "The most important is to take out the Orcish leader Karak, along with his four sons. They may well be on the front lines, but It's a fair guess Karak himself will be near those tents. The second objective, is to retrieve the Hammer of Castra."

"What does it look like?" asked a cavalryman.

"It's big and hammery." said Brightspark to the nervous laughter of his troops. "It's covered in runic symbols. Apparently you'll know it if you see it. But ready yourselves gentlemen, for today, we will be like a dagger thrust into the enemy's heart. There for a sudden, violent moment, to change the course of history. Are you ready men?"

"Yes sir!"

"Then charge!"

Four hundred horses surged forward as spurs jabbed into flanks. This caught Babs off guard. She'd been waiting for Brightspark to follow up with 'Are you ready woman?' Apparently the feminine version of the question wasn't coming, so she spurred her horse forward too.

Exhilaration replaced nervousness as the charging cavalry surrounded her, making a sound that drowned out even the orcish war drums. Babs couldn't imagine how any force could stop so many mounted warriors.

As they barrelled towards the rear guard of Orcs, the sight in front of her aided her imagination.

They say that no sand sculpture survives first contact with a toddler. They could also say that no battle plan survives first contact with the enemy.

Four hundred orcs of both genders were arrayed on the high ground. There were no archers, however a decade of battling with the Elves had helped their battle planning, compensating for their low intelligence. As the horses approached, the front rank lifted ten-foot, thick spears as an unwelcoming party.

Sharpened wood and steel punctured flesh everywhere in front of her. She dismounted and moved forward. It was bizarre seeing Orcs for the first time. It was like meeting a lost side of your family tree and suddenly realising where you got all your funny homicidal quirks from. In Barbidon's case, those included neck snapping, ball ripping, defootenising and penis chomping.

Late to the fray, Babs attacked Orcs already engaged, quickly finishing them off. She glimpsed Brightspark ahead, still mounted. Using him as her north star, she waded through the dead and dying, adding more to their number every few strides.

They were breaking through, but at a terrible cost. She spotted Brightspark again, now dismounted. He and ten men surged upward towards the tents. Four huge orcs in fearsome armour rushed forward to meet them.

Her heightened senses detected a faint sound behind her. It was so subtle, that in the midst of the raging battle, she had no right to hear it. She also should not have had time to spin around and deflect the thrown axe with her sword. Thanks to the priest's blessing and her ring, she did.

The thrower, a female Orc with a stupefied look on her face, continued to stare blankly. As if by waiting, the last few seconds would replay properly, with the axe striking Babs in the back. Babs instead rushed her assailant, who realised, too late, that the throw had left her unarmed.

"Half-Orc!" she spat.

A moment later, it also left her unlegged, as the black sword cleaved her body into two, roughly equal portions.

"Who's a Half-Orc now, Bitch?" Said Babs, rather pleased with that comeback.

She turned, frustrated at the distraction. Babs was just in time to see Brightspark, the most wonderful man she had ever met, crushed under a fatal hammer blow. It seemed too simple, too quick an end for such a hero, but she was in no doubt that it was his end.

The men with him were also dying in quick succession. She would never reach them in time. Tears streamed down her face as she absentmindedly reached for a small red vial at her waist pouch. A vial her dwarven friend had blown all his savings on at Potion Pete's in Wagrum.

She remembered Clamax's words. *'Promise me you'll save it for when all seems lost.'*

This probably meet the requirement. She drank the contents, feeling the sweet, warm liquid heat her throat as it raced down.

The impossible energy of the potion immediately coursed through her muscles. She could scarcely have been more ready for battle.

Blessed for alertness,

Magically ringed for nimbleness,

Wielding the sharpest weapon on the battlefield,

And now...as strong... as a

Mother.

Fucking.

Giant.

Death rushed to accompany her and collect the souls she would surely feed it.

Rage had overcome her before. Now, for the first time in her short life, she controlled it.

Babs walked up to the four males who had slaughtered the cavalry remnants, including her beloved Brightspark. They looked at her, confused which side she was on as she casually wiped blood from her sword.

"Who are you?" The closest one asked, great axe held in semi readiness, pending friend or foe confirmation.

"Sorry, there was another human back there I needed to finish off."

"I said, who the fuck are-"

He never finished his sentence. Like a viper, she lunged forward, puncturing his rib cage. Opting for speed over thoroughness, she immediately engaged the next two closest opponents. Her sword danced like an industrial food processor blade.

The two Orcs repurposed offensive strikes into frantic blocks. But like kittens dancing in the aforementioned food processor, the end was pre-determined. Her sword cut one axe shaft clean through. An arm was severed off. A torso side strike landed 4 inches deep in flesh, then a severed leg artery sprayed blood into the air. Three of the four oversized Orcs lay dying.

Without registering why, Babs ducked, the way every decapitated duck didn't. There was a woosh overhead. She surmised that it was the hammer that had been used to kill her darling Brightspark. The thought was confirmed when she stood up to her full height. The beastly face of her final opponent was a full foot higher.

He held no weapon.

"Ready to die?" The Orc smiled, too wide for his predicament.

"You should've kept your weapon for that." Babs said.

She was about to charge, but the instinct to duck struck her again. It was certainly better to have been struck by instinct than the enormous hammer that rushed over her head again. It had somehow flown back to him.

A follow up strike immediately came at her head. Babs stopped the enormous momentum with her sword and pushed forward, knocking him first backwards, then prone with a thud. She rushed forward again with an overhead strike to cleave him from his chest to his groin. The strike was blocked by the shaft of his rune covered hammer. Transitioning to a spear-like thrust, Babs drove the tip under his jaw and into his brain before partially blending its contents with a quarter rotation.

In a gesture that was, literally overkill, she stepped over the vanquished Orc, bent down, ripped his head off with her bare hands and threw it a hundred metres down the hill. She let out a long, guttural scream, until there was no air left in her lungs.

Barbidon breathed heavily, surveying the carnage. She was the only survivor of eight hundred combatants on this hillside. To the question of Orcs vs humans: The answer had proven to be; a little from column A, and a little from column B.

The effects of the giant's strength potion ebbed as she willed her body over the undignified, crushed remains of Major Brightspark.

Before reaching her destination, a golden glow wrapped around her ankles, wrists and waist. Babs dropped her weapon to free herself, but they gripped her like manacles, lifting her mere centimetres off the ground and spinning her around.

"You are... incredible." Said a crowned, decrepit Orc, leaning on a cane. "Quite incredible."

A younger, shamanistic male with a scar that ran along his cheek attended him.

Babs struggled in vain to break free.

The regal figure looked at the four massive dead Orcs around her. "You met your brothers I see."

The words hit Babs with the power but also speed of colliding tectonic plates.

"What... do you mean, brothers?"

"Well, half-brothers." He lifted the cane to point at his visual aids. "There's Durz that you stabbed in the chest. Kurdan's over there with his arm chopped off. Mugdul has the crevasse in his chest. Finally, the one with the fancy hammer was your eldest brother, Matuk. Though he won't be as good with it now you've thrown his head away."

"How could you possibly know they were my brothers?"

"Because you," he now pointed his cane unsteadily at her "my incredible warrior, are my daughter."

Babs shook her head "Why do you think that?"

"I've only ever heard of one Half-Orc ever being born. And secondly, that sword. It was my gift to you."

Bab's head spun.

"Daddy?"

An orc warrior rushed from the other side of the hill, pausing to take in the sibling bloodbath around him before interrupting their reunion. "Chieftain, we are losing on the low ground to the humans archers."

Karak turned to the messenger, looking tired. The old chieftain opened his mouth, but turned to the shaman instead. "You deal with it Arrowglance. I would like to have a chat with my daughter."

"I would no longer be able to control the bonds that hold her?" Said the shaman.

"That's okay, I think we can release her now."

Without audible command, the bonds vanished and Babs plonked to the ground.

Arrowglance gave her an almost apologetic look before turning to the messenger. "Pull the warriors back. We'll consolidate on the high ground and make them come to us."

Now alone, father and daughter faced each other for an orcish eternity. Over these four seconds, Babs' eyes welled with tears until she could stand it no more. She rushed forward to hug him, clasping his frail back long before he gripped hers.

"I'm so sorry, I didn't know they were my brothers."

"My pride in my offspring is based on their ability as warriors. Today I have gained more than I have lost."

"But...." Babs shook her head to dislodge the strange statement. Then her eyes lit up. "Mother! You have to see her. I know you were driven out of the village by the racist men there, but I'm friends with the Queen. The Queen! You could be together again!"

"Yes, wouldn't that be interesting, but I'm in the middle of a war right now." Said Karak extricating himself from the embrace. "Sorry, I don't even know your name."

"It's Barbidon. And your name is Karak? It's strange that mother never mentioned your name to me."

"Yes, quite strange. Come, there will be plenty of time for us to talk later. Should we see how this battle is going? Bring Matuk's Hammer though, it is too valuable to leave lying out here."

Babs held his free arm, further surprised at his fragility, as a racking cough seized his chest. Her mother Milfandria was only thirty-four. Karak's stooped stature suggested he was close to the grave, even though it offered hints of past strength.

As she looked at the weapon her brother had wielded, she had a revelation. It was covered in runes, but more importantly, it was very big and hammery, just as Brightspark said it would be.

"This is the Hammer of Castra, isn't it?"

"Ah, you've heard of it? Yes, Matuk took it off some Elven noble. I think it should be yours now."

As they walked around in front of the two conjoined tents, she was greeted with a visceral vista of violence. The hill provided a commanding view of the Orcs pulling back, leaving a no-man's-land of corpses. Death loves an evenly matched battle, and it had loved this one. The inexperienced ranks of human footman had been ill prepared for the strength and experience of Grunts. The leveling factor though, was the superior range of human bows.

With the withdrawal to higher ground, the two sides breathed heavily. Darkness approached.

Babs saw disdainful looks towards Karak on the blood splattered faces of the returning orcs. The looks were short lived, but they were there, and there were many.

Karak turned to her, putting his other hand on her forearm. "We'll have a meeting soon. I'll hold it in my tent, that way they won't outnumber us too much. I need you to back me up. It's the job your brothers would have done."

Babs flushed "Oh, of course Daddy. How do I do that?"

"Just stand near me. Look intimidating but calm."

"I can try?"

"Thank you, and one other thing. Maybe don't call me 'daddy' in front of them."

42

Two tents

"They're angry." Arrowglance said, entering Karak's tent twenty minutes later. He did not have time to elaborate.

Soon Orcs packed the small area. They enlarged the space to allow even more, lifting the adjoining flaps of the two tents.

Babs noticed that her paternal race did not wear military insignia like humans, but the bone chains these twenty-five wore were uncommon amongst the rank-and-file grunts.

"Greetings. Well fought today. I would like to introduce my daughter, Barbidon. She was raised in the human world, but after reuniting, she has chosen to join us."

The assembled gave her looks varying from suspicion to curiosity.

"Now, what news Killgore?"

"We have lost over a thousand warriors Chieftain. If we were to push on, it would wipe both armies out."

"How did they organise so large an army so quickly?" Karak's voice was almost complaining.

Arrow looked at Babs, exasperation showing. "Chieftain, the humans population grows each decade through farming and trade. With lives little longer than ours, their numbers can multiply far more quickly than the elves. They also have scouts and were likely aware of our movements."

A large Orc pointed a finger at Karak. He had so many bones around his neck, they jangled as he moved. "You told us the humans would be easy pickings, but their bows rival the elves for range and now we have lost a third of our force for your ego old one." He stepped forward holding his axe menacingly.

The atmosphere in the two tents was getting too tense. Karak returned the warrior's look with a sigh.

"I'm sure you appreciate Arrow's neutrality in our petty squabblings. Arrow, would you mind telling those here what happened to my sons this afternoon?"

"Barbidon killed them all in a four to one fight."

Every pair of eyes in the room turned to her. She remembered her father's request though, *'Calm and intimidating, Calm and intimidating'*. Her sword stood planted point down in front of her and she met their gaze coldly. She must have done an ok job, no one laughed.

"And how long, did my daughter take to double handedly kill four of the finest Orc warriors."

"About twenty seconds."

"And what did she do with Matuk after killing him?"

"She ripped his head off with her bare hands."

It takes a bit to shock an Orc, but most jaws dropped and *everyone* took a little shuffle away from her.

Barbidon fought back a smile at sounding like such a bad-ass. *'Calm and intimidating, Calm and intimidating'* she said to herself again, before focusing her gaze directly at her father's challenger. She had mentally decided to call him Mr Bone Jangles.

To her relief, he lowered his axe and stepped backwards.

"Well, I am sure Tooruk Clan will arrive tomorrow. Then we will crush them." Said Karak.

Another Orc piped up, braving Barbidon's body amputation service. "Have we received an outrider? They never promised to join us."

Arrowglance turned to Barbidon, quickly starting a new line of enquiry.

"You must know something of the human's plans, what can you tell us?"

Babs hesitated, weighing up helping her father's people or her friends and mother's. She realised the truth might help both.

"They will have six thousand more men coming within the week."

This set off a round of angry murmurings. "If that many reinforcements arrive, they will wipe us out."

"Even if we hold the high ground." Said Arrowglance.

The Chieftain waved a hand. "We will wait for the Tooruk Clan, I know they will come." Said Karak to his lieutenants. "I know they will come." This time to himself. "Tell the men to bolster the rear of the hill. We will remain defensive tomorrow and see what the day brings. Good night Brothers."

The Orcs left the tents, Bab's heard one mumble, "Too old to lead." to another, they nodded.

Babs ate with her Father and Arrowglance that evening. Babs answered questions on her recent adventures. Her father laughed and looked at her with the undisguised pride of someone beyond seeing glory in their own achievements. Conversation shifted to his adventures and battles with the elves. He seemed less inclined to be drawn on that detail.

"Why didn't you take my mother with you? You are the leader of all these Orcs, you could have rescued her from loneliness. We could have been a family. You could have been my father…"

Karak shuffled uncomfortably on his seat "I'm sorry, but Orcs don't mingle well with other races, she would not have been happy here."

Babs wanted to press further, but his speech slurred and tired eyes drooped.

"Perhaps we should let your father rest Barbidon." Said Arrowglance.

Babs reluctantly got up. "Ok we can talk more in the morning father, Let's get you to bed."

Babs exited the tent after seeing him drift off to sleep. Arrow had waited to walk with her.

"Things are not good." He said.

"His health or being the chieftain?" Babs asked.

"Both. He ruled through his sons, and they by fear. Now all he has is you, and the momentum of incumbency."

"He has you? Doesn't he?" Babs looked at the Shaman, frowning.

Arrow looked to the horizon. "I serve my people. For my adult life, that has meant serving your father. Now I fear, the two goals are no longer the same."

"So you would abandon your chieftain at his weakest?"

"If that saves lives, thousands of orc and human lives? Then yes. Blind loyalty is never an admirable trait."

"Do you want to take over?"

Arrow's eyes bulged as a laugh struggled to stay in his lungs. "Me? Gods no. From an early age I realised I was a weakling in a race that celebrates strength. I instead worked hard to learn and serve through being an advisor. Your father was strong, but his *real* strength was listening to advice, in his old age he has lost both those traits."

"Maybe I could convince him to step down? He could find my mother and they could be together again?"

Arrow stopped and turned to face her. "Barbidon, I doubt your parents were in love. It is far more likely he raped your mother."

Babs turned rapidly to face him. "No! They loved each other. He was forced away by racists in the village because he was an Orc. Those same men hated me."

"Did your mother ever mention his name?"

"Well, no. She didn't talk about it much. But that doesn't prove anything. She might have just been too sad at the memory of him having to leave."

"Maybe, but ask him tomorrow what your mother's name is. That should give you the answer you need."

"I will, and I'll prove you wrong."

"I hope you do. Either way, I'd recommend deciding in advance what you'll do if there is a revolt tomorrow."

43

They asked me to give
you this...

Back in the Citadel, Vaginia strode her stolen regal body purposefully toward the chamber of planning. Her inherited secretary and four guards following at the upper limit of walking speed.

"Any news of Major Longsword's expedition?" she asked, head turned.

"Not yet I'm afraid, though I thought their return more likely this afternoon your majesty."

She groaned inwardly when she spotted Lord Erec of Tion waiting for her by the chamber's door.

"Your majesty." He said, eagerly.

"Lord Erec." She replied, uneagerly.

"I was hoping to have a word with you."

'Having a word' with the lover of her body's previous inhabitant was not high on her 'to-do' list. Unfortunately, her guards were only here to protect her from bodily attack, not whiney ex-lovers.

"What would like to discuss?"

He looked at her, perplexed. "It is a delicate matter, perhaps better discussed in private?"

"Very well, we will grant you a brief audience."

She moved towards an empty waiting room.

"What is it?" she enquired once he'd closed the door.

"*What is it?* Darling you've been so aloof since the assassination attempt. I have wanted to be there for you, to comfort you, to..." he trailed off.

More likely to fuck me. She thought. "Lord Eric, I'm sorry, but you were right to point out my hypocrisy. I have heard your wife and son are visiting Del. I think you should attend to their needs above mine."

"So, what, is that it? Is that us done? Just like that?"

"I know it seems abrupt, but the truth is I have not felt myself since the incident. Something in me has changed." *Like my entire personality, knowledge and intellect,* she thought. "We cannot continue."

He opened his mouth, shut it, then opened it again. "I understand. Well, thank you for the time we have had together."

He moved to the door, opening it for her.

~

Vag struggled to pay attention to the council's affairs all morning. Her concern for Clamax overriding all thoughts. After lunch, her secretary finally came through the chamber doors with news.

"Your Majesty," he announced, "A Private Hodgkins is hoping to report to the council of planning. He is back from the expedition tracking the heretical Priestess."

"A private?" said Virgun.

"Is my brother Major Longsword not with him?" Asked Lord Erec.

The secretary shrugged. "No my lord."

"Send him in then." Said Virginia, wringing her hands.

Hodgkins did not fit Virginia's expectation of a soldier. His body type was echidna, minus the spikes and fur. He was Red-cheeked and gasping for breath after ascending the stairs with the speed of a boulder trying to shrug off gravity, it took him a while to speak.

"You are welcome at court, Private Hodgkins. What news of your mission?" Asked Virgun.

"Lady Ovula was there as feared, your grace, rebuilding the phallus."

Virginia's heart sank.

"My brother, Major Longsword?" Asked Lord Erec.

"I regret to inform you that the priestess killed Major Longsword, along with the other men."

Vag looked to Lord Erec, who seemed pensive. She felt guilt at having broken up with him immediately before news of his brother's death.

Hodgkins lifted his face, looking more upbeat, having delivered the darkest news. "Prudishia be praised though, she again bestowed me with immunity to the High priestess's demonic powers. Thus shielded, I was able to end her life." He reached into a pocket. "This was her necklace."

Virgun stood up to inspect it. He took it almost gingerly from Hodgkins.

"I can confirm this was the necklace the priestess wore. I noticed it when I interviewed her."

Vag observed the High Priest. He smiled, but there was little mirth in it. He seemed decent enough to take little pleasure in the death of a nemesis.

"We are interested to know if there were other accomplices at the site?" Vag asked.

"No your majesty, she was alone. The phallus was half repaired, so I spent some time destroying it. Rest assured, your *majestic* plan to rid the world of the false god is firmly on track."

Did he say 'majestic plan'? Thought Vag. Yes, he did! And there was a look of emphasis to accompany his words.

"Private Hodgkins, you have performed your duties admirably. We are delighted with your success." Said Vag. "Though I am very sorry for your loss Lord Erec."

Vag stood up, followed by everyone else in the room. She got a kick out of that.

"We will retire for a recess now. Hodgkins, I would like to speak to you privately about your endeavours. Follow me outside please."

"Yes, your majesty."

Out of earshot, she turned to face him.

"You used the term 'Majestic plan'". Did you hear that phrase from someone else, someone who was perhaps short of stature?"

"Yes, your majesty." Said Hodgkins, exhaling in relief and smiling wide with the realisation that the Queen was in fact the Magus Vaginia, an ally of the High Priestess. "Clamax and Ovula are both alive. They asked me to give you this…"

44

Orc Hard

Barbidon awoke the next day in the Orc encampment. After breakfast, she went with her father to inspect the warriors. To Barbidon, it felt more like the warriors were inspecting him. Furthermore, they did not approve.

"I'm worried for you." She said, "I'm worried they are going to kill you."

"Things are delicate, but I have ruled these clans for ten years. I am also confident that with you by my side, no one will dare make the first move."

"You could just leave with me though? You are weak and old. I don't say it to be mean, I'm only stating the truth. Why not spend your last days with my mother looking after you? I am friends with the Queen, no one would hurt you."

They climbed atop a broad rock that crowned the hill. A fresh breeze at their back contained only a hint of the decaying corpses from yesterday's attack. In front, Jackhammer's troops were quiet, having also taken up a defensive formation.

Barbidon guessed they awaited the Duke of Tion's reinforcements.

"Thank you Barbidon, but my place is here. I know what is best for my people, so it should be me that rules them."

"Was invading the human lands and getting your warriors killed 'for the best'?"

Karak looked hurt and was about to respond, but Babs remembered her conversation with Arrow. She cut him off.

"My mother never mentioned your name to me, don't you think that's strange."

She watched her father's facial expressions carefully. He looked more and more uncomfortable.

"Yes, that is st-"

"What was her name?"

"Barbidon, it was 17 years ag-"

Babs' mouth went wide in realisation that Arrowglance had been right. "You raped her! Didn't you?" she hissed, so close that tiny droplets of spit sprayed into his face. "How could you?! How could you break into a defenceless woman's house and rape her?"

"I, er... There was a sign. It said 'Orc hard', and I guess... I guess it made me think of sex."

Barbidon let out a guttural scream. This ensured the few orcs *not* already observing the old chieftain and his hyperwarrior daughter were doing so now.

Her arm involuntarily shot out, finding his frail neck, just as it had done with the boy Arque that she'd killed in her village.

His eyes bulged in alarm.

"It said Orchard." She said with the ominous calm of a dam wall. A dam wall about to burst. "*Not*, ORC. HARD!"

The words 'Orc Hard' rang out across the valley. She grabbed his cloak with her other hand, lifting him off the ground with strength born of genetics, physical conditioning, a high calorie diet and white-hot anger. Her hand tightened around his oesophagus, ripping it out of his neck. Blood sprayed over Babs and the surrounding stone as she dropped the body of her father.

For a moment there was a stunned, unnatural silence. One orc began chanting, "Orc Hard! Orc Hard!" He was joined by another, then another, until the whole hill-load of Orcs chanted in unison at the mighty Barbidon. "Orc Hard! Orc Hard!"

She looked around, a little unsure what to do next. Arrow and the Bone necklaced leaders gathered below her.

Babs held up her hand, silencing the crowd. Bone Jangles spoke first. "Barbidon. Your father was once a mighty leader, but that was the past. You have proven through your actions yesterday that despite your human blood, you are the most capable warrior we've ever had. We need your strength to lead us out of the mess he led us into."

She looked down at her father's corpse, then back at the Orcish horde. They looked at her with a naïve hope, ill matched to their monstrous appearance.

"My Brothers and Sisters." Barbidon said. "You want me as your leader because I am good at killing. This is not one of the three things your leader should be good at though. They should be smart. I am not. They should know their people well. I was raised by humans, and know little of your ways."

"They should also care about their people above everything else. My lifetime spent with humans would make that hard."

Several senior Orcs frowned, unsure where the speech was going.

"There is one orc here who has all those things. He knows you well, cares about his people and is super, super smart." Babs turned to face the Shaman. "Arrowglance. Could you join me please?"

Arrowglance looked around uncertainly, like a nerd just voted prom king. Several Orcs encouraged him up though.

As he stood beside her, Babs addressed the crowd again. "I am friends with the human Queen. She is desperate for the hammer once wielded by my eldest brother. With Arrow as your leader and my connection to the human General, I am sure we can trade this hammer and bring about a peace that will leave you richer and far less dead than staying here to be target practice for their arrows. That is why your shaman, an orc who has already shown he can dodge an arrow should be your leader."

Discussion started immediately. The tone seemed positive though. She heard one say, "He'd be way better than Karak."

Eventually Jangles got up on the rock with them. Babs kept a cautious eye on his weapon, looking for a sudden move. Turning to face the army, he lifted his axe, holding it high in the air shouting, "Chieftain Arrow!"

"Chieftain Arrow!" Came the reply from two thousand Orcs.

Half an hour later in the human encampment.

"Still no Idea what that shouting was about Sergeant?" Asked Jackhammer.

"No sir. It's been almost an hour, they don't seem to be preparing to advance. Wait... do you see that General?"

Jackhammer squinted through the sun that had crested over the Orcs position. "Yes, I do... is that two orcs advancing?"

Within a minute, he made out that one held the white flag of truce, the other a large hammer. His hopes lifted. Were they bringing the hammer of Castra to him? Surely not. A minute later he recognised Barbidon. After losing all his cavalry, and presumably Brightspark with them, this was strange indeed.

"Sergeant Barbidon, what news?"

"Hi General. I almost don't know where to begin." She collected herself with a deep breath, before launching into the story at blistering speed. "It's been crazy. First, Brightspark died with all the rest of the horse soldiers. I was so sad and angry that I killed my four brothers. Then I found out they *were* my brothers. Then I got the hammer of Castra. Found out my father was the orc leader. I killed him, after discovering he raped my mother. Then they wanted me to be Chieftain. I said they should give it to Arrowglance here instead, cause he's a shaman and *way* smarter than me. Then we came to see you." She took another breath to book-end her synopsis, holding her hands out to either side. "Ta da?"

He looked at her, speechless.

The Shaman Arrowglance took a step forward, extending his hand.

"General, My name is Arrowglance. As of this hour I am the new leader of my people. I was an advisor to the late Chieftain. Please accept my sincerest apologies for my inability to stop the unnecessary bloodshed yesterday. I would like to discuss ways we could end our fighting and move tentatively towards a more mutually beneficial relationship."

Jackhammer had expected little more than a string of barely coherent grunts in the unlikely event of negotiations. This shaman spoke with an eloquence more befitting an Elven diplomat. "I would like that very much Chieftain. Very much indeed."

An hour later he was pleased to have secured an in-principle agreement that he felt would be sellable to the Queen. The Orcs would get a small land concession. In exchange, they would hand over the hammer of Castra and provide Orcish shock troops on rotation to bolster the human army. Both parties could also mutually benefit from trade between the two races in time.

Jackhammer turned to Babs "Barbidon. Do you intend to return to the capital? I would understand if you feel conflicted loyalty. This is the unfair burden placed on the children of mixed-race couplings."

To her credit, she didn't take too long to decide. "It's okay. I want to bring the Hammer through the city gates like Major Brightspark should have done." She turned to the Chieftain. "Thank you for helping me uncover the truth."

She gave him a kiss on the cheek, he flushed. "You are always welcome to visit." He seemed about to give her a hug, then she looked like she was going to give him a one, but it wasn't at the same moment.

As a result, they both awkwardly waved goodbye before Chieftain Arrowglance headed back up the hill. Jackhammer watched the exchange. He was as rule, disgusted by the cross-race relations, but decided if Barbidon was to find a partner it was better with an Orc, than to further sully his own race.

He turned to his aide-de-camp. "I want to dictate a letter to her majesty. Then you will gather the officers, we're going home."

45

Royal comforter

On the evening of the next day, Brightspark's wife Nadia heard the distinctive sound of armour approach her door. It preceded a heavy knock.

She opened it, expecting a soldier, but the Queen's Guard who'd knocked had retreated. In his place, on her doorstep, stood the Queen in all her resplendent glory.

"Your majesty." She dropped to her knee, as her mind raced to explain this visit. Her heart sunk as she guessed the reason.

"Please, you need not lower yourself."

Nadia stood, slowly, to delay the news. To keep him alive for a few more seconds.

The Queen had a look of abject sorrow on her face. "Lady Brightspark." then dropping her formal tone. "Nadia, your husband was an extraordinary man. It is with the heaviest of hearts I inform you, that he died on the field of battle two days ago."

Tears held in check, now flooded her cheeks. She was vaguely aware of the queen stepping inside, closing the door and wrapping her in a hug.

She sank into the embrace, too grief stricken to question how uncharacteristic the gesture was of the normally austere monarch.

They stood there, embracing, the Queen not pulling away. Eventually Nadia let go, meeting her monarch's gaze.

"Thank you for coming to see me personally. I do not deserve this attention."

"There are few men in the realm as good as him. It was the least I could do. I will make sure you are not disadvantaged financially by his loss, though I know that will provide little immediate consolation."

Nadia regarded the Queen, struggling to reconcile this gentle, unpretentious compassion with the cold woman her husband had described.

"I was becoming close friends with the magus Virginia you know."

Rather than frowning, the Queen kept looking at her with compassion.

"Yes. I know."

"Seeing the kindness you've shown me today, I can't imagine what possessed her to commit such a crime against you."

"The world is a complex place. Perhaps in time the fog will clear as to her motives. I..." she paused, looking like she was on the verge of saying something more. "I should get back to the palace now. Would it be okay if I occasionally checked in on you?"

"Of course. Though I would not wish you to trouble yourself on my account."

"Goodbye Nadia."

"Goodbye your majesty."

She left, and the shock of having the Queen in her parlour faded. Now the Monarch's devastating news rushed back into Nadia's thoughts. She spent the evening without supper, her muffled cries spent on a pillow soon sodden with tears.

Two days later.

A cheering throng packed the streets of Del. The General insisted that Barbidon, on her mottled grey mare, ride right alongside his white charger. He looked happy to share the honour, which was very out of character for the limelight loving leader. Even when the crowd repeatedly shouted her name his smile remained in place. She stood in the saddle, lifting the hammer above her head to deafening applause.

Not everyone cheered with the same enthusiasm. Many anxious faces, often women, scanned soldier's faces for confirmation their love, or at least breadwinner, was not amongst the casualties.

Babs was glad to see the Queen, or rather Vaginia, standing alongside Virgun. Her eyes went to the hammer.

"Excellent work General, and you too Barbidon." The Queen stepped forward, inspecting the hammer of Castra which Babs held out for her. She gave Babs an unqueenly wink, before re-donning her regal persona. "After you have rested, we will hold a banquet where you can regale us with tales of your exploits."

"Your majesty does us a great honour." Said the General with an efficient bow.

"Come now, modestly ill suits you General, and we both know a celebration is owed."

"Should we discuss the proposed peace terms with the Orcs?" asked Virgun.

"That can wait till tomorrow morning I think. In the afternoon, I will lead a ceremony where we will destroy Orgasmodan's god stones. Perhaps Barbidon should have that honour, having been so instrumental in securing both the Hammer of Castra and Anvil of Tion."

"Thank you V... I mean, your majesty" said Babs.

Jackhammer gave her a curious look.

The Queen turned to her secretary. "I want everybody of note in the city assembled in the palace courtyard at four pm. This will be a momentous occasion."

Climax.

THE HAMMER OF CASTRA,TION's ANVIL.

It was a glorious early autumn afternoon the following day. The sun had lost its aggression and now bathed the large palace courtyard in a warm glow. One could've happily walked around naked with the only discomfort being the screams of witnesses. By four pm, almost a thousand people packed the conically shaped palace courtyard. There were courtiers, palace maids and cooks, officers, nuns & members of the merchants' guild. Those of rank sat on five rows of long wooden benches, whilst the masses stood behind. General Jackhammer had taken his place in the first row of seated dignitaries.

On one side sat the promoted Sergeant Hodgkins, vanquisher of Orgasmodan's high Priestess. For some unknown reason he had a focused yet nervously distracted expression on his face, like someone masturbating under a guillotine.

On his other side sat the downcast Lord Erec of Tion. It surprised Jackhammer how much the death of the arrogant Longsword had affected his brother. He reflected though, that death had a way of polishing the memory of a person even as it rotted their flesh. On the other side of Erec, sat his wife Lady Menstra of Tion and son Master Bae of Tion, a fidgety lad of ten and six.

There was also the Dwarven ambassador Airola Clevage. She did not look pleased with the ceremony, but was smart enough not to voice her disapproval. Finishing up his row of seating was Nadia Brightspark, dressed in mourning black. Looking at her filled his heart with guilt. The guilt of a commander who'd ordered a husband to his death.

There was a general excitement in the courtyard. Mortals had never before banished a god from the world. Jackhammer felt the significance of the occasion more than most. It had been a decade since he'd killed his childhood abuser, the Elven man once his mentor. Today however, would be the *real* culmination of his struggle. The abomination of inter-racial and homosexual lust would surely vanish from the entire world once they banished Orgasmodan's sick presence.

Barbidon, Virgun and the Queen stepped out from a palace door and onto to a makeshift stage. It had the air of an executioner's platform, fitting, given the task at hand. A hush descended over the masses as the Queen took centre stage behind the Anvil of Tion. The Queen had requested children not attend the ceremony. This enabled a level of hushed solemnity to descend over the crowd that seemed incongruous with it's size.

Vagina looked at that enormous crowd from the stage, nervously clearing her throat.

This was it.

She placed the god stones atop the anvil. These were not the god stones of Orgasmodan, as everyone assumed. Thanks to her access to the vault of relics, she and Babs were about to publicly destroy Prudishia's link to the world. All to the unwitting applause of her loyalest followers.

"Ladies and Gentlemen. For too long our society has been at war with itself over religious conflict. The Orcish invasion has shown the importance of staying united in the face of larger, external threats."

"For too long, the worship of the false god has led to unhealthy relationships and unnecessary suffering. Today that conflict will end as we destroy the god stones of this divisive deity. Several important figures joined us today that have made this momentous occasion possible...."

Twink listened to the Queen's speech impatiently. His eyes focused on the god stones. It still seemed surreal that he alone knew it was Prudishia's god stones that rested on the Anvil of Tion. That, thanks to his extraordinary effort in switching them, the Half-Orc was about to publicly destroy Prudishia's link to the world. All to the unwitting applause of her loyalest followers. The Queen finally finished her formalities. She stepped back for the warrior Barbidon, who held the enormous Hammer of Castra in her hand.

As she was about to lift it, Twink felt a pair of eyes upon him. It was High Priest Virgun, smiling stupidly in his direction. Knowing his hypocritical power as a priest of Prudishia was about to end, Twink saw no harm in warmly smiling back at the old man. *Enjoy your last moments of power,* he thought.

As Barbidon stepped up to the Anvil, Jackhammer noticed Virgun smiling strangely at someone further back in the crowd. On a whim, he followed his gaze. It took a moment to find the recipient, but he was alarmed when he did. Standing against a wall at the side of the crowd was a young, effeminate looking lad, who was smiling just as broadly back at Virgun. A terrible, horrifying thought occurred to Jackhammer. As Barbidon brought the hammer down, he shouted.

"Stop!"

No one heard him. As the hammer struck, an epically deep 'bouje' shock wave emanated from the anvil. It was the sort of descending, subwoofery bass a sound engineer would use if this book was ever turned into a movie.

Two hours earlier...

Virgun excused himself from lunch and now sat in his room with hands cupped over nose and mouth. He was almost hyperventilating, rocking back and forth. It was ninety-four years before the invention of the rocking chair, so his rump acted as the fulcrum in this endeavour. He stared intently at the key before him. In two hours, the Queen would retrieve Orgasmodan's god stones from the vault of relics, by then, it would be too late. He thought back to the words of the deceased Orgasmodanic priestess Ovula; *"Virgun, you don't choose to be homosexual. You of all people should know that."*

He thought of his time with Twink. Oh Twink. The name itself was sweeter than a Jaldurian fruit tart. He could still smell his scent from the times he'd massaged him in this very room. He longed for those times again, but how could they be together, be *truly* together, away from Prudishia's judging gaze. Could he walk away from it all? To go from High Priest, First Counsellor to the Queen, to just Virgun, old man of no importance.

Yes. For he could do anything, suffer any hardship, with Twink by his side. It was beyond doubt that the young chef cared for him too.

He remembered the worried anguish written so transparently on the boys face after he'd rushed to his chambers, the night of the queen's attempted murder.

He remembered Twink's breathlessness, his faltering words to him that night: *'I worried... I worried that something might have happened to you.'*

Most of all he remembered the embrace, oh how fleeting it had been, but to hold such beauty in his arms had been the most wonderful moment of his life.

Finding his resolve. He grabbed the key and headed to the Vault of relics. He would swap the god stones. He would change history forever.

-

Whilst Barbidon smashed both of Orgasmodans Stones with a single strike, Queen Vagina had pulled out a strange object from her clutch. She laid the circular inky black portal Hodgkins had returned to her on an angled portion of the platform built at her particular request. She then dropped a silk handkerchief through it.

-

On the other side of the portable portal, High Priestess Ovula sat astride the now armed and fully operational Phallus of Felicity. She had been 'edging' the two metre Phallus for over an hour. It was with great relief that she saw the signal. Vag's white silk handkerchief dropped through her side of the portal, positioned exactly at the tip of the head, on a wooden frame Clamax had built for the occasion.

She let the power of the ecclesiastical ejaculate finally flow. A monstrously powerful jet of Orgasmodan's sacred fluid flew into the inky black void.

-

Back in Del, everyone was recovering from the hammer blow shock wave, when an enormous fountain of fluid shot up from the platform one hundred and fifty metres into the air. It shot out where Vag had placed her side of the portable portal on the stage. This was not visible to the crowd though. To them it looked like it emerged from the stage itself. So much fluid flowed, that it drenched everyone in the courtyard for a full minute. People stood laughing, dumbfounded at where this geyser had cum from. Sorry, had *come* from. They turned their faces upwards in merriment, as the slightly salty water rained down upon their open mouths. One by one, libido increased and inhibitions plummeted faster than a feather in the gravity well of a black hole.

Lady Menstra of Tion put her hand atop her husband's. Their relationship had seen its cycles, but it had ebbed lowest of late. Yet when Erec looked at her now, it seemed the passion in their relationship was back. What was more, it needed to be expressed *RIGHT. NOW.* He clasped her hand and took her immediately to his private quarters in the keep. This left his teenage son behind, fidgeting a lot more than usual...

Virgun felt his powers vanish the instant Barbidon's hammer hit Prudishia's god stones. He did not care. He began walking trancelike off the stage towards Twink. Towards his future. A heavy sun shower came on suddenly, but he barely noticed it.

Entering the maelstrom of the crowd, Virgun searched for the one beautiful face that was more important to him than all the other's combined. After a while, his searching became frantic, then a break in the crowd formed, like Orgasmodan herself had parted the mass for him. Twink was talking excitedly to another young man as Virgun confidently strode up to him, face beaming.

"Twink! I have done it. I have switched the stones, broken Prudishia's connection to this world and renounced my power. I have done this because..." he felt the words catch in his throat. It was as though they carried too much emotion, too much weight to pass through his windpipe. "because I love you. Most ardently, and I want to spend the rest of my days devoted to you."

Rather than smiling and leaping into his arms. Twink frowned "What do you mean *you* swapped the stones? I was the one who swapped them, I was the one who had to massage you every night, to borrow the key until eventually I had my chance to swap the stones *myself*."

"But if you swapped the stones as well, how did..." The implication of Twink's words sunk in.

"What do you mean 'had to massage me'? Did you only pretend to care for me to get my keys?" Twink remained unyielding as tears queued up in Virgun's ducts. "But... I love you." It was all he knew how to say in that moment.

The young man's face softened. "I am sorry, your grace. My point was never to hurt you. It was to stop people of our persuasion from being executed simply for expressing a love like the one you've shown me today."

"Virgun."

"I'm sorry what?"

"You don't need to call me 'Your Grace', just call me Virgun." Said layman Virgun Blueballus again, already turning away to lose himself in the crowd.

He kept walking. His old legs felt frailer with every step. In the shadow of the Castle's courtyard gate, he slumped against the outer wall and gave permission for his tears to come. They could never stop for all he cared.

The Dwarven Ambassador Airola stood in wonder at the geyser spirting high into the sky. She'd not expected this from the ceremony. Soon it didn't even feel like a ceremony at all. As the liquid rained down upon the crowd, many started showing affection to one another. A *lot* of affection. Truth be told, she felt like some affection right now too. Airola lamented the absence of any partner for her, particularly a stout Dwarven man who she could hold in her arms.

As abruptly as it started, the geyser stopped. A sturdy Dwarven man appeared a moment later out of the same strange black circle, as if her imagination had conjured him into being. He was magnificent, simultaneously radiating an aura of power and humility. It was intoxicating to her, even at a distance. He gave the Queen a friendly embrace, then turned to look at the crowd, to look directly into her eyes.

Clamax watched in wonder, as Ovula drained half the lake by firing the phallus non-stop through the portal. He climbed up the portals makeshift supporting scaffold, then headed through the void, as soon as the pulsating member was spent.

He was eager to see its effect. Vaginia, with her new, majestic body and Babs helped him up. They embraced.

"It worked!" Vag said "All of it. It all worked!"

"You achieved the impossible Vag, and you too, Babs. Well done to both of you."

"You look different, Clamax." Said Babs, appraising him. "Like you're *really* fancy and powerful."

"That might be because I'm a Paladin now." Said Clamax, sounding almost embarrassed at the title.

"Really? Like the hero from the story you told me?"

"The real deal."

"That's awesome!" Said Babs, holding out her hand for a high five. When he raised his eyebrows, she realised her high five was *too* high. Lowering it to a Dwarven friendly height, he returned the gesture with a smile.

Clamax turned to look at the crowd that was embracing free love with gusto. Then he saw her, barely fifteen metres away, the first dwarven female he had seen since childhood. Her cheeks had a beautiful fine down of hair on them, and she was so.... so... *squat*. It was beguiling. He stepped off the platform and strode towards her.

"Ser Clamax at your service."

"Ambassador Clevage at yours."

They embraced in unspoken agreement and were soon servicing each other.

-

Sergeant Hodgkins had sat anxiously next to the general. The Queen made it clear that Jackhammer was not on their side and would need restraining if he realised something was up.

Somehow, he did realise things were amiss. Fortunately, by the time he yelled 'Stop', it was too late. He started rushing the stage, but Hodgkins tripped him. He face planted, then stared up in horror as the water rushed out. He looked back at Hodgkins, the Queen then Virgun in rapid succession. "I'll make you pay for this you fat shit! I'll make all of you pay!" But as the water reached it's zenith, Jackhammer looked at it with wide-eyed dread. He turned and ran, desperate to avoid the fluid as it rained down. This left Hodgkins free to move towards the platform.

The bukkake Bapjism eventually ended, and Hodgkins saw the powerful Dwarven Paladin emerge from the portal. As Barbidon and the Queen greeted Clamax, Hodgkins edged his way into the portal. It was a tight fit, but he had the help of a slender hand on the other side guiding him.

His foot slipped as he was almost through. Clutching desperately, he accidentally pulled Ovula off the Phallus with him. They both splashed into the waist-high crystalline waters. Getting to their feet, she began laughing. It was a sound gentler and sweeter than any bird song. He began laughing too, like a child ignorant of anguish or heartache.

Soaking wet and with the afternoon sun glistening off the surrounding water, they looked into each other's eyes. In that moment, he was just a twenty-eight-year-old boy, standing in front of a six hundred and fifty-two-year-old girl, asking her to love him. And love him she did.

Nadia Brightspark had felt numb ever since hearing the news of her husband. The attentiveness of the Queen had surprised her, visiting her again the day after delivering the news. She had trouble talking openly of her feelings with the monarch. In the absence of her husband, she wished Virginia was alive to comfort her.

Her numbness ended with the shock wave sent out by the god stones destruction.

The enormous fountain of water was the first hint of a divergence from official proceedings. She saw Jackhammer panic, running off, seemingly paranoid of the water raining down. The Queen then helped Vaginia's Dwarven friend up and out of a strange portal and the two embraced. Nadia stood up, realisation dawning on her. She looked intently at the Queen, noting her mannerisms. They reminded her of..."

The Queen met her gaze.

"Virginia?" Mouthed Nadia silently.

The Queen smiled tentatively and nodded.

Nadia ran to her and they embraced.

"How?" she asked in a whisper.

"It's a long story. I was desperate to tell you."

"Well, I'm just glad I still have you."

"I'm glad I have you too." Said Virginia, tightening her embrace.

47

⚬⚬⚬

Into the arms of true kin

Barbidon enjoyed smashing Prudishia's god stones, knowing she would now have the right to love, and be loved, by anyone. The spirting water had been amazing, seeing Clamax as a Paladin was incredible and super happy at the same time.

The nicest thing perhaps was seeing Nadia and Vaginia hugging each other. Babs realised that perhaps all those times she had seen them laughing together wasn't because they were laughing at her. Maybe it was just that sometimes, two people find such joy in each other's company that they need to let the laughter out, lest they burst with happiness.

As Vag had warned her, the water made everyone think about having sexual intercourse. It was working on her too. Many men, including a lot of the Queen's Guard, lined up to proposition her. This took equal parts sexual drive and foolhardiness on their part, given the only two penises she'd ever touched had either been ripped or bitten off.

She turned all of them down politely. The truth was, there was one person she wanted to hold above all others, and they weren't in this thousand strong crowd of humans. They weren't even in this City.

Babs left the courtyard, grabbed some supplies, and headed straight to the stables where she found her mottled grey mare. Despite the late hour, she made her way out of the city gates, taking the same western road she'd returned on the day before.

The next day she spotted her turnoff. It was quite an achievement given she had the navigational ability of a tree. This path now took her southwest, close to necromancer's house, and lake Youval, where she had first met Clamax.

Babs spent the following day passing through forests with familiar looking trees. She'd exhausted her poor horse, so frequently walked beside it, her excitement like a whip at her own back. As a cool southerly change pushed away the heat of the day, she emerged from the edge of the same forest she'd run into four weeks ago. The valley below held an orchard with a tiny hut, that until recently had been her entire world.

Walking closer, Babs eventually spotted her walking along a row of apple trees.

Her mother spotted Babs also, and there was no need for words. Milfandria dropped her basket, Babs dropped her sword. They ran for each other and embraced, tears streaming.

"Where have you been? You shouldn't be here. If they find that you've come back..."

"It's ok mum, I have a letter of pardon from the queen. She's a good friend of mine."

Her mother snorted, then her jaw dropped as Babs produced an ornate scroll.

"How did you become friends with the Queen! What in God's orchard did you get up to in your time away?"

"*So much. it was incredible mum! Though...*"

"Though what?" asked her mother, searching her daughter's eyes for the end of the sentence.

"I met my father."

"Oh."

They stood, holding each other's forearms, each unsure what to say next.

"Why didn't you tell me he raped you?"

Her mother looked at the ground. "I didn't want you to think you were unwanted, that I loved you less because of it."

"Mum, I could never think you don't love me."

Milfandria smiled, and they embraced again, before walking back to the hut. "Did you get along with him?"

"Not really, I ended up killing him."

"Wow. I can't say I approve, but I'm not sad either."

"I also found out I had I four brothers."

"Really? What were their names?"

"I can't remember, I killed all of them too." Said Babs, pausing as she saw the look of shock in her mum's eyes. "It's okay, it was in a battle."

"A battle?"

"Yes. Battles are when everyone decides killing people is a good thing for a while."

Her mother reached out, cupping her daughter's cheek in her hand. She was smiling, but also shaking her head.

"I know what a battle is, I was just surprised you were in one. Still, I think we need to work on your temper."

"I know. I snap too easily." Said Bab's, walking past the large sign her grandfather had erected twenty years ago.

It was a simple sign, with only one word on it: 'ORCHARD'.

She had to admit, now that she examined it, there was a bit of a gap between the C and the H.

THE END...

If you have enjoyed this book, Babs will give you a big hug* if you leave a review on the site you bought it from!

*hug subject to inter-planar travel at hug-ee's expense.

www.ingramcontent.com/pod-product-compliance
Lightning Source LLC
Chambersburg PA
CBHW070052120726
47909CB00002B/371